"It has to be done," Kane told Grant flatly. "Someone has to find a solution to this insanity. Right?"

"Yes, I know." Grant's deep voice was surprisingly gentle.

"Someone has to save humanity or what's left of it. We have to act for mankind...and even if we die in the attempt, at least the world will survive to judge us."

Grant said nothing. He stared at Kane across the table, not blinking, not moving, or even appearing to breathe. Kane felt some of the tension drain away from himself. He was right and he knew Grant was sure of it. Then he saw a tiny glitter of moisture within Grant's deep-set eyes.

Grant lifted one hand in a gesture. He spoke one word: "Tomei."

Kane caught only a blurred, fragmented glimpse of gleaming metal from behind him, then the edge of the female guard's butterfly sword touched his throat, forcing his head back.

"I'm sorry, Kane." Grant's voice was a hoarse whisper of anguish. "Give me the memory cards without an argument, and I'll arrange for you to get back home safely. But I don't ever want to see you here aga

Other titles in this series:

James Axler
Outlanders

TALON AND FANG

Heart of the World
BOOK 1

A GOLD EAGLE BOOK FROM
WORLDWIDE®

TORONTO • NEW YORK • LONDON
AMSTERDAM • PARIS • SYDNEY • HAMBURG
STOCKHOLM • ATHENS • TOKYO • MILAN
MADRID • WARSAW • BUDAPEST • AUCKLAND

First edition May 2003

ISBN 0-373-63838-8

TALON AND FANG

Rent by talon and fang,
Death comes without a pang;
But where its black shadow lay
All of love and hope were torn away.
                              —Justin Geoffrey

The Road to Outlands—
From Secret Government Files to the Future

Almost two hundred years after the global holocaust, Kane, a former Magistrate of Cobaltville, often thought the world had been lucky to survive at all after a nuclear device detonated in the Russian embassy in Washington, D.C. The aftermath—forever known as skydark—reshaped continents and turned civilization into ashes.

Nearly depopulated, America became the Deathlands—poisoned by radiation, home to chaos and mutated life forms. Feudal rule reappeared in the form of baronies, while remote outposts clung to a brutish existence.

What eventually helped shape this wasteland were the redoubts, the secret preholocaust military installations with stores of weapons, and the home of gateways, the locational matter-transfer facilities. Some of the redoubts hid clues that had once fed wild theories of government cover-ups and alien visitations.

Rearmed from redoubt stockpiles, the barons consolidated their power and reclaimed technology for the villes. Their power, supported by some invisible authority, extended beyond their fortified walls to what was now called the Outlands. It was here that the rootstock of humanity survived, living with hellzones and chemical storms, hounded by Magistrates.

In the villes, rigid laws were enforced—to atone for the sins of the past and prepare the way for a better future. That was the barons' public credo and their right-to-rule.

Kane, along with friend and fellow Magistrate Grant, had upheld that claim until a fateful Outlands expedition. A displaced piece of technology…a question to a keeper of the archives…a vague clue about alien masters—and their world shifted radically. Suddenly, Brigid Baptiste, the archivist, faced summary execution, and Grant a quick termination. For Kane there was forgiveness if he pledged his unquestioning allegiance to Baron Cobalt and his unknown masters and abandoned his friends.

But that allegiance would make him support a mysterious and alien power and deny loyalty and friends. Then what else was there?

Kane had been brought up solely to serve the ville. Brigid's only link with her family was her mother's red-gold hair, green eyes and supple form. Grant's clues to his lineage were his ebony skin and powerful physique. But Domi, she of the white hair, was an Outlander pressed into sexual servitude in Cobaltville. She at least knew her roots and was a reminder to the exiles that the outcasts belonged in the human family.

Parents, friends, community—the very rootedness of humanity was denied. With no continuity, there was no forward momentum to the future. And that was the crux—when Kane began to wonder if there *was* a future.

For Kane, it wouldn't do. So the only way was out—way, way out.

After their escape, they found shelter at the forgotten Cerberus redoubt headed by Lakesh, a scientist, Cobaltville's head archivist, and secret opponent of the barons.

With their past turned into a lie, their future threatened, only one thing was left to give meaning to the outcasts. The hunger for freedom, the will to resist the hostile influences. And perhaps, by opposing, end them.

Chapter 1

From the flatlands, the old blacktop road looked like a frayed ribbon stretched across the grassy plains to the foothills of the Bitterroot Range. Deeply cracked and furrowed, the road was dotted with thistles and weeds that sprouted from the countless splits in its surface. When the crumbling strip of asphalt reached the foothills of the mountains, it began looping and curving like a snake crazed by heatstroke. The ancient two-lane highway wended its way up toward the chain of mountain peaks that comprised the Continental Divide and formed the natural boundary between Idaho and Montana. Twisting in a serpentine trail through a tumble of chert outcroppings, the road climbed toward a hogback ridge. Against the blazing glory of fusing sunset colors loomed great crags of granite.

At the crest of the pass, Tanvirah stumbled and fell to her knees. Her lungs burned as if they were on fire, and her breath came from her open mouth in rasping pants. Sweat stung her eyes as she looked northward toward a parallel mountain range, the Beaverheads. Its highest peak, the Garfield, was snowcapped, and she desperately wished for a sudden wind storm to blow in and cool her off.

A deep, thickly wooded gully yawned below the crest on which she knelt. The forest was a riot of early autumn tints, orange and red and gold. On her left, beyond the tree line, rocky ramparts plunged straight down to a tributary of the Clark Fork River a hundred feet below. The tall trees were fir, pine and aspen. The shadows between them were very dark and coolly inviting.

She could see how the road leading up from the foothills to the Cerberus plateau skirted hell-deep chasms and sheer cliffs. Acres of the mountainside had collapsed during the nuke-triggered earthquakes more than two centuries before. The path was far more rugged than even her father had described, but more than a quarter of a century had passed since he had even seen it, much less walked it.

For the past six hours, she had been dragged behind the eight survivors of the Pischaca war party, two of whom were seriously wounded. They left a wet red trail in the road dust, but they continued to march. The Pischacas had attacked the company of half a dozen Magistrates her father had assigned to escort her to Cerberus.

When the Sandcat reached the edge of a rockfall blocking the road, the driver was forced to brake. The entire group disembarked to see what could be done about finding a way around or through the barricade. Tanvirah's father had described a camouflaged egress. When everyone had left the safety of the vehicle, the Pischacas attacked. One group of the stunted, ugly goblin-men had lain hidden in the tall grasses in the tree line. They rose and loosed a shower of arrows on the astonished Mags. Tanvirah caught only glimpses of the creatures she had been told were extinct for the past fifteen years.

As the Magistrates tried to retreat to the Sandcat, more Pischacas shoved up from shallow pits in the ground, discarding the cut sections of grassy turf they'd used to disguise themselves. Like the others, they carried axes and war hammers, swords and clubs, and attacked without fear.

Greasy, greenish-gray skin sagged around their frames, loose and thickly knobbed with fist-sized warts, tough as leather armor and proof against a poorly aimed blaster shot. The clots of hardened flesh gave them a half-formed appearance, as if their creator had forgotten to smooth out their bodies—something that Tanvirah knew was possible. The hairless, gorilloid faces of the Pischacas were broader from side to side than their heads were deep from front to back.

Their mouths were straight horizontal gashes, with almost no trace of lips. Their deep-set eyes had hazel irises and tiny pupils, like black beads. Shaggy animal hides covered their genitals. Knife and sword sheaths were crudely woven into them. They carried primitive war hammers and stone axes, as well as bows and arrows.

There were scores of the creatures—they sacrificed at least two dozen of their brethren to draw the fire of the Magistrates, waiting until their Spectre autoblasters were emptied before swarming out in a howling wave. They pulled the black-clad men down one by one, wrenching off their helmets and splitting their skulls with blows from their sledgelike war hammers or battle-axes. The latest version of Mag armor—jet-black BDUs composed of a Nomex-Kevlar-Neoprene weave and charcoal-colored porcelain helmets with face masks that covered everything but the eyes—provided only temporary protection from the assault.

But the Magistrates weren't accustomed to fighting adversaries as strong and as fierce as the Pischacas. The creatures courted death so they could deal death. Tanvirah had often heard her father decrying the poor combat skills of the postwar generation of Mags.

The Pischacas spared Tanvirah's life. She knew the reason why; she was a woman, young, fresh and, by their standards, beautiful. She doubted the Pischacas knew she was the daughter of the Imperial Authorities of High River—or if they did know, they wouldn't care. In fact, it was best they didn't. When one of them began to bind her wrists with rawhide thongs, she drew a knife from a sheath in her boot and stabbed at its side, but the point of the blade only scraped against one of the cartilaginous knobs, barely scoring the surface.

The goblin-man had laughed at her attempt to kill him and easily disarmed her. While he tied her, he indulged in a bit of rough fondling, which she silently endured. The Pischacas were taller than her, and their oil-sheened flesh gave off a virulently repulsive odor.

To keep from getting sick, she had to breathe through her mouth.

Tanvirah was forced to run behind the survivors of the war party as they loped off toward the mountains, arms laden with salvage. She fell several times but her captors didn't stop for her. She scrambled to her feet, abrading her hands and knees. She knew if she didn't rise, she would be dragged until she died.

She had never known fear, despite the tales her father had told her of the Pischacas—or at least the body of myth from which their name derived. According to him, the Pischacas were part of the unholy family of Rakshashas of Hindu India. The lord of all of the Rakshashas was Ravana, who had ten heads and twenty arms that grew again as soon as they were cut off and a hideous body sporting scars and open wounds. Like all the Rakshashas, the Pischacas were dedicated evildoers and the vilest branch of the family.

But these Pischacas weren't demons spawned from Hell. Rather they had been birthed from stainless-steel wombs filled with synthetic amniotic fluid. They weren't mutants, either, not the distorted caricatures of humanity accidentally spawned by the toxic residue of the long-ago nukecaust.

Tanvirah recalled tales her father told her of how, in the first century following the atomic megacull, mutants were feared and hated, particularly the stickies. They were monstrous, mutagenically altered human beings with sucker pads on their fingers and toes and a great hatred for normal people. The Pischacas' hatred for humanity was no less intense than that of the stickies.

If the goblin-men didn't take pleasure in her pain, they were certainly oblivious to it. Every breath she took was agony. The torture of the tight thongs half buried in the flesh of her wrists soon ebbed to numbness, but the rest of her body was not lost to feeling. Tanvirah cried out sharply as she stumbled and fell to her knees. The Pischacas dragged her the last few yards, the rawhide bindings biting so deeply into her wrists that blood oozed out around them. The Uma stone and its coil of silver chain hidden in an inner pocket of her bodysuit cut into her right hip.

The Pischaca who held the plaited length of leather cast a glance over a shoulder at her and grinned at her, exposing stumpy, discolored teeth. He tugged on the tether as if to urge her to rise, but no strength remained in Tanvirah's legs. Sharp rocks rasped against her thighs, stomach and breasts.

When they reached the crest of the pass, the war party stopped. A rocky crag thrust out seven or eight feet above the roadside, like a crooked shelf. Tanvirah struggled dizzily to her knees, blinking at the descending sun as it turned the blue-gray panorama of the sky into crimson-hued dusk.

The Pischaca dropped the length of leather to the ground and swaggered toward her on bare, splay-toed feet. He didn't seem the slightest bit out of breath, despite dragging her and other heavy items salvaged from the Sandcat. She lifted her chin and met his yellow gaze defiantly. The goblin-man contemptuously kicked her in the left side, just between her hip and ribs.

Tanvirah folded, writhing in the dust, hearing the Pischaca's hoarse laughter over her own gasps. She struggled to her knees again. This time the creature's thickly callused foot caught her on the side of the head. The kick made a thousand multicolored stars flash before her eyes. She fell again, only dimly aware of the Pischacas laughing uproariously.

She lay on the roadbed, tasting blood and gasping through an open mouth. One of the warriors knelt beside her and pulled her arms back and up, peeling the rawhide thongs from her wrists. Before circulation could return to her hands, he pinned them against the ground, which she knew didn't come close to requiring all of his strength. Her legs were left free and a Pischaca knelt between them. Gripping her knees, he forced them apart effortlessly.

Deeply socketed eyes gleaming, the Pischaca fumbled with his loin covering. He inhaled deeply through his open mouth, and the loose flesh at the base of his neck swelled. The swelling rolled down his chest. His stomach muscles flexed in wide, regular ripples that slid down to his groin. When the undulation reached his pelvis, his penis engorged and curved out in an erection of monstrous proportions.

Tanvirah stared, horrified into immobility for a long second by its greenish color and wart-encrusted length. It reminded her of a bludgeon, the inflamed crown looking almost as large as her fist. The testicles sagging beneath it were correspondingly huge and equally revolting in appearance. She had believed the Pischacas were bred without organs of reproduction at all, much less functional ones.

The creature apparently understood her astonishment, because he winked at her conspiratorially. The wink broke her paralysis, and she cried out in fear. Tanvirah didn't have much leverage with which to power a kick, but she tried, straightening her legs out and up like springs. The Pischaca caught her by the ankles and wrenched her violently forward. Her back scraped along the rough surface of the road, her elbows digging little grooves in the dirt.

Heedless of the zipper, the creature ripped open her bodysuit, from the collar to just above her pelvis. Arching her back, Tanvirah twisted her body to one side, freeing her right leg with a fierce tug. She kicked him with all of her strength in the lower belly. The Pischaca grunted and she kicked him there again, this time pistoning her heel into his sagging testicle sac. The creature didn't appear to feel the blow.

Panic overwhelmed Tanvirah, causing her to thrash and flail madly at him with her free leg. She smashed the sole of her foot into his face, then into his throat and chest. The Pischaca took it all, grunting softly with each kick. He allowed her foot to smash him until she was utterly exhausted, panting and covered with sweat. When she felt his thick fingers squeezing her breast, she barely mustered a feeble foot nudge, much less another kick.

Tanvirah lay limp, her respiration labored. She couldn't rise or fight anymore. She decided to let the monsters rape her or kill her or whatever the Pischacas did to human women they seized. She kept her eyes closed, waiting for the entrance of either a blade or a disfigured male organ.

Neither occurred. The Pischaca removed his hand from her breast, and she heard the creatures muttering uneasily to one another. She didn't understand a word of what they said. In fact, she felt a distant quiver of surprise that the creatures even had a language.

The Pischaca restraining her wrists released her. She sensed and heard the creatures shifting and shuffling all around. Opening her eyes, Tanvirah carefully raised her head from the roadbed and looked around. On the crag overlooking the crest of the pass stood a tall man.

She couldn't see him clearly, since he was backlit by the fiery setting sun, but she could tell he was six feet or more in height and as lean as a spear. He wore a long coat that appeared to be made of supple black leather. A wide, wing-tipped collar was tugged up high around his neck.

Tanvirah slowly hitched around to face the man, half expecting one of the Pischacas to cuff her. But they were as entranced by the silent apparition as she. The man grimly looked over the eight Pischacas and the girl on the road. The creatures eyed him nervously, but the man neither moved nor spoke. Sunlight winked dully on a strange object cradled in his arms.

By squinting, Tanvirah could just make out a skeletal, riflelike shape. The sectionalized barrel terminated in a long cylinder, reminiscent of an oversized sound suppressor made of a crystalline substance.

The man met her gaze. Tanvirah suppressed a shiver when she looked into his cold, pale eyes. They were almost the same color as the high western sky, blue with just a touch of gray. They blazed in a gaunt, bearded face. Tanvirah absently noted how the man's face was too harsh and hard to be handsome, even without the long, jagged scar cutting like a lightning bolt from left to right across his face, from hairline to jawline. His dark, silver-stippled hair hung loose past his shoulders, stirred by a touch of the wind.

He was a lone man, outnumbered and apparently underarmed, yet he exuded an ominous, menacing aura that was almost supernatural. That aura kept the Pischacas from mounting an attack or even challenging him. They muttered and grunted apprehensively among themselves. Tanvirah received the distinct impression they knew the man—if not by sight, then by reputation. She realized if the bloodthirsty monsters had encountered any other human on the mountain road, they would have gleefully dismembered and disemboweled him on the spot.

But the Pischaca apparently knew this man. He wasn't a legend to the creatures, Tanvirah knew. He was more of a ghost story. The greasy green goblin looming over her swallowed noisily and uttered a word that Tanvirah understood.

Gutturally, the Pischaca murmured, "*General*. General Kane."

Chapter 2

Kane found himself staring fixedly at the vision of dark beauty lying on the road. Even though she was in a half-prone position, he could tell the young woman was tall, with a voluptuously curved body. Much of it was visible through her torn open garment. Her blood-bedrabbled face was full cheeked and bold nosed, her skin the rich brown of coffee and milk, her eyes large and black and flashing.

Despite the fresh blood staining them, her wide, sensuous lips were set in a defiant line. Her sleek, straight hair was a thick, ebony cascade sheening over her shoulders from a part in the middle of her scalp. There was something familiar about her, but because of the dimming light and the poor vision in his right eye, he couldn't be sure. She looked to be in her early twenties. It had been a long time since Kane had been so close to a woman so young and beautiful—or a woman at all, for that matter.

When the Pischaca with the deflating penis grunted his name, Kane couldn't help but smile coldly. "That's my name. You have the advantage of me."

The Pischaca slapped his chest. "Sweet William. I served under you in the battle of Snakefish."

Kane snorted as if he didn't believe him. "Right. Release the girl, Sweetums."

Sweet William performed a passable imitation of his own snort. "Kiss my ass. One man with no blaster—I don't care how bad they say you be, Kane. You ain't givin' us no more orders."

The other Pischaca growled slobbering agreement with Sweet William's declaration. The goblin-men apparently didn't recognize the pulse-plasma rifle in his arms as a weapon, or if they did, they didn't consider it much of a threat.

"I wasn't giving you an order, Sweetums." Kane pitched his voice low. "I was giving you a choice. Release the girl or die."

The Pischaca chief laughed scornfully, lips peeling back to reveal his discolored, tusklike teeth. "Funny guy."

Then Sweet William's temper changed in the mercurial way of his kind. The grin became a ferocious snarl, and he narrowed his eyes. He grabbed the girl by the back of her neck with one hand and clasped his softening organ with the other. "She's mine! I'll fuck her brains out with this and then let my clan have what's left!"

Kane didn't move, keeping the surge of revulsion he felt from showing on his face. He noted how the girl grimaced in pain but didn't cry out. The breeze blew the foul stench of the creatures to him. He knew their noisome smell had less to do with matters of poor hygiene than with an essential biological characteristic of the genetically engineered race.

"Well?" Sweet William challenged.

"Well…" Kane narrowed his eyes. In a voice barely above a whisper he said, "Set the girl free and get off my mountain, shit-spawn."

Sweet William sneered. "Or what? You kill us all?"

"That'll be up to your clan, Willy-boy, whether they want me to kill them or not. But I sure as hell will kill you."

It wasn't a boast, not even a threat. There was a quiet, confident ring of a promise in his tone and words, and Sweet William didn't like the sound of it. He didn't release his grip on the girl, but he loosened it, judging by the relief that showed on her face.

Sweet William growled, "You and me got no reason to fight, Kane. The war is over. All the barons are dead, and you're not an imperial general no more."

Kane shook his head as if he found the Pischaca's words so pathetically stupid, he could scarcely believe the creature had even uttered them. "We're not talking about what we were in the past, Willy-boy. It's just me and you and your piss-breathed crew here on my mountain. It's the next twenty seconds you should be worrying about, not the last twenty years."

Sweet William had narrowed his eyes to slits. Kane could easily guess the kind of thoughts lumbering through his brain. Regardless of what else was said, the Pischaca chief intended to attack him. He had no choice. If he backed down in front of Kane, his clan would not forget and his position as their leader was doomed.

"This isn't necessary," Kane said softly. "No more of your kinsmen's blood has to be spilled here."

The Pischaca's swart, greasy face contorted at the mention of blood. He released Tanvirah and shoved her away as if she were of no more use to him. She sprawled on her face. Moving in an unintentional but ludicrous parody of dignity, Sweet William closed up his loincloth and rose to his feet. Kane knew the goblin-man was no longer intimidated by him, and his finger caressed the firing plate of the plasma-pulse rifle in his arms.

Sweet William stared unblinkingly, directly into his face, inhaled deeply, then roared, "Kill him!"

Before the echoes of the goblin-man's bellow had begun to fade, Kane swung the barrel of the rifle in a short arc, depressing the trigger switch. Lightning bursts pulsed from the small, bell-shaped bore in a blinding blue-white flare. There was no recoil. The crackling torrent of incandescence engulfed the Pischaca, and he instantly burst into flame, transformed into a flailing, fire-wreathed scarecrow. Then Sweet William's body exploded from within, and his viscera splattered the ground for twenty feet all around.

The other Pischacas recoiled from the spray of warm flesh and ruptured internal organs. They snatched at their weapons and squalled with fury. As one, they lurched toward the outcropping on which

Kane stood. He noted with approval how gracefully the captive girl rolled to one side, getting out of their path.

Kane kept his finger tight on the trigger switch of the pulse-plasma rifle and sprayed the wave of blue-white light as if it were water from a hose, swinging the muzzle in a wide field of fire. The energy charge sliced through a pair of Pischacas standing shoulder to shoulder, carving them open at their waists. The two halves of their bodies fell away from each other and thumped wetly to the roadbed amid bright showers of blood.

The five remaining Pischacas cried out in horror and dismay and retreated from the shelf of rock, then the rifle in Kane's hands emitted a sputter and the beam of plasma disappeared. He quickly consulted the small LCD window near the trigger plate. Three zeroes glowed redly against a black background. The weapon was drained of energy. With a curse, he tossed it aside. It was far too lightweight to be of much use as a bludgeon.

The Pischacas growled in bloodthirsty gratification when they saw him discard the rifle. The growls turned into mutters of surprise when Kane reached up behind him, over his head with both arms, then snapped them up and out with a swift, sharp gesture. Sunlight flickered briefly on the polished surface of the flat sword blade.

Kane cut a figure-eight pattern in the air, the razor-keen steel of the *katana* humming. He didn't really want to stain the sword with foul Pischaca blood, so he gave them the chance to rethink their attack and retreat. The samurai sword was a wedding gift from Shizuka, made by New Edo's reigning craftsman. It hadn't been forged to draw the blood of submen and he didn't want to sully either Shizuka's memory or that of her sword smith.

At the same time, Kane recognized the feeling coming over him, an emotion he hadn't experienced in a long time. It was rage, white-hot rage that filled his soul. The very notion that these unclean things would invade his home territory, bringing both a captive and loot plundered from the dead, drove almost all rational thoughts from his mind. From within and without he began shaking with fury, with the compulsion to cleanse from the face of the mountain the filth shambling below him.

Kane leaped from the ledge. He landed on the road and almost went to one knee, wincing at the sudden spurt of pain stabbing through his ankles. Still, he managed to hold the *katana* before him, hands locked around the intricately inlaid handle in a two-fisted grip.

The goblin-men gaped at him, then three of them rushed him in a cluster. Feinting to the left with the sword, Kane spun on the ball of his right foot and came around facing the middle Pischaca. The Pischaca had his heavy war hammer lifted over his malformed head, holding the four-foot-long shaft in both hands. Teeth bared in a snarling grimace, the half-naked creature brought down the stone head of the mallet.

Kane shifted, a mocking smile on his face. He whipped the *katana* forward. Already committed to the move, dragged by the weight of the fifty-pound hammer, the Pischaca squealed in panic as he saw Kane step lithely out of the way, pivot on the heel of a foot and whirl back, leading with the blade in a side swing.

The edge of the sword chopped into the Pischaca's midsection with a sound like a melon splitting. The creature's guts seemed to burst out from the long, vertical gash in his belly. They spilled to the ground, worming in all directions. The goblin-man tripped on a blue-sheened loop of intestines, feet sliding out from under him.

Kane wheeled again, slashing backhanded with the sword. The keen edge sliced through a Pischaca's squat neck, popping the head free of his sloping, wart-pebbled shoulders. For an instant, the malformed skull seemed to bob atop a fountain of blood. Before Kane could move again, the third Pischaca was on him, roaring in wild madness and swinging his ax as hard as he could.

Desperately, Kane lifted the blood-filmed sword, the edge meeting the ax head. Flint rang against steel, and sparks jumped from the point of the impact, hot enough to burn Kane's skin. As he leaned away from the weapon, the edge of the ax swept down and opened a rent in his shirt and the flesh beneath, tearing through the skin on his right side. Fiery pain streaked through his torso. Only a backward wrench of his body kept the ax blade from crashing through his third and fourth ribs.

Kane moved again, instantly on the attack, knowing another Pischaca was already shifting into position on his left. His movements with the samurai sword were quick and sure, parry and thrust, burying the point deep in the Pischaca's chest, between a pair of the knoblike growths, and piercing his heart. The scream that issued from the creature's mouth was surprisingly high-pitched and piping. He raised the ax in one hand, as if hoping to split his foe's skull as his final act.

Kane lifted his leg and kicked the goblin-man in the groin, getting rid of his last dying threat, as well as freeing his sword from his body. The Pischaca's corpse stutter-stepped backward, blood spewing from his chest.

Ducking under one of the remaining Pischaca's bare-handed attacks, Kane rammed him low with his left shoulder. It was like body-blocking a Sandcat, and he staggered backward, falling to one knee. Before he could regain his footing, the Pischaca lashed out with an arm, knotting a hand in Kane's shoulder-length hair, holding on tight.

Kane gritted his teeth, clamping his jaws shut on a cry of pain. The creature hissed at him, its long, mottled gray tongue flicking out for his eyes and face. He twisted his head, barely able to keep the Pischaca's barb-tipped tongue from puncturing his eyes. He whipped the sword up between them, first cutting the slithering tongue in two, then placing the edge against the creature's throat. He slashed upward.

Pischaca flesh parted instantly at the relatively tender underside of the jawline. Hot blood splashed across Kane's face. He made a swift sawing motion with the sword, feeling the edge bite more deeply, rasping against the Pischaca's vertebrae. The goblin-man's severed arteries spouted a scarlet fountain, briefly blinding Kane. He managed to wrench out of the creature's grasp and step back, trying to clear his vision with desperate swipes of his free hand. The Pischaca fell heavily, strands of Kane's hair clutched within his gnarled fingers.

The last Pischaca didn't attack Kane. Instead, he whirled on the girl and thrust at her with a crude spear, evidently obeying the vindictive impulse that if he and his clan couldn't have her, neither would Kane. The sharpened flint shard fitted into a notch at the end of the wooden shaft jabbed toward her face. She shifted aside and delivered a surprisingly expert snap kick to the monster's groin that drove his pendulous testicles almost up to his navel.

The goblin-man dropped the spear and staggered away, bent double and clutching at his crotch. Blinking blood from his eyes, Kane saw the girl snatch up the spear and thrust with all her might, burying the sharpened end into the warrior's chest and shoving the creature away from her.

The dying Pischaca tripped over one of his brethren and toppled backward, clasping the wooden shaft in one hand as he clutched at his crotch with the other. The girl threw her entire weight against the spear, trying to drive the shaft completely through him and impale him against the ground. One of his flailing feet sent her stumbling backward.

Before the creature could rise, a long-legged bound brought Kane to his side. He lifted the *katana* over his head and brought it down in a swift, two-handed, cleaverlike chop. The Pischaca's head rolled free of his shoulders like an awkward ball.

As he watched the goblin-man's body sag limply to the ground, Kane felt like doing the same. The rage drained out of him, leaving him weak and trembling. He leaned against the bulwark of stone, taking inventory of his aching muscles and joints. He was disgusted to hear how loudly he wheezed from the unaccustomed exertion.

The Pischaca corpses lay huddled close together on the pass. The fresh mountain air of early evening was astringent with the stench of burned flesh. He dragged the sleeve of his coat over his face, wiping blood from it.

Kane watched the dark girl striding toward him, picking her way over the bodies. She didn't even try to close up the torn bodice of her bodysuit. Her full breasts strained at the lace-edged cups of her brassiere. She was long limbed and fairly tall.

Without preamble, without a words of thanks or so much as an inquiry about his physical condition, she said crisply, "Most of these genetically engineered warriors weren't bred for intelligence...which is a lucky thing for the rest of us.''

"Yeah," he said dryly, surreptitiously probing at the cut on his side. He brought his hand out from beneath his coat and examined the blood glistening on his fingertips. "I know I feel blessed.''

The girl eyed him speculatively. "Did I hear that monster right? You're General Kane?''

He shook his head. ''Just Kane now. The war's long over.''

The girl didn't acknowledge his reminder. ''My name is Tanvirah Singh. Daughter of Mohandas Lakesh Singh. He sent me to find you, sir.''

ABOUT THE BEST THING Tanvirah could say for the bearded, long-haired man was that he had been punctual in the timing of his rescue and gone about it very efficiently. Still, she was barely able to conceal her shock when she saw how old and scarred the man was. She had seen pix of him when he was much younger, of course, but all the softness of youth was long gone, replaced by scar tissue and deep lines of hardship.

Tanvirah was certainly aware of his reputation, of the legend that had sprung up around him. No single man in the past two hundred years probably had a reputation to equal Kane's, but in Tanvirah's view, reputations didn't resolve long-standing matters of state.

Kane's reaction to her announcement was not what she expected or hoped for. His expression didn't alter.

Casually, he reached into an inner pocket of his coat and extracted a blunt cigar. He carefully severed the tip against the red, wet edge of the sword blade. Placing the end of the cigar in his mouth, he set it afire with a simple flint-and-steel lighter that looked very old. He began smoking with a preoccupied intensity.

Tanvirah didn't care for the odor of tobacco, but the smoke at least softened the harsh stink of charred goblin flesh. She demanded, "Sir, did you hear me?"

Kane rolled the cigar from one corner of his mouth to the other. He squinted at her with one pale blue eye. "It's my eyes that are going bad, not my ears. I should've guessed you were some relation to Lakesh. You have his nose."

Her face tightened as he added, "And your mother's height and figure. How is Erica nowadays?"

Tanvirah checked the self-conscious impulse to cross her arms over her breasts. She was used to being ogled. "She's probably the same as the last time you saw her."

Kane grinned, removed the cigar from his mouth and blew a wreath of gray smoke toward the sky. "I doubt it. The last time I saw her, she was about seven months pregnant. With you, I presume."

"If it was twenty-three years or so ago," Tanvirah replied waspishly, "then you presume correctly. Sir."

On impulse, Tanvirah ran a hand over her hip, making sure the Uma stone was still safe in its pocket. Kane caught the movement and his eyes narrowed. "Lose something?"

Tanvirah shook her head. "No."

When she declined to elaborate, Kane hesitated a moment then asked, "What did she tell you about me?"

"Not a thing. She didn't need to. Everybody knows about the great General Kane. You're a legend. You fought in every major engagement in the Consolidation War and probably a few minor ones nobody ever heard of. You destroyed the Scorpia Prime and the Nirodha movement. Then you turned down an authority position offered by the imperator himself, to live alone up here like the old man of the mountains."

Tanvirah paused, then said quietly, "And according to my father, you've been conducting illegal temporal-fault-line experiments, too."

"Ah," Kane said, nodding in satisfaction. "So that's why he sent you up here—he thinks I'm getting too close to finding a resolution."

"No, sir," she retorted. "He sent me to bring something very valuable back from Cerberus."

Kane's eyes narrowed in sudden suspicion. "There's nothing in there your father wants. The place was cleaned out of anything of value long before you were born."

Tanvirah drew in a long breath. "Except for one thing, sir. You."

Chapter 3

Before Kane could formulate even a banal response, Tanvirah's face suddenly twisted and she turned away from him. She walked about four steps before she dropped to her hands and knees and vomited. Or tried to, dry-heaving convulsively and painfully as her belly strove to empty itself. Nothing was ejected but strings of bile-laced saliva.

Kane watched her, not surprised by the delayed reaction to the violent events of the past few minutes—or the ordeal she had obviously suffered on the way to the mountain pass. He had already figured out that she was the only survivor of a larger party, since not even Lakesh would dispatch his daughter on a lone mission into the Outlands.

After a minute or two, the shudders that racked her frame stopped, but she didn't stand. She remained on all fours, hanging her head, her hair screening her face. Kane sheathed his *katana* and went to her side, helping her to her feet. "Can you walk or should I carry you?"

Tanvirah laboriously raised her head, raking her hair out of her eyes. "To where? Are we that close to the redoubt?" Her voice was hoarse and weak.

He nodded in the direction of the mountain peak.

"We won't make it before nightfall, but there's a cave up there. I use it as a hunter's blind. I have food and water."

She swayed, leaning gratefully against him, her left breast against his arm. Kane could feel her heart pumping hard and fast. She murmured, "Thank you, General."

He started to correct her, but decided it wasn't worth the effort. He didn't bother retrieving the pulse-plasma rifle from the ledge. It was worthless now, since he had no power packs left for it.

As they walked up the road, Tanvirah feebly gestured to the corpses behind them. "What about their bodies?"

Kane lifted a shoulder in an indifferent shrug. "There are plenty of animals around here that don't mind the taste of Pischaca flesh—raw or overcooked."

Tanvirah clapped a hand over her mouth as if she feared she was about to throw up again. Kane paused, but she managed to get control of herself. After a few moments of deep breathing, she felt confident enough to walk on her own. She tilted her head back, looking at the forbidding array of serrated black crags, broken black rock and cliffs towering ahead of them. The narrow road looped up through the slopes, wending its way around basalt bastions and granite pillars.

Squinting against the great bright furnace of sunset gold burning the sky, Tanvirah said, "So these are the Darks. They don't seem so dark to me."

Kane didn't explain to her how nearly two centuries

earlier, the few people who lived in the region held the Bitterroot Range—colloquially known as the Darks—in superstitious regard. Due to their mysteriously shadowed forests and deep, dangerous ravines, a sinister body of myths had grown up around the Darks.

The enduring legends about evil spirits lurking in the mountain passes to devour body and soul were a form of protective coloration that every exile in the Cerberus redoubt went to great pains to maintain. Of course, nobody cared one way or another any longer about the superstitions. The nearest neighbors of the installation, Sky Dog's band of Sioux and Cheyenne, were long gone.

"Tell me how you got here," he suggested.

Tanvirah tossed her black hair back over her shoulders, curtly explaining about the Sandcat journey from High River and the successful ambush staged by the Pischacas, despite the well-armed Magistrates.

Kane listened without comment, recalling how the Pischacas' favorite tactic was the ambush, usually sprung in mountainous areas. He retained vivid memories of an ambush in the Sierra Madres—only then he had been commanding a combined troop of imperial soldiers and Pischacas. An entire division of baronial infantry had been wiped out in minutes.

About five years after that incident, the Western Pischacas who had survived the Consolidation War turned to outlawry and began preying on their former masters. Kane had led a squadron of troops to clean out a particularly vicious Pischaca clan bolt-holed in the Black Hills.

Kane had lured the Pischacas out by allowing them to rout a small group of troopers who acted as stalking horses. When they pursued the soldiers through a canyon, they found themselves facing not a disorganized and demoralized party, but rather a contingent of disciplined troops who had lain hidden, waiting for the goblin-men to leave the rocky ramparts and stage a frontal assault.

The Pischacas had never truly functioned as soldiers even during the war, but as guerrillas, ruthless hit-and-run bushwhackers. So when they realized they had been duped, they broke and ran. Very few of them escaped alive that day, nor were any prisoners taken.

Kane didn't feel any pride at the memory of the battle, since it had been primarily a slaughter—genocide pure and simple against sentient creatures who had been created solely to mete out death and destruction to baronial forces. Once their purpose was served, they were hunted into extinction.

Just as full night fell over the road, the two people reached the cave. It wasn't deep or particularly spacious, not much more than a cavity punched into the stone bulwark of the mountain, but it afforded some protection from the chill wind. The walls were decorated with faded, crude paintings and petroglyphs, representations of bizarre figures and shapes.

Kane lit a small campfire with wood stacked against one wall. From a rucksack he took out a blanket, which Tanvirah draped over her shoulders, a self-heat MRE package and a bottle of distilled water. She dampened a cloth with the water and dabbed at the dried blood on her face, then rinsed out her mouth and spit toward the cave opening.

With his back to her, Kane tended his wound with the contents of a small first-aid kit. The bleeding had stopped some time before, but his shirt was stiff with dried blood. He set his teeth on a groan as he poured antiseptic into the cut and then bandaged it as best he could with a field dressing saturated with antibiotic gel.

The ration package contained chicken à la king that had the flavor and texture of wallpaper paste. From previous experiences, Kane knew it was a pretty poor substitute for a meal, particularly after what the girl had experienced. But Tanvirah ate the bland food without complaint or any sign she even tasted it. They sat on opposite sides of the fire and ate in silence for a minute. Kane couldn't help but be impressed by the girl's proud, fearless demeanor.

Glancing around the rock walls of the cave, Tanvirah said, ''A hunter's blind, you said. What game do you hunt?''

Kane's reply was uninflected. ''Not animals.''

''Mutants?''

''The Pischacas aren't mutants.''

Tanvirah nodded as if she understood completely. Kane assumed Lakesh had raised her to believe that the mutie species that had once roamed the length and breadth of the postnuke world was less the accidental by-product of radiation and environmental changes than the deliberate practice of pantropic science—a form of genetic engineering devoted to creating life-forms able to survive and thrive in the postnuke world.

But genuine muties hadn't been much of a threat for a very long time. The animal mutations hadn't lived long. Many species were extinct, and had been even before the first mushroom cloud had billowed up from embassy row in Washington, D.C., more than two centuries earlier.

The few animals that survived the freezing temperatures of skydark had mutated into grotesque imitations of their progenitors. The first two or three generations of mutant animals had run toward polyploidism, a doubling or tripling of the chromosome complement. Their increased size greatly reduced their lifespans; only a few of the giant varieties survived more than three or four generations.

"Do you have a lot of problems with the Pischacas?" she asked.

Kane shrugged. "Ever since the end of the war, they've been drifting down north from the reservations. First they came in small scouting parties and kept away from the settlements. They usually went back. Then some of them stayed."

"I didn't think they could reproduce," Tanvirah commented. "There was only supposed to be one generation of the ghastly things."

Kane smiled dourly. "Yeah, so your old man said.

But me and a lot of other people told him that nature always finds a way. But he had the blessing of the imperator and so…'' His words trailed off.

Tanvirah's face locked in a hard mask. "My father will be enraged when he hears how the Pischacas attacked us. He'll want to find their main settlement.''

Kane chuckled, but it sounded forced. "I wish him luck.'' Then he scowled and demanded, "Why did Lakesh send you overland to bring me back?''

"Because you altered the transit-feed harmonics of the Cerberus gateway,'' Tanvirah answered stiffly. "Otherwise I would have gated in normally.''

Kane rolled his eyes in weary exasperation. "Oh, please. Lakesh invented the damn things. Everything I know about the units I learned from him or Bry…who also learned from him. He could have figured out the right phase modulations and transported you to the redoubt. Or circumvented it altogether with the interphaser.''

Tanvirah nodded. "True enough,'' she admitted. "He was afraid you'd kill anybody who gated in unannounced—particularly him.''

"So he told you how I feel about him?''

Tanvirah took another mouthful of food and chewed it slowly and thoughtfully. She washed it down with a swig of water and said quietly, "He said you hated him, sir. That you blamed him for the death of a woman.''

Kane's pale eyes brooded on the dancing flames. "That's not quite accurate.''

She looked at him quizzically, hopefully. "No?"

"No. I blame him for the deaths of *several* women…and men, too."

Anger flashed briefly in Tanvirah's dark eyes. "It was war, wasn't it? Causalities were inevitable."

Kane's lips quirked in a humorless smile. "Coming from someone who probably never even saw a dead body until today, that's quite the piece of arrogant presumption." He stopped smiling. "Lakesh saw to the creation of the Pischacas so they would die in greater numbers than human beings during the war. Instead, they ended up killing more of our own people after the war was won."

"He said you blamed him for that, too."

"That and many other things."

Tanvirah lifted her chin haughtily. "He also said you never respected him or my mother…or their decision to marry."

Kane looked at her, admiring the way the firelight sculpted her features. The manner in which she held her head was familiar. A memory ghosted through his mind—of lying in a tangled bedspread, his lips trailing across the sweat-damp neck of Erica van Sloan.

Tanvirah went on. "My father said you were embittered because your own true love went to her grave after spending only a short time with you. You were jealous of him and my mother, that they had a child and you did not."

Kane didn't answer. The issue of Tanvirah's parentage wasn't one he was ready to address. Even a quarter of a century after the fact, he still felt betrayed by Lakesh's machinations and his temper rose. It rose so high that it took all of his self-restraint to keep from turning Tanvirah over his knee and sending her back to Cobaltville—High River, he automatically corrected himself—with the imprints of his hand on her backside.

He knew a good deal of the anger should have rightly been directed at himself for not stopping Lakesh from turning traitor, when he first deserted Cerberus to join Sam the imperator. Of course, in strict terms, Lakesh hadn't deserted Cerberus or him. It wasn't as if he had turned his back on a glorious cause, after all.

But then, none of the work of Cerberus could be defined as glorious. It had been brutal, bloody and soul wearying, from the first foray against the barons until their final defeat. There were no fanfares, no victory parades, no medals for the lives he and the people there had led first as exiles, then as insurrectionists and finally as soldiers.

Kane had lost count of the people he had killed during those years, but he remembered those who had displayed admirable courage, particularly his allies in the war against the barons. In some instances, he had even admired the ideals of his enemies. More than once, he had found his sympathies lying primarily with his adversaries.

He never blamed the outlanders or the Roamers for fighting against the forces of the imperator. Had he been them, he would have fought just as hard. But he was pledged to end the reign of the nine barons, and the only way to do that was to make their Outland territories useless as either refuges or staging grounds.

He shook his head to drive the memories back into the cobwebbed corners of his mind. "You still didn't answer my question. Why did Lakesh send you here?"

Tanvirah smiled wanly. "To bring a final peace. So you can be the hero again, sir."

Kane stared at her, surprised into speechlessness for a long moment. At length, he repeated incredulously, "'Final peace'? I thought that's what the world, the new adaptive Earth has been wallowing in for these past twenty-odd years. Seems to me your old man and the imperator himself accused me of trying to plunge the world back into war. That's why I was exiled."

Tanvirah's shoulders stiffened. "Your exile was your own, sir."

He waved away her words. "That's immaterial."

"You objected to the formation of the Consolidated Confederation of States." A note of accusation edged her voice. "You claimed the imperator was corrupt and the CCS was maintained by naked power and coercion."

"I objected to a form of government that answered to a single authority," Kane replied matter-of-factly. "At best, the CCS is a monarchy. At worst it's a dictatorship."

"The imperator brought peace," Tanvirah said doggedly. "He ended the tyranny of the nine barons. You fought with him to attain that goal. Why couldn't you accept those victories and live within the new structure?''

"Because I wasn't a fool," Kane shot back.

"Like my father, my mother were fools—like all of your friends and allies? Fools like them?''

Kane sighed, trying to keep his mounting anger in check. He ran both hands through his hair. "They were fools because they confused what they *wanted* to be true with what *was* true.''

"And that is?'' she asked curtly.

Quietly, calmly, he said, "The real history of our world, instead of the fake one, arranged over two hundred years ago. That truth.''

Tanvirah tossed aside the empty MRE pack. "Who are you," she asked grimly, "to decide what is our real history, what is not real? Why do you fancy yourself as the final arbiter of the real from the unreal?''

Kane looked into Tanvirah's face and cast his mind back over the history he knew. He could easily imagine Lakesh taking her outdoors when twilight ended a day and pointing toward the buildings of the High River and the land beyond and saying, "Look yonder, daughter. The world is finally ours again. We fought long and hard for it, spilled and shed much blood. Many good people died to regain our planet. The old ways of living by violence, by talon and fang, are past. To stop those ways from returning, you must keep the faith and never question the how and why.''

And Lakesh, ever the scholar, ever the historian,

ever the pedant, would have probably told the young and wide-eyed Tanvirah how, more than two centuries before, increasingly hostile relations between the United States and the Soviet Union culminated in an all-out nuclear war.

No one knew who had won or lost the war, because no government statisticians remained to conduct body counts. Conservative estimates calculated that more than two-thirds of Earth's population perished during those first two hours and forty-five minutes. Since, by then, the entire planet was a smoldering cinder, there was no sure way of differentiating between the victors and the vanquished.

Sometime late that afternoon, nuclear winter—or skydark—began. Massive quantities of pulverized rubble had been propelled into the atmosphere, clogging the sky for a generation, blanketing all of Earth in a thick cloud of radioactive dust, ash, debris and fallout. After nearly thirty years of endless nights, of freezing temperatures even in subtropical climates, of fallout storms, well over another million people had perished.

When the survivors and the children born after the nukecaust climbed out of their shelters, their bunkers, their caves, they knew only one dream—to survive.

The old cultures were gone, burned down to their foundations. New societies were formed, with their own laws, their own rules, their own beliefs and even their own dialects.

These only dimly reflected the changes of the planet itself. Most of North America was known as the

Deathlands, an aptly named home to mutated forms of animal, vegetable and human life, radioactive hot spots, marauders and scattered settlements of people trying to scratch out an existence in a hostile environment. Human culture in the seething hellpits of the Deathlands existed at its lowest level since the Dark Ages.

Shortly after the worst of the skydark was over, some descendants of the original survivors decided they had outlasted the aftermath of global devastation for a reason. These families knew people would revert to primitive levels, so they determined to force some sort of order on barbarism. They were better educated, better bred and better armed than almost anyone else who shambled across the Deathlands. The families became ruling hierarchies, and they spread out across the ruined face of America.

The territories they conquered became baronies. At first, people retreated into the villes ruled by the barons for protection, then as the decades went by, they remained because they had no choice. Generations of Americans were born into serfdom, slaves in everything but name.

Many of the most powerful, most enduring baronies evolved into city-states, walled fortresses whose influence stretched across what became known as the Outlands for hundreds of miles.

In decades past, the barons had warred against one another, each struggling for control and absolute power over his or her territory. Then the barons realized that greater rewards were possible if unity was achieved, in common purpose and organization.

Territories were redefined, treaties struck among the barons, and the city-states became interconnected points in a continent-spanning network. A Program of Unification was ratified and ruthlessly deployed. The reconstructed form of government was still basically despotic, but now it was institutionalized and shared by all the former independent baronies.

Nine baronies survived the long wars over territorial expansion and resources. Control of the continent was divided among nine barons. The pretenders, those who weren't part of the original hierarchy but who arrogantly assumed the title to carve out their own little pieces of empire, were overrun, exterminated and their territories absorbed. The hierarchical ruling system remained, and the city-states adopted the name of the ruling baron.

Technology, most of it based on predark designs, appeared mysteriously and simultaneously with the beginning of the reunification program. There was much speculation at the time that many previously unknown Continuity of Government Stockpiles were opened up and their contents distributed evenly among the barons. Though the technologies were restricted for the use of those who held the reins of power, life overall improved for the citizens in and around the villes. Manufacturing industries, totally under the control of the villes, began again.

What was left of human history belonged to the

Outlands, the baronies and, by proxy, the Archon Directorate.

That was the history Kane knew, the history Lakesh had told him. He had implied that agents of the Archons had been the true architects of much of that history, pulling the strings to trigger coups, assassinations, natural disasters, wars and the overall destabilization of the entire world.

That was the history he knew, but Kane found fault lines within it. In fact, he found so many fault lines, he had devoted the remainder of his life to tracing them down, to finding where they led, to following them to the fracture points, regardless of the consequences.

It wasn't as if he could not recognize the inevitables of life. He was too used to them—deprivation, hardship, loneliness, the emptiness of dreams, the death of hope. He had accepted many inevitables in his life, but the one thing he had never resigned himself to was surrender, not when even the most remote possibility of a victory remained.

There was only one possibility of reversing defeat, and he explored it. If the inevitability of history could be altered, even slightly, then his future—humanity's future—could be changed.

Kane allowed a slow, taunting smile to play over his lips. "That's really why you're here, isn't it, Tanvirah? Lakesh is afraid I've finally found the main temporal fault line, and in that case, I *am* the man who can make the determination between real history and that which the imperator helped to manufacture."

Chapter 4

When Tanvirah awoke the next morning, she was alone in the cave. The fire had burned to cold ashes sometime during the night, but she slept warmly in the insulated sleeping bag Kane had given her.

Smothering a yawn, she folded back the top layer of the sleeping bag and got up, wincing at the aches and pains in various parts of her body. She averted her eyes from the raw red welts encircling her wrists. They were very tender and twinged with each movement.

She found a water bottle and rinsed out her mouth, spitting as discreetly as she could into the ashes of the campfire. Her lips were swollen, but the cuts didn't seem deep. They had already scabbed, but inasmuch as she doubted she would be kissing anyone soon, she wasn't concerned.

It was Tanvirah's custom to sleep naked, but she hadn't removed her torn bodysuit, since she didn't want to bare herself before Kane. She had expected to be brutally raped and then murdered by the Pischaca warriors who had seized her; she didn't want to tempt the man who had saved her life, regardless of his reputation for being honorable. She had no idea how long

Kane had lived in the mountains alone and presumably celibate. She knew he had incurred a wound in the fight with the Pischacas, but she wasn't sure if it was painful enough to overwhelm any amorous energy her presence might stimulate.

She wasn't a virgin—no priestess of the Shakti sisterhood could be, particularly when the Sati rites were practiced—but she didn't find Kane attractive. She preferred young men with fair coloring, who treated her with the deference due a daughter of an authority. Kane reminded her of a grim, gray timber wolf, always stalking in search of prey. Her father had said Kane's Lakota name was Unktomi Shunkaha, which meant Trickster Wolf. His manner was certainly as dark and harsh as that of a grizzled old wolf.

Thinking of Kane made Tanvirah wonder where he was. He wasn't in the cave, and for a moment she experienced a surge of fear that he had gone on to Cerberus and left her on her own.

She found him sitting outside the cave in the dew-wet grass, picking through the items the Pischacas had stolen from the Magistrates. She realized he had risen early and gone down into the morning mists to salvage what he could from the scene of the battle with the Pischacas.

"Good morning," she said, shivering a little in the postdawn chill.

He grunted and examined a Spectre side arm, checking the action. He didn't turn toward her or rise.

"If you're hungry, there are more ration packs in the cave."

Tanvirah thought about the taste of the MRE of the night before and decided to pass, at least for a while.

He uttered a wordless noise of disgust and tossed the weapon aside. "The firing pin is broken."

Kane picked up another pistol and began examining it, popping the ammo clip from the magazine. It contained several rounds, and with a murmured "Ah" of approval, he slid it back home.

"You don't really need that, do you?" Tanvirah asked, not particularly interested but trying to make conversation.

Studying another firearm, Kane answered distractedly, "Your old man cleaned out the Cerberus armory at the beginning of the war. The only weapons there now are the ones I salvaged from various battlefields."

Before she could stop herself, she said curtly, "In clear violation of the law. Like the plasma rifle from the Moon base. Sir."

He swiveled his head toward her, regarding her with an eyebrow arched at a challenging angle. "Just how much do you know about what went on in Cerberus?"

She started to shrug, then realized the gesture would expose more cleavage than she cared to under the circumstances and instead crossed her arms over her breasts. "I've been helping Dad with his memoirs. I've just about finished transcribing the first couple of years' worth of his exploits."

"*His* exploits?"

Tanvirah nodded. "Of course. It's a historical record, so we're very accurate."

Kane opened his mouth as if to reply, then shook his head in disgust and returned his attention to the Spectre. Tanvirah hesitated, then began "General—"

"Just plain old Kane," he broke in.

She nodded. "Sir—"

"You can drop that, too."

"All right," she snapped, louder and more impatiently than she intended. "Will you go with me to High River? We can gate there from Cerberus."

"I can't spare the time." He smiled sourly when he said it.

Tanvirah sighed wearily. "You don't trust me or don't trust my father?"

"I don't know you well enough to make a decision about your trustworthiness one way or the other. But I don't trust Lakesh or your mother. And even if I did, you haven't given me a sound reason to gate to New Edo, much less to High River."

Tanvirah smoothed her hair with nervous gestures of both hands. "It's complicated."

"Then—as your old man liked to say when he *was* an old man—bottom line it for me."

Tanvirah frowned. "Bottom line—the Nirodha conspiracy, which arose following the war, appears to have been the tip of the iceberg. The entire governmental structure might be compromised by a cabal of fanatics. Traitors who will stop at nothing to prevent humanity from achieving a secure and peaceful future.''

Although Kane's expression didn't otherwise alter, she saw his hand instinctively reach up to touch the scar on his face. She felt encouraged by his reaction and went on, ''You remember them, of course.''

Kane nodded. In a faraway voice, he said, ''*Nirodha* is a Sanskrit term meaning complete destruction or the utter cessation of existence. Nihilism in its purest form...nothing from nothing and into nothing.''

His thoughts flew back to what he remembered of the Nirodha movement, if it could be called that. The roots of the organization took seed in India during the Consolidation War. The loose affiliation of fanatics had emerged fifteen hundred years earlier from the steamy jungles of India to loot and pillage everything from settlements to merchant ships. Its members adhered to the cataclysmic teachings of a thirteenth-century prophet known as Scorpia Prime.

Its most public incarnation had been in late-twentieth-century Japan, surfacing as a doomsday cult known as the Aum Shinrikyo. That particular version was a heavily financed movement that infiltrated almost every aspect of Japanese life. Its followers were rumored to have been intimately involved in the development of doomsday weapons to hasten Armageddon. The nuclear holocaust of 2001 was a fulfillment of their prophecy, but it hadn't gone far enough, since humanity as a species survived.

In the two centuries following the nukecaust, the

cult slowly revived. The movement regained its former strength during the chaos and carnage of the Consolidation War. It fell under the control of a female Sikh militarist who took the title of Scorpia Prime. No one knew where the title originated other than the obvious fact the name translated as Royal Scorpion or Scorpion Queen.

By the conclusion of the war, the Nirodha had managed to insert its pincers into virtually every city-state on Earth. It was single-mindedly devoted to achieving one goal—the attainment of perfection by the annihilation of humanity, both old and new.

To meet this new threat, the imperial army didn't disband, but acted as a bulwark both against the menace of the Pischaca and the Nirodha movement. In the early stages of the struggle, Scorpia Prime's role was a covert one.

Kane had suspected for years there was not a single Scorpia Prime, but several people who played the part. More than one Scorpia Prime was reported killed. As one of their last acts as partners, he and Grant had blown up the armory and munitions dump of the movement's centralized headquarters, obliterating their stronghold in Assam. Both men had fervently hoped they had annihilated the movement itself.

As if sensing his thoughts, Tanvirah said, "The Nirodha acted on that philosophy by believing humankind was fundamentally evil, base, worthless and deserving only of destruction."

"Yeah." A hint of anger tinged Kane's voice as he

turned to look at her. "They learned the underpinnings of that philosophy from the barons."

Tanvirah didn't dispute him. An important part of the Program of Unification of a century earlier was that humanity was far too primitive and irresponsible to govern itself. The ville bred had been taught from birth if they made themselves helpless, believed themselves to be miserable sinners, then the barons would shower them with rewards. Of course, the people didn't have the ability to evaluate anything outside of their limited fields of experience. The barons and the laws they espoused saw to that.

"It was a philosophy you helped enforce," Tanvirah gently reminded him.

Kane's eyes narrowed. "I tend to have a vague recollection of that."

Tanvirah felt a surge of anger at his sarcasm. "The Nirodha have embarked on a series of terrorist acts over the last year, each one more destructive and violent than the one preceding it."

"That was always their pattern."

She nodded grimly. "Yes. Back then they were building to an act of final destruction, but you stopped them by killing Scorpia Prime."

"Then stop them again," he said coldly. "Me and Grant showed you how the first time. Track them down and burn them out."

"True enough. But the tactics that worked over twenty years ago won't be effective now."

"Why not?" he demanded.

"The Nirodha learned from their first defeat," she declared calmly. "They aren't attacking from without. They don't really exist as a centralized movement any longer, either. Pockets of believers survived on every continent. They've already invaded the body politic of the CCS like a virus. In every city, high places and low, there are people who seem to work for the furtherance and advancement of humanity, but who in fact have sworn allegiance to only one belief—the Nirodha.

"They lead double lives, whether they're administrators or simple farmers. Their rank in our world doesn't coincide with their standing among the Nirodha. A street cleaner in High River could be the Scorpia Prime. A cabinet minister in New London could be no more than a clerk among the Nirodha. But all they care about is the Tandava, the Dance of Shiva, the destruction of all creation. As Shiva dances, he brings about the time of Praloya, the destruction of the universe. Everything disintegrates into nothingness...even the ego is consumed and everyone is rendered pure and without spiritual blemish. That is the philosophy of the Nirodha."

Kane nodded impatiently throughout Tanvirah's melodramatic dissertation. "You not only inherited Lakesh's nose, but you also got his flair for the theatric. I know they're willing to wipe out humanity. As I recall, the barons were willing to wipe us out, too, if they lost. That still doesn't tell me why I should go with you."

Tanvirah nodded, closing her eyes briefly as if wearied by the talk. "Would you not agree that one reason the Nirodha were relatively easy to defeat was they were technologically outmatched by the forces of the imperator?"

Kane's mobile mouth curved in a patronizing smile. "Define 'relatively easy.'"

Tanvirah shrugged. "Losses weren't as high—"

She caught herself when she saw Kane's smile disappear. Softly, she said, "I apologize."

"Get to the goddamn point, if there is one." His voice was pitched to little more than a growl.

"The point," Tanvirah declared, "is that the Nirodha are no longer technologically inferior. They've found a way to destroy the future of humankind."

"How?" Kane demanded.

"By the same method you've been studying to change it. Temporal manipulation."

Kane stared at her blankly, bleakly, for a long moment, then rose swiftly to his feet. "Bullshit," he grated between clenched teeth.

She remained seated, regarding him calmly. "I am afraid it is not."

"There's only once place on Earth where functional Operation Chronos tech can be found," he declared. "And nobody has touched it in the last twenty-seven years but me."

"I didn't say anything about Operation Chronos. There are other methods by which to tamper with time, as you are aware."

Kane didn't reply, but he knew the girl spoke the truth. Operation Chronos, a major subdivision of the twentieth century's Totality Concept, had been devoted to manipulating the nature of time, building on the hyperdimensional transit breakthroughs of Project Cerberus. During development of the mat-trans gateways, the Cerberus researchers observed a number of side effects. On occasion, traversing the quantum pathways resulted in minor temporal anomalies, such as arriving at a destination three seconds before the jump initiator was actually engaged.

Lakesh found that time couldn't be measured or accurately perceived in the quantum stream. Hypothetically, constant jumpers might find themselves physically rejuvenated, with the toll of time erased if enough "backward time" was accumulated in their metabolisms. Conversely, jumpers might find themselves prematurely aged if the quantum stream pushed them further into the future with each journey. By studying these temporal anomalies, Operation Chronos found its starting point, using the gateway technology, to develop time travel.

"Are you telling me the Nirodha have found a new way to travel through time?" he demanded.

Tanvirah slowly rose, wincing at the stiffness in her limbs. "That is my father and mother's fear...not to mention that of the Consolidated Council. But it's not exactly new."

"How can that be?" Kane's tone was challenging, commanding.

"I'm not a physicist like my parents," Tanvirah answered, "but I know enough of the bare bones to grasp basic principles. According to Einstein's theory of gravity, anything that has mass or energy distorts the dimensions of space and the passage of time around it, like a bowling ball dropped on a trampoline. By circulating laser beams in the right way, by slowing them down and shooting them through anything from fiber-optic cable to special crystals, they might create a similar distortion that could theoretically transport someone through the quantum field to different times."

Kane eyed her skeptically. "I've read about that theory. It's very old. As far as I know, it was never tested."

"My mother claims that early Operation Chronos efforts explored a number of different methods. She was attached to Overproject Whisper. She herself created a chronon-energy manipulator—the Sloan Spatiotemporal Dissociator. You might have heard of it in your researches."

Kane knew of it, but didn't reply. Overproject Whisper was an umbrella division of the Totality Concept, and one of its subdivisions was Operation Chronos, along with Project Cerberus and a few others.

Tanvirah continued, "She said that a device was built to test whether it was possible to transport a subatomic particle, like a neutron, through time. The energy from a rotating laser beam warped the space inside the ring of the light so that gravity forced the neutron to rotate sideways. With even more energy, it was believed possible for a second neutron to appear. The second particle would be the first one visiting itself from the future."

"Did it work?" Kane asked.

"Apparently," replied Tanvirah.

"Then why was Operation Chronos not successful until Project Cerberus made its first breakthroughs?"

She smiled wanly. "Sending anything larger than a subatomic particle through time required more energy than physicists back then knew how to tap into or harness. However, if it was possible to use light to send a neutron through time, a feat that doesn't require as much energy as sending a human, it wouldn't have been long before engineers figured out a way to send a person."

"Except," Kane interjected, "your old man's discoveries made it unnecessary."

She nodded. "Pretty much, yes. But if the Nirodha employ this method to find the same temporal fault lines as you claim you have, they will try to fracture them…not repair them." She paused and regarded him with suspicion. "At least, we were assuming you wanted to repair them."

Kane turned toward the cave. "That was the general idea. Let's get ready to move out. It's about a three-hour hike to Cerberus. I hope you're in as good a shape as you appear to be…it's uphill all the way."

Tanvirah repressed a smile and a sigh of relief.

Kane hadn't made any promises, but now she detected a softening of his attitude. She had feared he might be so embittered that once he learned of her parentage he would send her back down the mountain to find her own way to return to High River. At the very least she could now gate back home.

Under the circumstances, she figured it something of a victory. And with a distant sense of dismay, she realized she didn't find Kane quite so unappealing as before.

Chapter 5

Tanvirah stumbled to a halt. She swept her eyes from left to right and in a tone of awe mingled with horror, she husked out hoarsely, "Almighty God."

Kane stood beside her, his long coat slung carelessly over a shoulder, his *katana* sheathed at his back. The long walk had opened up his wound, and the right side of his khaki shirt was soaked through with blood. He impatiently brushed away a few flies buzzing around it. He didn't so much as glance at Tanvirah when he said, "If it's any consolation, it *is* a lot worse than it looks. But you should've seen it before I cleaned it up."

He started walking again, onto the plateau. On the far side, a mountain peak lifted gray stone crags and broken turrets to the blue midmorning Montana sky. After a moment of gazing around with wide, shocked eyes, Tanvirah hurried to catch up to the man as he strode purposefully toward the Cerberus redoubt.

On the far side of the plateau, the broad tarmac tumbled into an abyss. The precipice dropped a thousand feet to a riverbed. The ragged remnants of a chain-link fence ran around the plateau. At one time, steel guardrails had bordered the rim, but only a few rusted metal stanchions remained.

Very little of the original outside structure remained. Craters a yard wide and nearly twice that deep pocked the surface of the tarmac. Chunks of asphalt, metal and other less identifiable objects were scattered around.

The gutted shell of a Manta transatmospheric ship was pushed up against the rocky abutment at the base of the peak. Although the hull was overgrown with tangled vines, the burned out wreckage of a Deathbird could be identified enfolded within the Manta's extended alloyed wings. The rust-edged rotor vanes thrust up at thirty-degree angles, giving the entire mass the look of a black windmill sinking into a quagmire.

Her eyes following the line of the slope, she saw triple rows of headstones and grave markers projecting up from the grassy covering. The markers bore only last names, and Tanvirah could make only a few of them out—Farrell, Falk, Wegmann, DeFore. The others were obscured by high grasses and discoloration.

A broad-axled SPIDE assault vehicle lay on its left side a few yards away, completely burned out. As they strode past it, Tanvirah stooped to peer through the cracked, soot-black windshield. The charred skeleton of a human being lay within, the exposure to searing heat contorting him into a fetal position. His armor had melted down to slag and permanently welded him to the inner hull. She repressed a shudder.

Kane commented mildly, ''It took me twenty years

just to get to this point of cleanup. I'll get around to separating that poor bastard from his wag one of these days."

Kane and Tanvirah crossed the plateau to the massive vanadium alloy sec door recessed into the peak. It opened like an accordion, one six-inch-thick panel folding over another. It stood partially ajar, as it had for the past twenty-seven years, ever since the opening battle of the Consolidation War had irreparably damaged the controls.

When Cerberus was built in the late twentieth century, the plateau had been protected by a force field, powered by atomic generators. Sometime during the century following skydark, the energy screen had been permanently deactivated, so Lakesh saw to the installation of new defenses. Although they couldn't be noticed from the road, an elaborate system of heat-sensing warning devices, night-vision vid cameras and motion-trigger alarms surrounded the mountain peak.

Planted within rocky clefts of the mountain peak and concealed by camouflage netting were uplinks with an orbiting Vela-class reconnaissance satellite and a Comsat. For several years, Lakesh safely assumed that no one or nothing could approach Cerberus undetected by land or by air. But when his assumption was proved incorrect, it was proved wrong in a very big way.

Kane paused at the sec door, fishing around in his coat pocket and removing a flashlight. To Tanvirah, he said, "I never did get the lights back on in this section. So watch your step."

He stepped over the threshold, the white-yellow rod of incandescence piercing the darkness. Tanvirah followed closely. Kane noticed she seemed too shocked to speak, even though he was sure her father had told her about what befell Cerberus and most of its personnel on the day the combined forces of Barons Cobalt, Samarium, Thulia and Mande had all converged on the mountain plateau.

Constructed primarily of vanadium alloy, all design and construction specs had been aimed at making Project Cerberus an impenetrable community of at least a hundred people, although Lakesh had always preferred to think of the trilevel, thirty-acre facility as a sanctuary for exiles. The redoubt contained a well-equipped armory and two dozen self-contained apartments, a cafeteria, a decontamination center, a medical dispensary, a swimming pool and even detention cells on the bottom level. The facility also had a limestone filtration system that continually recycled the complex's water supply.

The Cerberus redoubt had weathered the nukecaust and skydark and all the subsequent earth changes. Its radiation shielding remained intact, and its nuclear generators provided an almost eternal source of power. At least they had done so until twenty-seven years before.

Painted on the wall just inside the entrance was a large, luridly colored illustration of a three-headed black hound. Fire and blood gushed between yellow fangs, and the crimson eyes glared bright and baleful. Underneath it, in ornate Gothic script was written Cerberus.

Kane recalled that when Brigid once asked about the artist, Lakesh opined that one of the original military personnel assigned to the redoubt had rendered the painting sometime prior to the nukecaust. Although he couldn't be positive, Lakesh figured Corporal Mooney was the artist, since its exaggerated exuberance seemed right out of the comic books he was obsessed with collecting.

Lakesh had never considered having it removed. For one thing, the paints were indelible, and for another, it was Corporal Mooney's form of immortality. Besides, the image of Cerberus, the guardian of the gates of Hell, represented a visual symbol of the work to which Lakesh had devoted his life. The three-headed hound was an appropriate totem for the installation that, for a handful of years, housed Project Cerberus, the primary subdivision of the Totality Concept's Overproject Whisper.

The researches to which Project Cerberus and its personnel had been devoted were locating and traveling hyperdimensional pathways through the quantum stream. Once that had been accomplished, the redoubt became a manufacturing facility. The quantum interphase mat-trans inducers, known colloquially as "gateways," were built in modular form and shipped to other redoubts.

On the few existing records, the Cerberus installation was listed as Redoubt Bravo, but the people who made the facility their home had never referred to it as such, even during the height of its power and influence following the immigration of colonists who had fled from Manitius base on the Moon. At that point in time, the Cerberus personnel included specialists in almost every field of human endeavor or science—physics, electronics, medicine and even astronomy.

Tanvirah reached out and tentatively touched the illustration of the three-headed hound. She murmured, "The Trimurti."

Kane squinted toward her. "The what?"

"The Trimurti," she replied. "In Hindu myth it means the trinity. The combined essence of divinity."

Her finger touched the snarling heads one at a time, and she intoned, "Brahma, the Creator. Vishnu, the Preserver and Shiva, the Destroyer. One body with the heads of three gods. Alone they could do nothing, but together they were all-powerful."

Kane nodded. "One created, one preserved and one destroyed the work of the others. Pretty much a symbol of what went on here."

Her eyes flashed with dark anger. "It's the doctrine of unity."

"Yeah," he drawled with unmistakable sarcasm. "I've had a little experience with it before."

Tanvirah sighed in weary exasperation. "Dad told me you tended to oversimplify things."

"I had something of a reputation for that," Kane said agreeably.

"He also told me it was a pose...that you enjoyed pretending you weren't as intelligent as you really were. You did it to piss him off."

Kane smiled sourly. "It was hard to have fun in a place like this, but I tried."

"Don't try to have that kind of fun with me," she retorted sharply. "I've been forewarned."

Kane and Tanvirah moved carefully along the wide passageway beneath great curving ribs of metal that supported the high rock roof. Traversing the twenty-foot-wide corridor was slow work due to the tons of stone and twisted metal that had fallen from the ceiling and turned the passage into an obstacle course.

Kane could never walk down it without remembering the long-ago dawn when he was awakened by a series of loud explosions and rolling echoes. He recalled with unpleasant clarity how he ran out of his quarters wearing only beard stubble and into a choking cloud of dust and smoke that billowed in from the entrance.

The entire mountain peak shuddered with violent volcanic convulsions that shook loose avalanches of granite, concrete and steel support beams. Kane remembered trying to get to the operations center, when a boiling blizzard of dust and stone chips came down on him. He had turned and begun to run, but his lungs became clogged with grit.

Nearly blind, succumbing to a coughing fit, he dived

into the first open doorway and barely avoided being buried by the collapse of the ceiling. Domi had rendered him aid—

"Kane?"

Tanvirah's querulous voice brought him back to the present. He turned toward her. "What?"

"Do you really live here?" Judging by the tone of her voice, she found sad beyond words the concept that the place truly was his home.

Kane carefully considered his words before answering. Sometimes the sense of alienation, of isolation, was sleeping within him, and then he was reasonably content to be separated from the society of those who he barely believed were his fellows. But sometimes the ache of loneliness, of futility he saw in his future, was so acute it possessed him utterly. During those periods, he found the notion of walking off the edge of the plateau congenial.

Brusquely he said, "The rent is cheap enough."

He continued on. The scattering rubble became less dense the farther they walked. By the time they reached the entrance to the operations center, the floor was fairly clean of debris.

Kane fumbled for the light switch just inside the open door and thumbed it into the on position. Tanvirah wasn't able to bite back a gasp of dismay at what she saw. Naked light bulbs dangled from a crisscross network of wires and cords crudely affixed to the high ceiling. The vanadium alloy walls were smeared with scorch marks and perforated with bullet holes.

The two people stood at the open doorway of the central control complex, the command center, essentially the brain of the Cerberus installation. A long room with high, vaulted ceilings, the walls were lined by consoles of dials, switches and readout screens. A double row of computer stations formed an aisle, but no circuits clicked, no drive units hummed, nor did any indicator lights flash.

All the consoles had been blasted into twisted masses of metal, plastic and broken glass. Every piece of equipment had been shot, smashed and torn. There didn't appear to be a single intact microprocessor within any of the computer casings or chassis.

Through an open doorway at the far end of the center, in a separate antechamber, stood the redoubt's gateway unit. The brown armaglass walls atop the elevated emitter array housing gleamed dully. As the first fully debugged matter-transfer inducer built after the prototypes, it served as the basic template for all the others that followed.

Most of the gateways were located in Totality Concept redoubts, subterranean military complexes scattered over the face of America. Even during the height of the Totality Concept researches, only a handful of people knew the redoubts even existed, and only half a handful knew all their locations. The knowledge had been lost after the nukecaust, rediscovered a century later, then jealously, ruthlessly guarded. There were, however, gateway units in other countries—Russia, Mongolia, Tibet, England, South America.

But not all installations containing a gateway were connected to the Totality Concept. The gateways mass-produced as modular units were sent all over the world. Not even Lakesh knew how many were manufactured or to where they were shipped.

Kane bowed and made an elaborate "after you" gesture. "Find a seat, if you've a mind to, Miss Singh."

Not moving, Tanvirah seemed to have trouble speaking. When she did, her voice was a hoarse whisper, full of pain. "So this is where the Consolidation War, the final war, began."

Kane regarded her with a slit-eyed glare, but he didn't refute or rebuke her. In most ways, the important ways, she was right, even though her definition of "final war" was open to challenge.

It had been almost twenty-nine years since Sam, the so-called imperator, had first appeared and factionalized the nine barons—and, in the process brought a new order to the face of the world. The ancient Roman Empire was governed by a senate, but ruled by an emperor, sometimes known as an imperator. This person served as the final arbiter in matters pertaining to government. The baronies acted dependently, unified in name only. The arrival of the imperator changed all of that.

During a council of the barons in Front Royal, Baron Cobalt put forth the proposal to establish a central ruling consortium. In effect, the barons would become viceroys, plenipotentiaries in their own territories. They were accustomed to acting as the viceroys of the Archon Directorate, so the actual proposal didn't offend them.

Each of the fortress-cities with its individual, allegedly immortal god-king was supposed to be independent. Cooperation among the barons was grudging despite their shared goal of a unified world. They perceived humanity in general as either servants or as living storage vessels for transplanted organs and fresh genetic material.

The barons were less in favor of the Baron Cobalt's proposal than his intent to be recognized as the imperator. However, they really didn't have much of a choice—Cobalt had established a monopoly over the medical treatments the barons needed to reverse their autoimmune weaknesses and stay alive.

Because of those congenital metabolic deficiencies, the barons lived insulated, isolated lives. The theatrical trappings many of them adopted not only added to their semidivine mystique, but protected them from contamination, both psychological and physical.

Although all the hybrids were extremely long-lived, cellular and metabolic deterioration was part and parcel of what they were—hybrids of human and Archon DNA. Just like the caste system in place in the villes, the hybrids observed a similar one, although it had little to do with parentage. If the first phase of human evolution produced a package of adaptations for a particular and distinct way of life, the second phase was an effort to control that way of life by controlling the environment. The focus switched to cultural rather than physical evolution.

The hybrids, at least by their way of thinking, represented the final phase of human evolution. They created wholesale, planned alterations in living organisms and were empowered to control not only their environment, but also the evolution of other species. At the pinnacle of that evolutionary achievement were the barons.

When Baron Cobalt dangled the medical treatments before his fellow barons like a carrot on a stick rather than shared them freely, war was the inevitable result—particularly after Sam hijacked not only Cobalt's plan, but the title of imperator. A series of battles began, known as the Imperator Wars. The conflict was short-lived and ended with the siege of Cobaltville and the ousting of its baron. But peace didn't come with the imposition of imperial rule. To the contrary, it sparked dozens of smaller wars and a succession of plots and counterplots.

The Cerberus exiles weren't oblivious to these machinations occurring in the Outlands and in the villes, but they weren't particularly disturbed by them, either. Baron Cobalt, the only hybrid lord who bore Cerberus a personal grudge, was missing and presumed dead.

Sam, the imperator, was fixated on unification, as the barons were, but with a different objective. His stated intent was to end the tyranny of the barons and unify both hybrid and human and build a new Earth.

In the months following his appearance, the entire structure of the baronies changed. He made considerable inroads into toppling the old order and enfranchising his forces even though not all the barons supported him.

The general consensus among the Cerberus staff was that even the barons who withheld their support wouldn't undertake organized resistance against him. Even if all the baronies united against the imperator, it would require months to prepare any kind of military campaign and they had to do so in secret, else they would not have access to the medical treatments. For a short time, an uneasy peace prevailed.

However, Cobalt wasn't dead. No one really knew where he had been or why he hadn't died when his metabolic treatments were denied. But he had been setting the stage for a major, winner-take-all confrontation between the imperator and his allies and the disenfranchised barons.

Cobalt viewed Cerberus as a wild card that needed to be dealt out of the equation before Sam could be challenged. The vengeful baron and his anti-imperial forces did just that, by essentially neutralizing the redoubt, destroying the majority of its personnel and the advanced tech available to them.

The battle raged for less than an hour, and the plateau literally became sodden with blood, spilled by defender and attacker alike. Kane remembered with startling clarity how for one glorious moment after Philboyd crashed the Manta TAV into the Deathbird, the Cerberus warriors swept the plateau clear of black-armored Magistrates. But the Mags regrouped and charged forward and swarmed into the redoubt.

Even after nearly thirty years, Kane felt a surge of pride at the memory of how the people fought back with anything they could get their hands on. They shot, hacked and stabbed until they themselves were shot, hacked and stabbed. No one gave up, not even the few personnel Kane had once contemptuously dismissed as cowardly "teeks," technical geeks.

There were survivors, of course—Grant, Brigid Baptiste, Bry, Lakesh and a handful of Moon base émigrés. They had no choice but to join the imperator in his China stronghold. Even before the smoke had cleared from the Cerberus battlefield, they planned and launched the first counterattacks against the barons that became known as the Consolidation War.

By harnessing the energies of the Heart of the World, Sam implemented a long-range strategy that eventually culminated in the systematic and utter destruction of everything baronial. The Consolidation War was won by the sheer determination of the newly formed Consolidated Confederation of States. By war's end three years later, the armies of the barons were not only broken and scattered to the four winds, but the entire feudal system of god-kings was dismantled.

Thus America was united again. But soon afterward there were rumblings of new threats, new menaces to the hard-won peace. Kane couldn't help but suspect these new enemies were manufactured to keep him and a few others from turning their attention to the unresolved questions of the Battle of Cerberus—

When he felt the hand clap onto his shoulder, Kane whirled, instinctively raising his arms to draw his *katana*. Tanvirah recoiled from him, fear registering on her face. He felt his own face contort in a silent, lupine snarl.

"I didn't mean to startle you," she stammered. "I asked you a question and you didn't answer me so I—"

"Never mind," he broke in harshly, feeling a flush of shame warming the back of his neck. "I get preoccupied sometimes. Guess it has something to do with my age."

She nodded in understanding. "My dad drifts off, too, once in a while." She paused and added quietly, "I've seen him crying when he thinks nobody is looking. I've heard him say 'Domi.' Do you remember her?"

Kane felt his chest clench in a painful spasm. His "Yes" was a ghostly echo in the big room. "She died on the day Cerberus was attacked…trying to save a woman and her unborn child."

Tanvirah said nothing, but her long sweeping lashes veiled her eyes for a moment.

Unbuckling his scabbarded sword, Kane asked, "What were you asking me?"

"I wanted to know if I could take a look at the gateway unit…make sure it's operating."

Kane hesitated and Tanvirah interjected curtly, "I won't break it, if that's what you're worried about. Dad gave me training in its hardware."

Shaking his head, Kane replied, "I'm not concerned about you damaging it. I've been using it for something a little different than hyperdimensional travel, and I don't want you to disturb its new settings."

Tanvirah smiled wanly. "We know the new settings. You've been trying to turn it into a temporal dilator."

"Actually," Kane said, "I call it a spatiotemporal dissociator."

She raised a sardonic eyebrow. "*You* call it that?"

Kane shrugged, placing his coat and *katana* on a desk. "To be precise, its technical name is the Sloan Spatiotemporal Dissociator, but your mom was pretty pissed at me when I stole the plans for it from her." He smiled slightly, but without much humor. "When you get home, you can tell her we finally got the damn thing working."

Startled, Tanvirah swung her head toward him. "'We'? You said you lived here alone!"

Kane began walking toward the anteroom. "No, *you* said that. Do you want to meet my roomie?"

Chapter 6

The stamp of years and suffering accentuated the skull-like contours of the old man's face. Waxy white and deeply seamed, it was the face of a man nearing the conclusion of his life. He wore large dark glasses with heavy rims. What little hair he had was no more than tufts of tangled coppery curls. His frail, emaciated body was hunched over in a wheelchair. He wore a patched gray bodysuit that looked as if it had been stripped none too carefully from a vagrant scarecrow.

The man grasped the wheels of his chair with claw-like hands and turned it. Behind the gray-tinted lenses of his glasses, his eyes darted up and down Tanvirah's form with an aggressive intensity. She tried to meet his gaze with an intimidating one of her own, but his eyes didn't stop on her face; they continued flicking from one part of her body to another. In a hoarse, scratchy voice, he declared, "You're Lakesh's daughter."

He made it sound like an accusation, and Tanvirah snapped, "I don't believe I've had the pleasure."

Doing a poor job of repressing a grin, Kane said, "Meet Donald Bry, Tanvirah."

Her shoulders jerked in reaction to his words.

"Him?" she shrilled. She bent forward slightly, studying the wheelchair-bound man closely. "You?"

"Me," Bry said with a short nod.

Eyes wide with astonishment, Tanvirah exclaimed, "I heard you were dead!"

Bry's seamed face seemed to collapse in a network of wrinkles. It took Tanvirah a moment to realize he was smiling. "Pretty damn near it, I can't deny. But I pulled through."

Tanvirah struggled to regain her composure. "Mr. Bry, if my father knew you were alive, you would enjoy a high position in High River. He has often spoke of his deep respect and affection for you."

Bry's lips writhed as if he were either trying to laugh or to spit. "That's why he was willing to let me rot in Scorpia Prime's stronghold, I suppose. Respect and affection."

Angrily, Tanvirah retorted, "He believed you were dead."

Bry's body quaked, his gnarled fingers flexing and unflexing on the armrests of the wheelchair. "Apparently he didn't give much of a shit one way or the other."

Tanvirah opened her mouth, but Kane said quietly and firmly, "That's enough from both of you."

She turned her dark, furious eyes on him. "I don't think it is, sir. If Dad had any idea Mr. Bry was up here, alive—" She broke off, groping for words.

"He would have arranged for his repatriation?"

Kane inquired quietly. "It was fine with your old man for me to live up here alone, but not Bry?"

Tanvirah cast her eyes downward for a moment, then raised them to stare steadily into Kane's face. "That's not exactly how I would have phrased it, but yes."

"I didn't want that fuckin' Lakesh to know I was up here!" Bry's voice rose in a strident bray of outrage. "I never wanted to see him again."

He turned furious eyes on Kane. "What the hell is she doing here in the first place?"

Kane quickly explained to Bry how Tanvirah came to be in the redoubt. As he did so, she gave the mattrans unit a swift visual inspection. Just as her father had described, on a small plaque above the keypad encoding panel, imprinted in faded maroon letters, were the words Entry Absolutely Forbidden To All But B12 Cleared Personnel. Mat-Trans. Even Lakesh didn't know who the B12 cleared personnel had been and what had become of them, though he had opined they had probably jumped from the installation after the nukecaust, desperately searching for a place better than Cerberus and doubtlessly not finding it.

Tanvirah frowned at how the metal plate on the elevated jump platform gaped open, exposing the confusing circuit network of the emitter array. From the aperture stretched a web of fiber-optic cabling, terminating in a control console spanning the far wall. The console was crescent shaped, surrounding a single operator's chair in the center. It bristled with thousands of tiny electrodes and complexities of naked circuitry, leading to a switchboard containing relays and readout screens. Below the console rested a small square generator bolted to a wheeled pallet. She guessed it was there to provide power to some secondary systems.

Projecting above the inner horseshoe curve of the console, attached to a stanchion, revolved a model of Earth around three feet in diameter. The contoured surface showed rivers, lakes and oceans in blue, forests in various shades of green, deserts in beige and light gray for mountain ranges. Cities were rendered in pale yellow. The carefully detailed surface was mostly beige.

"So this is it?" Tanvirah demanded. Her tone held a ringing note of challenge, of deep skepticism. "Your homemade version of a temporal dilator?"

"You don't sound impressed," Kane observed dryly.

"Should I be?"

Bry shrugged. "This isn't the first time the gateway unit was altered to act as a time machine. Your father used the fundamentals of the quantum interphase mattrans inducers to break through the chronon structure, utilizing the quincunx effect to its full potential."

Tanvirah regarded him coldly with an over-the-shoulder glance. "It looks like you cobbled it together from odds and ends found in—"

"Tom Edison's basement?" Bry interrupted sardonically. "That was one of your father's favorite expressions. It got really tiresome."

"The truth *can* be, sometimes," she shot back.

Kane smiled wryly. "Bry and your old man cobbled this particular thing together many years ago."

Tanvirah took a sharp, startled breath. "For the Omega Path?"

"Exactly," Bry confirmed smugly. "So it's more than a piece of junk. It's a historical artifact."

Tanvirah couldn't argue with Bry, even had she wanted to. She retained very vivid memories of what her father had told her about the Omega Path program, his one attempt at temporal manipulation.

Without access to the specs and data of Operation Chronos, Lakesh was unable to duplicate their accomplishments, so he decided to circumvent them. He saw to the creation of the Omega Path program and linked it with the mat-trans gateway.

The concept was sound—to dispatch Kane and Brigid back through time to a point only a month before the nukecaust, so they could hopefully trigger an alternate event horizon and thus avert the apocalypse.

The Omega Path had worked, at least insofar as translating them into a past temporal plane, but they came to learn it was not their world's past, but another's, almost identical to it. Any actions they undertook had no bearing on their world's present or future.

Lakesh could only speculate on what had happened, and on the system of physics at work. Operation Chronos had functioned on the "chronon" theory, that time wasn't continuous, but made up of subatomic particles jammed together like beads on a string. According to the theory, between each bead, each individual unit of time might exist in an infinite series of parallel universes, fitted into the probability gaps between the chronons.

Tanvirah retorted stiffly, "It's an artifact that you've probably damaged beyond all hope of repair with your tinkering."

"We followed Erica's specs," Bry said defensively.

"As best we could, anyway," Kane interjected.

Tanvirah said grimly, "My mother said it would never work...you can't recapture something that was. That's like lighting a candle and trying to get the same flame on the wick as the time before."

"That's because you look at time from a single perspective," Kane countered. "Just like I was raised to believe. I've had to alter my consciousness over the last fifteen years to be able to accept that the passage of time is like a perpetual motion machine, which depends a great deal on subjectivity."

Tanvirah narrowed her eyes. "That's metaphysical claptrap."

Bry chuckled, a sound like pieces of dry parchment being rubbed over violin strings. "We know Earth is in motion, don't we? We have measurable phenomena and reference points that tell us so. We are moving in relation to something else, the universe at large. But we can't feel Earth turning at twenty-five thousand miles per hour, can we? We can't feel the fact that the world is going around the Sun or that the Sun is going around the galactic center. But we know it to be true, both subjectively and objectively."

"So you're saying," ventured Tanvirah, "that since we're moving forward at the same rate of speed, we can't actually relate to time except as a subjective phenomenon?"

Kane nodded. "Pretty much, yeah."

She shook her head impatiently. "Time is also relative to mass and velocity."

"Which makes it exist as a continuum," Bry stated, "a series of events running in a continuous stream from the instant of the Big Bang all the way to the future, when entropy catches up with it. The only way we can perceive separate moments of time, the events, is subjectively. We believe in the flow—ergo we have the flow. Remember what Einstein said, that the distinction between past, present and future is only a stubbornly persistent illusion."

Tanvirah gave the appearance of pondering Bry's words, but Kane received the distinct and uneasy impression she was only pretending. "So if you don't believe in the flow, then you can alter time?"

Bry nodded. "Essentially."

"Then what keeps you stuck in one place and one era?" she challenged triumphantly.

"The chronon wave," Kane replied promptly. "We're riding it, surfing it."

"Think of humanity as a glob of mercury on a sheet of glass," Bry suggested. "It runs across the glass when we tilt it at either slow or fast speeds, depending on the angle of the tilt.''

Tanvirah cast her glance from the console to the model of Earth to the upright gateway unit. She didn't say anything, but Kane saw the unease flickering in her eyes.

Kane said calmly, ''None of this is really beyond your understanding. If you inherited even a fraction of your parents' IQs, everything we've said here must sound pretty childish.''

Tanvirah turned her face toward him but didn't meet his gaze. He continued with a harder edge in his voice, ''You're doing a poor job of pretending we're not onto something. And I'm going to assume the Nirodha are onto something similar.''

Tanvirah sighed heavily. ''I admit it. The Nirodha research dovetails with yours. They are trying to ride a time wave, as well. But they intend to ride it over the edge of the sheet of glass Mr. Bry mentioned. And the edge is where time ends, the sum of all existence.''

Bry's eyebrows crawled toward his bald pate. ''How can they do that? What tech are they employing?''

''We're not sure,'' she replied. ''And the equations they're employing are so esoteric that even I have trouble following them. Hyperdimensional physics depends on the directed acceleration and deceleration of subatomic particles, but they don't seem to have a propagation medium.''

''Then they'd have a singularity,'' Bry said confidently. "And if they do, they don't have it work-ing...otherwise none of us would be here to debate the possibility."

Tanvirah nodded, but she didn't appear convinced or comforted. "What do you intend to do once your device is completed?" she demanded. "Search through all of human history for the point at which to change the course of technical development and keep *now* from happening?"

"We've found that point already," Kane replied with a trace of smug satisfaction.

Tanvirah nodded again, as if she had expected the answer. "So have the Nirodha. And whatever method they're using would require enormous power. And there's only one place on Earth that has the power to harness the chronon waves and it must be secured."

She directed a level gaze at Kane. "It's forbidden to everyone on Earth. Except you."

Kane nodded, feeling not in the least victorious that Tanvirah had confirmed his earlier suspicions. In an uninflected voice, he intoned, "Thunder Isle. But your news is old...the place is off-limits even to me."

Chapter 7

Although she wanted to, Tanvirah didn't protest when Kane took her on a short tour of the Cerberus redoubt. She had seen vids of the entire complex, taped by her father before the assault. She knew about the machine shop, the nuclear-generated power and the armory with its grenades, machine guns and all the deadly toys men of Kane's generation loved so much.

The installation was a mere shadow of what it had been, barely a rough sketch of the sprawling, bustling underground city of steel and glass as envisioned by Lakesh.

Acceding to her request, Kane took Tanvirah down the emergency stairs to the engineering department on the third level. Within a huge wire enclosure were three ovoid, vanadium-shelled generators. If the central complex two levels above had served as the brain of Cerberus, the subterranean room was its heart, pumping life and power to it. Opposite the cage stretched a long operations and monitoring station. Although a few liquid crystal displays glowed, only a couple of needle gauges wavered. Only one of the generators still functioned. She knew that the reactor itself was buried an additional hundred feet below the engine room, beneath rock and shield concrete.

Kane escorted her to the cafeteria, where so many briefings, planning sessions and schemes had occurred. He gestured to the pair of big industrial-sized refrigerators. "You're welcome to look over our supplies, but I warn you our menus are pretty limited. We used to trade food with what was left of Sky Dog's band, but they relocated a couple of years ago. They never were much into farming anyhow."

Tanvirah didn't request clarification about the people in question. She was at the point in her father's memoirs where he had gone into great detail about the band of Amerindians who had been the Cerberus installation's nearest neighbors—its only neighbors, for that matter. Direct contact hadn't been established between the redoubt's personnel and the tribespeople until shortly after the arrival of Kane, Grant and Brigid Baptiste. Kane had managed to turn a potentially tragic misunderstanding into a budding alliance with Sky Dog.

Not so much a chief as a shaman, a warrior priest, Sky Dog was Cobaltville bred as they were. Unlike them, he had been exiled from the ville while still a youth, due to his Lakota ancestry. He joined a band of Cheyenne and Sioux living in the foothills of the Bitterroot Range, and eventually earned a position of high authority and respect among them.

"Dad told me about the alliance you struck with

Sky Dog," Tanvirah said as she opened a refrigerator door. "What happened to them?"

"They were the first causalities of the war," Kane replied. "Baron Cobalt ordered their extermination so none of Sky Dog's people could warn us up here. He felt he owed them a massacre."

Tanvirah didn't know what to say, so she opted to remain silent, although she mentally kicked herself for not remembering the fate of the Amerindians. Many years before, a squad of hard-contact Mags from Cobaltville made an incursion into the Bitterroot Range as part of a ville-wide cooperative effort. The squad's mission was to investigate the Cerberus redoubt and ascertain if it was playing host to three wanted seditionists—namely Kane, Grant and Brigid.

The Magistrates were stopped and soundly defeated by Sky Dog's band of Amerindians in the flatlands bordering the foothills. Grant and Kane were instrumental in the victory, although they managed to keep their involvement concealed from the invading Mags.

Tanvirah found the makings of a simple salad in the crisper drawers of the refrigerator. At a loss for anything pertinent to say about Sky Dog, she commented, "Dad told me you were very popular with the Indians. That they adopted you into their tribe."

"That's true."

Tanvirah knew that most of the people who had lived in the redoubt—with only a few exceptions—were ville bred and they were accustomed to an artificial environment, particularly the Moon base émigrés. Rarely did any of them stray more than ten yards from the edge of the plateau.

Her father had often remarked with amusement how Kane frequently complained of suffering from redoubt fever. He would requisition one of the vehicles to drive down the treacherous mountain road to the foot-hills to Sky Dog's permanent encampment.

No one had ever asked what he did down there among the Amerindians, where he was known and ad-mired as Unktomi Shunkaha. It was a name the band of Sioux and Cheyenne had bestowed upon him, first conceived as something of an insult. It became syn-onymous with cunning and courage after he orches-trated the Indians' victory over a Magistrate assault force.

After remaining with the band for a few days, Kane would return to the redoubt, often dirty and dishev-eled, but always relaxed. Lakesh and others wondered if Kane had a willing harem of Indian maidens who always looked forward to a visit from Unktomi Shun-kaha, but everyone knew better than to inquire about it.

Tanvirah shut the refrigerator door and carried the bowl of vegetables to a table. Striving for a bantering tone, she inquired, "Were there very many blue-eyed Indian children left in the wake of your visits?"

She glanced toward Kane. Cold steel eyes looked back at her, unblinking and without a glint of emotion. She sat at the table and shifted her feet uncomfortably.

"I apologize. Dad wanted me to learn absolutely everything about you I could."

"And have you?" His voice was pitched low, barely above a whisper.

"I don't know. You keep looking at me like a wolf about to devour a rabbit in one gulp." Tanvirah forced herself to meet his gaze. "Frankly, you scare the hell out of me. Sir."

The man's lips quirked slightly beneath his mustache in what she hoped was a smile. He turned away from her and went to a nearby table. He dropped into a chair and stretched out his legs, propping his feet up on another chair. As he crossed his ankles, she saw that hard glint in his eyes had softened somewhat. "Did what you learned about me scare you?" he asked in a tone that suggested he was only mildly interested. "Or have I only been scaring the hell out of you since we met in the flesh?"

Tanvirah mixed the lettuce, carrots and what she hoped were snap peas together in the bowl with her fingers. She pretended to be totally engrossed in the simple task when in reality she was summoning all of her willpower to lift her head and gaze directly into Kane's eyes.

"I don't care for your manner very much," she blurted, surprised by her sudden angry vehemence.

Kane shrugged. "Most don't. I've had complaints about it before."

"I don't like it," she said between gritted teeth.

"What's there to like?" he countered. "Here's the

way it works—you're the interloper here. The only reason you made it this far is because I allowed it. The only reason you're sitting there eating our food is because I allow it. And I can disallow it pretty much when I feel like it.''

"Shove your threats up your ass," Tanvirah snapped.

He sighed with a forced, patronizing weariness. "You apparently didn't learn as much about me as you thought, otherwise you'd know I don't threaten. I make simple statements of fact.''

Tanivrah shoved a few scraps of lettuce in her mouth, disregarding the fact some of them were limp and rusty. She chewed slowly, trying to regain control of her temper. She had been warned by both her mother and father how infuriatingly contradictory Kane could be, but she still hesitated between letting him know about her outraged dignity or maintaining a relatively indifferent facade.

She was accustomed to a certain amount of informality from her advisers and colleagues. She had never insisted upon the full rendition of imperial rights, even though she and her parents were certainly worthy of them, due to their status. But Kane's deliberately disrespectful and casual manner showed her that no one had ever really been at ease in her presence before, even the lovers she had taken during the orgiastic Sati rites.

"We were talking about Thunder Isle," she said with a cold calm.

"I don't know about 'we,'" Kane reminded her. "I mentioned the place. That's as far as it went."

Tanvirah ignored the gibe. "It's the only place where Operation Chronos technology was fully functional. You cannibalized that tech to build your own backyard time machine."

"You seem to know a great deal about what I've been up to," he said genially. "How can that be?"

"My mother and father have reports of what you took from Redoubt Yankee on Thunder Isle years ago."

Kane nodded. "And I'm sure they told you I've been monkeying around with the Chronos equipment without understanding any of it, using the trial-and-error process."

When she didn't immediately respond, Kane arched a challenging eyebrow. "Didn't they?"

"Yes," Tanvirah retorted. "Both of them told me how you tended toward recklessness."

"A tendency," he admitted. "I can still be reckless, I won't deny—and it's a damn good thing too, or you wouldn't be sitting there."

She rolled her eyes in frustration. "All right, all *right!* You saved my life, thank you, thank you! Now can we get back to—"

"And the way I learned *not* to be reckless," he interrupted, "was through the study of any given situation. I studied the Chronos temporal dilator and read everything in Redoubt Yankee's database pertaining to it, particularly that written by Torrence Silas Burr. I'm sure you've heard your mother speak of him.''

Tanvirah nodded in grudging assent, but said nothing. Her mother, by her own admission, had been beautiful, haughty and arrogant when she earned her Ph.D in cybernetics and computer science at the age of eighteen.

Before she was twenty, Erica van Sloan had accepted a position with the Totality Concept. In the vast installation beneath a mesa in Dulce, New Mexico, she served as the subordinate, lover and occasional victim of a man who made her own officious personality seem mousy and shy by comparison.

According to what her mother had said, Torrence Silas Burr was brilliant, stylish, waspish and nasty. He excelled at using his enormous intellect and equally enormous ego to fuel his cruel sense of humor. He delighted in belittling and degrading not just her, but other scientists assigned to Overproject Whisper. The one scientist he could not deride was Mohandas Lakesh Singh, the genius responsible for the final technological breakthrough of Project Cerberus, which permitted Operation Chronos to finally make some headway.

"The main thing I learned," Kane continued, "is that the nature of time is very, very difficult to handle. Change one major thing, you wind up with approximately the same mess you were trying to fix—or you make a worse mess.

"Change a bunch of small things in the hope it'll

end up changing the one major thing, and you'll find out you've just shuffled probabilities around, not averted anything. The disaster—like the nukecaust—will still happen, only the causes and effects will be different. All the factors that contributed to whatever you hoped to change are still present in the timeline. Understand?''

Tanvirah nodded impatiently throughout Kane's dissertation. ''Yes, yes. Causality I understand.''

Kane's eyes widened in mock admiration. ''Oh, really? Can you by any chance explain it to me, then?''

A little sullenly, Tanvirah shot back, ''What does it mean to you?''

''Causal law, conservation of energy and mass to energy ratio involves more than continuous functions. A spatial and temporal discontinuity is entirely possible, just like Burr and your mother always suspected.''

Tanvirah pushed the bowl of vegetables away from her. ''Possible, but not something that can deliberately be engineered.''

''Of course it can,'' Kane said matter-of-factly. ''That was your old man's whole thesis, the bones of his recruitment speech to me, Grant, Brigid and Domi back in the day.''

Tanvirah knew exactly what Kane referred to, since her father had often spoken of that particular encounter, stemming as it did from a conversation with none other than Silas Burr nearly two centuries before. In the Dulce facility, Burr had confided to Lakesh that his staff had used the Operation Chronos technology to peep through a gap in the chronon structure into a future date, January of 2001.

They discovered that a nuclear holocaust had, for all intents and purposes, obliterated the world. That news was horrifying enough, but what was worse was that further peeping experiments had shown that not only was the holocaust preventable, but it wasn't supposed to happen. Operation Chronos had disrupted the chronon structure and triggered a probability wave dysfunction. They had created an alternate future scenario for humanity—or so Burr had postulated.

Tanvirah said defensively, "My father didn't fully understand the nature of the continuum, the quantum field back then. Nor did Torrence Silas Burr. It wasn't until my mother—"

She broke off when she saw how Kane's eyes narrowed. He bit out, "Until your mother waggled her ass at Lakesh and lured him over to the imperator's side. I still don't know who was the primary seducer…Sam or Erica."

Tanvirah felt the hot flush of anger warming her cheeks. She was barely able to restrain herself from hurling the bowl of vegetables at Kane's head. "You're a stubborn fool," she said, her voice sibilant with spite. "And an ignorant one. The continuum isn't as easy to distort as my dad once believed. The resilience of the chronon structure was unknown to him."

"But not to Sam, apparently," replied Kane. "After

deserting us here, Lakesh gave up on trying to correct the probability wave dysfunction.''

"Because he came to understand there wasn't one, you idiot!'' She despised the shrill, petulant note in her voice, but she couldn't help herself. "What happened was *supposed* to happen! There never was an alternate event horizon. Time and events moved correctly. We now have a world at peace.''

Kane seemed to take no offense at being called an idiot. Tanvirah guessed he had heard far worse epithets thrown his way. Quietly, he intoned, "I didn't much like the world before it was at peace. But I really dislike it now. And I know damn and good well it wasn't supposed to be this way. Whether the Nirodha or Sam or the Archons are responsible, it *will* be changed.''

Tanvirah sat straight up in her chair. "You *do* want another war! Just like the imperator said!''

Kane shook his head. "I'm not going to pretend that pre-imperial Earth was a nice place. It was damn ugly. The cost in human suffering was enormous, but the so-called adaptive Earth the imperator wants is far worse.''

"How can that be?'' Accusation edged Tanvirah's question like sharpened steel. "What can be worse than annihilation?''

"There can be different degrees of annihilation, Tanvirah. A spiritual one, with all free will bred out of humanity, the entire population changed into drones adapted to fulfill various needs, and all of us working for a nonhuman overlord.''

He paused and declared grimly, "*That* is worse than annihilation. That's what I intend to rectify with my homemade temporal dilator."

Tanvirah's eyes flashed like polished orbs of onyx. "Let's stop dancing around the real issue, shall we? Even quantum physics has its natural laws. *You* can't go back in time and coexist at any point in the past where you already existed. So even if you've found the temporal fault lines, there's nothing you can do to repair them."

A lazy, almost contemptuous smile played over Kane's lips. "Who said anything about me?"

Chapter 8

Kane refused to answer any more questions or continue the debate. He led Tanvirah out of the cafeteria and down the corridor. He directed her to turn into the first door on the left. It opened up onto a wide, white-tiled shower room. Each of the six stalls was enclosed by shoulder-high partitions. Rad-counter gauges were affixed to the walls beneath the showerheads. Outside of every stall were shelves holding folded towels and terry-cloth robes.

"You can use a shower," Kane said, absently fingering his nose. "Both of us can."

Tanvirah was too emotionally drained to even wonder if he was making a snide comment about her hygiene or lack thereof.

"This used to be decam," Kane continued. "It's the only place in the whole redoubt where the plumbing still works perfectly. The en suite bathrooms are iffy."

He strode to the far end of the decam facility, unbuttoning his shirt as he went. Tanvirah stepped into the tiled enclosure and peeled off her clothes, placing them on an empty shelf near the front of the cubicle. She turned on the faucet. A spray of water jetted from the nozzle, and she adjusted it so it was a needle-like rain.

When the water was hot enough, almost at the tolerance level, she stepped beneath the flow. She used a liquid-soap dispenser affixed to the wall to work a lather all over her aching body, even making a shampoo of it for her hair. Although her limbs bore contusions and a few abrasions, they weren't particularly noticeable on her dusky complexion.

The entire room filled quickly with billowing clouds of steam, and she contented herself with luxuriating beneath the driving jets of hot water, letting them soothe the muscle ache. She reveled in them, turning to feel their impact on her breasts and belly, back and buttocks. After a few minutes, she adjusted the faucet and streams of cold, clear water gushed down and rinsed the soap from her body.

She watched the water drain away, down into a natural limestone filtration system built under the redoubt. According to her father, once it passed through and the chemicals, including the lilac scent, had been leached out, the water returned to the complex's water supply.

Stepping out of the cubicle, Tanvirah pulled on a long robe, glad to be rid of the dirty and torn bodysuit. The robe was of old satin and almost diaphanous. She removed the Uma stone from her clothes and placed it in the voluminous pocket of her robe. She started to leave decam, but she heard a faint grunt, full of annoyed pain. She moved toward the furthermost shower stall.

A naked Kane stood there, body glistening with water. His back was turned to her, and she winced at the mementoes of past violence scattered all over his lean, long-limbed body. She saw the stellate scars of bullet punctures, the thin and jagged white lines of edged steel that had sliced into his flesh and the swirling weal of a long-ago burn between his shoulder blades. She repressed a shudder at the sight of whip tracings etched into his lower back, buttocks and thighs. Her mother had told her how Kane had been cruelly scourged when he was a prisoner of the Scorpia Prime.

Now he stood in frowning reflection, trying to peel away a blood-encrusted bandage from his right rib cage. He had reopened the wound in the process, and a thin stream of scarlet trickled down his hip and across his thigh.

She started to turn away when Kane cursed again as the bandage finally came loose. Impatiently he wadded it up and tossed it away with an angry snarl. As he reached toward an open medicine cabinet bolted to the stall wall, she glimpsed the raw wound on his side, a gaping cut surrounded by bruised, blue-black flesh. As she gazed at the injury, he glimpsed her. He made no move to cover himself. His expression didn't change at all.

Tanvirah, feeling like a combination of voyeur and naughty child who had been caught sneaking a snack, stepped boldly into full view. She gestured toward the medicine cabinet. "Would you like me to help you dress that cut? I have medical training."

"It's more than a cut," Kane replied gruffly. "I think some of the intercostal cartilage has been ruptured." He hesitated, then said, "Yes, thank you."

Tanvirah entered the cubicle. "Let me see."

Kane raised his arms and held them high to each side and began a slow turn toward her. Tanvirah, as both a student of medicine and a Shakti priestess, was not unaccustomed to observing the naked male body. But Kane produced a startling effect, evoking such a strong sexual response within her she was both dismayed and enthralled.

Tanvirah's gaze of carefully calculated clinical detachment passed over his body. The way he earlier reminded her of a wolf returned to the forefront of her mind. He was built with a stripped-down economy, with most of his muscle mass contained in his upper body, much like a wolf. His musculature was long and flowing, like stretched-out bundles of piano wire covered by a pale brown lacquer.

The smooth symmetry of the lacquer was spoiled by a number of scars, one of which cut down from his almost hairless chest across his muscle-ribbed stomach to a couple of inches above his pelvis. The scar came to stop just above his thick thatch of pubic hair. She tried to stop herself, but her eyes strayed down and paused on his penis. It was long, and thickly veined, looking almost as sinewy as the rest of him.

Despite his age and the scar tissue, Kane's body was

that of the classic warrior, of the gladiator. She reflected that the ancient Romans built statues to honor men like him and women murmured at their feet.

Ashamed of her own frivolity of thought, Tanvirah concentrated on efficiently cleansing the wound. Under the shower spray, the water swirling down the drain turned red, then a pale pink. Her fingers were deft, probing, and she heard the hiss of indrawn breath as she parted the edges of the wound.

"Just epidermal tissue slashed," she said. "If the cut was deeper, you'd have broken and exposed bone. I don't think you have ruptured cartilage, though, just some bruising."

"Can you treat it?"

"Easily."

Tanvirah sterilized the wound with a mixture of sulfa and antiseptic. While she worked, her robe fell open, partly revealing the hollow between her full breasts. She didn't bother closing it up, knowing the tantalizing glimpse she permitted him was less a brazen invitation than a silent declaration she felt safe with him now.

She struggled to keep her respiration steady and her expression composed as she applied the bandage to his ribs, making sure the adhesive strips didn't adhere to the edges of the wound.

She kept casting surreptitious glances downward, but neither Kane's breathing, demeanor nor the condition of his manhood changed. She, on the other hand, felt a dew of sweat gathering at her temples and she realized she was moist elsewhere. Looking down at herself, she was shamed and a little shocked to see her nipples, hard and hot, poking against the thin fabric covering her breasts.

Tanvirah felt a surge of angry humiliation when she realized her touch and near-naked proximity was having no apparent effect on the man. More than once during the Sati rites when she danced the sacred steps of Kali while dressed in traditional garb she had seen men aroused to jetting climaxes simply when she moved her body in the ritual motions of divine lust.

She glanced down at his organ, imagining it hard and erect, visualizing him during a Sati celebration, throwing her down on the altar stone, pushing her legs apart and plunging his iron-hard member violently into her—

"Done?" Kane asked mildly.

Tanvirah nodded, straightening and closing her eyes against a brief wave of dizziness. She was startled by her shortness of breath and pounding heart. She said faintly, "In a few days you should be pretty much healed."

Face neutral of expression, Kane stepped around her and took a robe from a shelf. He donned it, saying, "Thank you. You're very good."

She cast a him a quick, suspicious glance but there was no hint of mockery in his eyes or tone. He strode briskly toward the door. "Let's find you some quarters so you can rest up."

Following him out of the decam facility, Tanvirah

hurried to catch up. The wing that held most of the apartments was as poorly lit as the rest of the redoubt, although most of the debris had been cleared or pushed to one side of the corridor.

Tanvirah passed an open door and stopped to look at what lay beyond it. She saw a simply, but nicely appointed, living room, lit by a dozen long tapers. By their flickering light she saw a sofa, several chairs and a coffee table upon which rested a stack of oversized hardcover books. Atop the stack lay a pair of square-lensed, wire-rimmed eyeglasses, as if the wearer had carelessly tossed them there only a moment before. She knew that was not the case. In fact, she received the distinct impression she was looking into a shrine, not an apartment.

"What about this one?" she called to Kane, who was several yards ahead of her along the corridor.

Rocking to a swift, unsteady halt, Kane cast a glance over his shoulder and whirled. He stalked back to her and shut the door firmly. The tone of his "No" brooked no option for either debate or questions.

Mystified, but too tired to argue with the man any further, Tanvirah followed Kane farther down the corridor. He stopped before a door and pushed it open. A ceiling light strip flashed on automatically. "This used to be your old man's place. He took everything personal with him when he joined up with Sam."

Without further words, Kane turned and began retracing his steps down the passageway. "Wait," she said. "You haven't told me how I can get back home."

Not pausing, Kane replied, "That's because I haven't figured it out yet."

With that he marched away into the murk. Tanvirah clenched her teeth to keep herself from spitting an obscenity at his retreating back and entered the small apartment.

As Kane had said, there were no objects of a personal nature within, only the bare essentials of living quarters. She was disappointed that nothing remained of her father's long occupancy. Almost everything she knew of her father's past was an oral history, with very little in the way of actual artifacts or even memorabilia.

Going to the door, she peered out into the corridor, making sure neither Kane nor Bry was anywhere in sight, then she closed and locked it. From the pocket of her robe she removed the Uma stone and then shucked out of it. Nude, she sat in the center of the living-room floor, arranging her limbs in a lotus position. She unwrapped the slender silver chain from around the yellow diamond and held the pendant up before her eyes. The teardrop-shaped stone, no larger than the first joint of her thumb, had been cut into its present shape thousands of years ago.

Tanvirah placed the delicate silver chain over the crown of her head, arranging it so the diamond rested against her *ajina* chakra, her third eye at the bridge of her nose. The flawless diamond was both a symbol of her office as a Shakti priestess and served as a means of communication.

She closed her eyes, going through a relaxation exercise by balancing her breathing, her heart rate and trying to reduce the flow of adrenaline through her body. It wasn't easy, not with the memory of Kane's naked body so fresh in her mind.

Kane surprised and deeply unsettled her. Like her mother and father had said, he was undeniably a ruthless man, a trained warrior and killer. By the standards instilled in her since birth, he was a brutish relic of the bygone days of talon and fang. The general consensus of authority opinion about pre-imperial Magistrates was not high. They were viewed as egotistical, testosterone-saturated thugs lacking any qualities of mercy or abilities of higher thought. They were tools in the hands of the barons to batter and terrorize a recalictrant population into submission.

The design of the Magistrate's badge, a scales of justice superimposed over a nine-spoked wheel, symbolized the oath to keep the wheels of justice turning in the nine baronies. And the Mags turned them relentlessly, inexorably, grinding down anyone who stood in their way.

According to Lakesh, if events hadn't forced Kane out of Cobaltville, he might have still been a Magistrate when the Consolidation War broke out, fighting against the imperial forces instead of for them. Her father claimed that it had only been threats against Brigid Baptiste and Grant that had galvanized Kane into leaving. He hadn't left the baron's service of his own accord; he hadn't recognized how inherently evil the baronial system had been.

But now; Tanvirah doubted her father's rather contemptuous assessment of the man as essentially a blunt instrument. She sensed an unexpected depth of compassion in Kane—at one time, the man had cared deeply, not just for other people, but about principles of honor and duty. A killer he certainly was. He had gone about dispatching the Pischacas very efficiently, but he hadn't taken any overt sadistic glee in ending their lives, and he had offered them the chance to retreat, as well.

Desire rose in her again as she recalled how Kane's skin felt against her fingers, the feel of a man who had fought and shed blood in her defense. She tried to tell herself that she was simply reacting to the pheromones of a warrior, the masculine scent exuded by an alpha male who had killed for her. But in this instance, the male had denied himself the fruits of his victory.

Even if Kane had spent the past twenty-odd years celibate, Tanvirah doubted if it was due to a physical problem. She knew from what her mother and father had told her that Kane was secure in his virility. Certainly his now legendary captivity in Area 51 had proved that beyond any shadow of a doubt, not just to him but to anyone who had ever heard the tale.

Area 51 was the predark unclassified code name for a training area on Nellis Air Force base. It was also known as Groom Lake, but most predarkers preferred to call it Dreamland. Contained in the dry lake bed was a vast installation, extending deep into the desert floor.

More than two decades before, Baron Cobalt had proposed to use it as the staging ground for a grand experiment in hybrid-human relations. Since Area 51's history was intertwined with rumors of alien involvement, Baron Cobalt had used its medical facilities as a substitute for those destroyed in New Mexico.

He reactivated the installation, turning it into a processing and treatment center, without having to rebuild from scratch, and transferred the human and hybrid personnel from the Dulce facility—those who had survived the destruction, at any rate.

Still and all, the medical treatments that addressed the congenital autoimmune system deficiencies of the hybrids weren't enough to insure the continued survival of the race. The necessary equipment and raw material to implement procreation had yet to be installed. Baron Cobalt had unilaterally decided that the conventional means of conception was the only option to keep the hybrid race alive.

Kane was unaware of the baron's decision when he and Domi penetrated the Area 51 facility. He didn't learn the full extent of the plan until he was apprehended. During Kane's two weeks of captivity, he was fed a steady diet of protein, laced with a stimulant of the catecholamine group. It affected the renal blood supply, increasing cardiac output without increasing the need for cardiac oxygen consumption.

Combined with food loaded with protein to speed sperm production, the stimulant provided Kane with hours of high sexual energy. Since he was forced to achieve erection and ejaculation six times a day every two days, his energy and sperm count had to be preternaturally high, even higher than was normal for him.

She knew that her father had taken a personal hand in breeding into Kane a number of superior adaptive traits. Resistance to disease and exceptionally potent sperm were only two of them.

Lakesh had consulted the findings of Overproject Excalibur, the division of the Totality Concept that dealt primarily with bioengineering, to find in vitro genetic samples of the best of the best human DNA. In the vernacular of the time, it was referred to as purity control.

Everyone who enjoyed full ville citizenship was a descendant of the purity-control undertaking. Sometimes a particular gene carrying a desirable trait was grafted to an unrelated egg, or an undesirable gene removed. Despite many failures, when there was a success, it was replicated over and over, occasionally with variations.

Some sixty years ago, when Lakesh determined to build a resistance movement against the baronies, he rifled the genetic records to find the qualifications he deemed the most desirable.

Despite all that, the main reason Kane was chosen to impregnate the female hybrids was for a more prosaic reason—male hybrids, even the barons, were physically incapable of engaging in conventional acts of procreation. They were unable to achieve erections, and even if they could, their organs of reproduction were so underdeveloped as to be almost vestigial.

Kane wasn't the first human male to be pressed into service. There had been other men before him, but they had performed unsatisfactorily due to their terror of the hybrids. At first the females selected for the process donned wigs and wore cosmetics in order to appear more human to the trapped sperm donors. It was a revival of an old "alien abduction" scenario, when a handful of Balam's people still existed and were forced to undertake extreme measures to stave off extinction. However, most of the men in Area 51 weren't volunteers and had to be strapped down. Even after the application of an aphrodisiac gel, they had difficulty maintaining an erection.

Kane had not suffered from such a liability. Many of the hybrid women who had been forced to cooperate with Baron Cobalt's experiment still spoke in hushed tones of Kane's totally uninhibited participation—like a demonic force of limitless priapic energy and powerful seminal discharge. And more shockingly, many of the females decided they actually enjoyed exploring the long dormant sexual aspects of their nature, as an adjunct to their high intellectual development.

In many ways, Tanvirah reflected, it was that experiment that proved the essential compatibility between old and new human. Even though only one pregnancy developed during that period, the divisions between hybrid and human were forevermore blurred. Since then, hybrid females and human males had been pairing off, and the past two decades had seen a rise in mixed-breed offspring, children bearing the best qualities of old and new human.

Tanvirah began the slow, deep breathing pattern in preparation for her communication, aligning the frequency of her SQUID implant with the vibratory harmonics of the Uma stone. It was a difficult melding, the joining and the working in tandem of psi energy, organic and inorganic matter, but the implant made it possible and her mother had made the implant possible.

When the world blew out on noon of January 20, 2001, Erica van Sloan was safely ensconced within the Anthill facility. But despite all of the safety precautions, radiation still trickled in. Bomb-triggered earthquakes caused extensive damage.

Since the military and government personnel in charge had no choice but to remain in the facility, it took them a while to realize they were just as much victims of the nukecaust as those whom they referred to as the "useless eaters" of the world. They had assumed that after five years or less of waiting inside the Anthill, a new world order would be in place, but the prolonged nuclear winter changed their ideas about any kind of order, world or otherwise. Even if the personnel managed to outlast the skydark, they would still sicken and die, either from radiation sickness or simply old age.

So they embarked on a radically daring plan. Cybernetic technology had made great leaps in the latter part of the twentieth century, and Erica herself had made some small contributions to those advances. Operations were performed on everyone living in the Anthill, making use of the new techniques in organ transplants and medical technology, as well as in cybernetics.

Over a period of years, everyone living inside Mount Rushmore was turned into cyborgs, hybridizations of human and machine. With less energy to expend on maintaining the body, the cyborganized subjects ate less and therefore extended the stockpile of foodstuffs by several years.

Since the main difficulty in constructing interfaces between mechanical, electric and organic systems was the wiring, Erica oversaw the implantation of SQUIDs directly into the brain. The superconducting quantum interface devices, one-hundredth of a micron across, facilitated the subjects' control over their new prostheses.

Although Erica herself had designed the implants and oversaw the early operations, she certainly didn't care for the process being performed on her. She knew the SQUIDs could be used to electronically control the personnel, and she wasn't fond of being turned into a biomechanical drone. However, she was even less fond of the alternative—euthanasia.

Over the past couple of decades, Erica had found a

new use for the SQUIDs, by employing them to facilitate long-distance silent communication that didn't depend on electronics, transmissions that couldn't be overheard or jammed.

As Tanvirah felt the pins-and-needles tingling of the implant and the Uma stone exchanging energy, a rich warmth blanketed her. She mentally followed the route of blood through her circulatory system, tracing the autonomic functions back to the controlling portion of her brain. She slowed her respiration rate even further as her mind went here and there through her body, examining it, adjusting it, honing her responses.

The warmth spread up from the center of her belly, flowed through her arms and legs and collected at her *sahasrara* chakra, the Wheel of Shiva's Seat at the crown of her head. In her mind's eye she saw a white blossom opening, the petals reaching out to engulf the universe. She felt as if she were floating, hovering between the solid material world and one made of warm, insubstantial light.

Within the white blossom shapes formed, geometric and pristine. Some might have called her vision that of a temple, a place built to house a god, adored, adorned by devoted priests. But she knew the vastness of the huge complex that lay beneath the Xian Pyramid in China. The mathematical form of the temple designed for maximum efficiency held the beauty of functional design.

She knew the huge domed space was actually a natural cavern. The unfinished stone of its ceiling gleamed here and there with clusters of crystals and geodes. The floor dipped at a gentle incline, and at the center, surrounded by a collar of interlocking silver slabs, was a pool. The inner rim was lined with an edging of crystal points that glowed with a dull iridescence. At first glance, the pool took up the entire chamber floor, except for a walkway around it, about five feet wide.

On the rim of the pool a lone man-shape stood. He looked like a relatively young man, perhaps only a few years older than she, but Tanvirah knew his appearance provided no guide to his true age. He was pale of skin, and the top of his head was swathed in a white turban with a blue Uma diamond emblem pinned to the front of it.

The face he turned toward her was as austere as if it were carved from marble. His high brow came down and out in a wide slope, culminating in a pair of sweeping arches. Beneath the brow arches, sunk very deep in his head, as if hiding from the light, haughty golden eyes shone like polished ingots. Below the crag of brows and probing eyes, his face seemed to taper down like a teardrop. A sharp, narrow nose and a long, thin mouth that never curved far from a straight line completed the face.

He was aware of her. A ghostly whisper insinuated itself into her consciousness, even though his lips did not move.

Sister. Your imperial brother welcomes you.

High Imperator, Tanvirah replied according to ritual, *Scorpia Prime greets you.*

Chapter 9

Kane stopped by his quarters only long enough to shuck out of his robe and get dressed. He sheathed his rangy body in the midnight-colored shadow suit that absorbed light the way a sponge absorbed water.

Although the black, skintight garment didn't appear as if it could offer protection from a fleabite, it was impervious to most wavelengths of radiation. The suits were climate controlled for environments up to highs of 150 degrees Fahrenheit and lows as cold as minus ten degrees Fahrenheit.

Composed of a complicated electrospin weave of spider silk, Monocrys, Nomex and Spectra fabrics, the garment was essentially a single crystal metallic microfiber with a very dense molecular structure. The outer Monocrys sheathing went opaque when exposed to radiation, and the Nomex and Spectra layers provided protection against blunt trauma. The spider silk allowed flexibility, but it traded protection from firearms for freedom of movement.

Kane had long felt the shadow suit was superior to the standard polycarbonate Magistrate armor, if for nothing else but its internal subsystems. Built around nanotechnologies, the microelectromechanical systems combined computers with tiny semiconductor chips. The nanotechnology reduced the size of the electronic components to one-millionth of a meter, roughly ten times the size of an atom. The inner layer was lined by carbon nanotubes only a nanometer wide, rolled-up sheets of graphite with a tensile strength greater than steel. The suits were almost impossible to tear, but a large-caliber bullet could penetrate them, and unlike the Mag body armor, they couldn't redistribute the kinetic shock.

The garment had no zippers or buttons, only a magnetic seal on the right side, and he put it on in one continuous piece from the hard-soled boots to the gloves. The fabric molded itself to his body, adhering like another layer of skin. He smoothed out the wrinkles and folds by running his hands over his arms and legs. It had been a long time since he had last worn it and he was again surprised by its light, almost insubstantial weight.

He struggled to keep the vision of Tanvirah's dark beauty from dominating his mind. He couldn't allow himself to be distracted, even by a woman who obviously wanted to make love. Even though it had been a long time, he recognized the signs of a woman wanting to abandon herself to her physical urgings, but he was maintaining a psychological distance.

He couldn't help but wonder about her, about her trustworthiness. Erica had been a conniving bitch who was only as loyal to the man whom she married as she was to the directives of the imperator. Kane assumed if Sam ordered her to leave Lakesh, she would do so with the same unquestioning obedience as she had shown when Sam ordered her to wed him. Kane didn't get the same sense of duplicity from Tanvirah, but as Erica's daughter, that made her the imperator's stepsister in a rather roundabout way. That tenuous familial connection was sufficient to prevent Kane from taking anything she said at face value.

He supposed the girl could have been conditioned by Sam as a precaution against her saying too much to Kane, or she simply could be displaying family loyalty as the new form of Unity Through Action.

More than a century before, Unity Through Action was the rallying cry of the early Program of Unification. It awakened the long-forgotten trust in a central government by offering a solution to the constant states of hardship and fear—join the unification program and never know want or fear again. Of course, any concept of liberty had to be forfeited in the exchange.

One of the basic tenets of the unification program involved taking responsibility. Since humanity was responsible for the arrival of Judgment Day, it had to accept the blame before a truly utopian age could be ushered in. All humankind had to do to earn this utopia was to follow the rules, be obedient and accept the new order without question.

For most of the men and women who lived in the villes and the surrounding territories, this was enough, more than enough. Long sought-after dreams of peace and safety had at last been transformed into reality. Of course, fleeting dreams of personal freedom were completely crushed, but such abstract aspirations were seen as nothing but childish illusions.

In fact, almost every tradition of the predark world that survived the nukecaust, skydark and the anarchy of the Deathlands was spit upon as an illusion. Even the ancient social patterns that connected mother, father and child were broken. That break was a crucial one in order for the unification program to succeed. The existence of the family as a unit of procreation and therefore as a social unit had to be eliminated.

But all that had changed with Sam's rise to power and the establishment of an imperial family. Now the family unit was viewed as the foundation of strength, a forward-looking symbol of the future, humanity's only salvation.

At one time, Kane had considered building a family of his own, but that was a long time ago. Tanvirah's presence reawakened those urges to procreate, but he wasn't sure why. Just thinking about her evoked memories of his previous lovers.

Kane snarled aloud, shaking his head furiously, tossing back his mane of hair. He had no time to entertain notions of love, romance or simple old-fashioned lust, and less patience with memories of all the women he had loved, fought and lost. Memories were the worst. They soured his stomach, quenched the fire in his spirit and took all the strength from his limbs.

He had loved Brigid Baptiste, with her long red-gold hair the color of an autumn sunset and eyes the hue of emeralds. She had loved him fiercely in return, although they had many differences between them.

She was a woman with a brilliant intellect he had admired, yet it was tainted by a streak of romanticism that had finally cost her life. It was a trait to which he had been irresistibly drawn, but now she was dead and he was alone. That was the reality he had forced himself to live with for many, many years, but it was one Kane had never fully accepted. If he had, he would have taken the plunge off the plateau's edge long before.

He knew now Brigid had attempted too much and undertaken too many risks, and he had remained silent when he should have objected to her plan of action. Even after they were married, he was too impressed by her courage and idealism to stand in the way of achieving her dreams. The lure of building a world free of baronial tyranny, the promise of equality between human and hybrid—even now Kane couldn't understand how she could have been such a fool as to believe the imperator's words, spoken first by Sam, then stridently expanded upon by Lakesh. Why hadn't she realized, like Kane, there had to be something wrong?

Kane felt the sting of unshed tears in his eyes and he began a deep-breathing exercise. He relaxed his neck and shoulders first, then worked all the way down to his toes. He concentrated on regulating his respiration, putting himself into a quasi-hypnotic state.

He was trying to achieve the "Mag mind," a technique that emptied his consciousness of all nonessentials and allowed his instincts to rise to the fore. He'd been trained to do it while a Cobaltville Magistrate, and had used it for handling pain when he'd been wounded, or for dealing with physical exhaustion. It wasn't quite as effective as dealing with emotional pain and stress, but he didn't want to risk medicating himself with the few sedatives still in the medical stores, not with the plans he had made for himself.

After a couple of minutes, the sharpest edge of grief had been blunted and he left his quarters, making his way swiftly to the workshop adjacent to the vehicle depot. He picked up a kit of tools, then reversed direction and went to the operations center. As he expected, Bry was still there, frowning at a monitor screen and the text scrolling across it.

He didn't look up when Kane entered, but he demanded harshly, "What are you going to do about her?"

"I haven't decided yet."

"She knows more than she's telling…a *hell* of a lot more."

Kane nodded. "I'm aware of that."

Bry pushed his wheelchair back from the desk and gave him an appraising glare. "We can't trust her."

"I'm aware of that, too."

As if he hadn't heard Kane's response, Bry went on, "Stupidity nearly got us killed before. We made the mistake of underestimating the Nirodha, and that's how I ended up in this chair." He patted his knees for emphasis. "Let's not underestimate the girl."

Kane said softly, grimly, "We have something Lakesh and Erica want...or we have something they fear. Something of tremendous value, at least."

Bry chuckled, a dry-wood-rasp sound with no real humor in it. "I wish I knew what it was."

"Me, too. That's why you're going to send me to Redoubt Yankee, so I can recover the last piece of hardware we need to finish the retrieval circuit."

Bry's eyes widened in astonishment, then narrowed in apprehension. "Have you gone insane? If you're caught there, monkeying around with what's left of the temporal dilator—"

Kane cut him off with a short gesture of impatience. "Yes, yes. I remember."

"And you think you're exempt from the death penalty?"

A corner of Kane's mouth quirked in a smile. "I guess if I don't come back, we'll find out once and for all."

He turned toward the antechamber and the gateway unit. "I'll disconnect the power couplings while you reset the controls. I only want to travel through linear space for the moment.''

"How do you know he didn't block our gateway's phase-transit signature?'' Bry demanded loudly. "If he did, best-case scenario is you'll be bounced back here with a bad case of jump sickness. At worst case, you'll just speed around the entire Cerberus network like a handful of electrons.''

With a disdainful snort, Kane entered the ready room and went to the base of the elevated jump chamber. "Remember who we're talking about.''

The acoustics of the operation center adequately conveyed Bry's deep sigh. "Right. I stand corrected. Give me a couple of minutes to reboot and reroute the wave-guide conformals.''

Kneeling before the elevated platform, Kane carefully removed the coaxial and fiber-optic cables from the various ports. Even after all these years, he was still slightly surprised by the intensity of anger Bry felt toward Lakesh. Learning that Lakesh had essentially framed him for a crime in order to recruit him to Cerberus hadn't embittered him.

Decades before, when Lakesh decided not to remain a key facilitator of the unification program's aims and goals but become its most dangerous adversary, he manipulated the political system of the baronies to secretly restore the Cerberus redoubt to full operational capacity. But having a headquarters for a resistance movement meant nothing if there were no resistance fighters.

The only way to find them was through yet more manipulation. Using the genetic records on file in villes, Lakesh selected candidates for his rebellion, but finding them and recruiting were two different things. With his authority and influence, he set them up, framing them for crimes against their respective villes.

It was a cruel, heartless plan with a barely acceptable risk factor, but Lakesh believed it was the only way to spirit them out of their villes, turn them against the barons and make them feel indebted to him.

By the time Kane had finished disconnecting the cables and sealed the access plate, Bry called out to him from the operations center, "Destination lock encoded. Ready to make the phase transit."

Kane glanced toward him, started to lift his right index finger to his nose, caught himself, then stepped up into the jump chamber. Using the wedge-shaped metal handle affixed to the armaglass, he closed the heavy, counter-balanced door. The lock clicked, circuitry engaged and the automatic transit process began. He briefly considered leaving the chamber and retrieving his *katana*, but decided it was best to make his trespass unarmed except for the tool kit.

He leaned against the far brown-tinted wall, folding his arms over his chest. A low hum rose from the floor, rising in pitch. As the pattern of hexagonal disks above and below him began to exude a silvery shimmer,

Kane wondered briefly if Lakesh ever wished he had taken this particular gateway unit with him when he left the installation for good.

He doubted it, since Lakesh's capacity for sentiment seemed to have been swallowed up by his pride and ambition to win the Consolidation War by any means necessary. But whether he cared about the unit or not, the fact remained Lakesh was the first human being ever to undergo the matter-transmission process, his body transformed to digital information, then transmitted along a hyperdimensional pathway and reassembled in a receiver unit. The first time, the receiver unit had only been a few feet away.

But even to accomplish such a short jump, both the transmitting and receiving mat-trans units had required an inestimable number of maddeningly intricate electronic procedures, all occurring within milliseconds of one another, to minimize the margins for error. The actual matter-to-energy conversion process was sequenced by an array of computers and microprocessors with a number of separate but overlapping operational cycles.

Matter transmission worked on the principle that everything organic and inorganic could be reduced to encoded information. The primary stumbling block to actually moving the principle from the theoretical to the practical was the sheer quantity of information that had to be transmitted, received and reconstituted without making any errors in the decoding.

The string of information required to program a computer with every bit and byte of data pertaining to the transmitted subject, particularly the reconstruction of a complex biochemical organism out of a digitized carrier wave, ran to the trillions of binary digits.

The process had been found to be absolutely impossible to achieve by the employment of Einsteinian physics. Only quantum physics, coupled with quantum mechanics, had made it work. As the physicist who had made the final breakthrough in reconciling relativistic and quantum mechanics, Lakesh should have been as famous and as admired as Einstein. Instead, he had labored not just in obscurity, but in government-ordered anonymity.

But he was by no means the first to make this discovery. The forebears of Balam's people possessed the knowledge of hyperdimensional physics. The so-called Archons had shared this knowledge in piecemeal fashion with the scientists of the Totality Concept.

But they hadn't shared their knowledge that the gateways could accomplish far more than linear travel from point to point along a quantum channel. When Lakesh realized he was only rediscovering ancient scientific principles—and only those that had been laid out for him to stumble over—his ego had been severely wounded.

And perhaps, Kane reflected, that bitterness had driven him to reach for even greater goals, even if he had to not just compromise his principles to achieve them, but also bury them six feet under. Heaving a profanity-seasoned sigh, Kane decided Lakesh's motivations really didn't matter and hadn't for a very long time.

The plasma wave forms resembling white, early-morning mist began wafting from the emitter array above and below. Lakesh referred to the wreaths of vapor as a by-product of the quincunx effect, an infinitesimally short period of time when lower dimensional space was phased into a higher dimension.

Kane closed his eyes, waiting to be swept up in the nanosecond of comfortable nonexistence.

Chapter 10

With a faint hum vibrating against his eardrums. Kane blinked and the world swam mistily back into reality. He swayed on unsteady legs, a bit surprised to see he had ended the gateway jump in the same standing posture in which he had begun it.

Usually, no matter how jumpers arranged themselves before a transit, they arrived at their destinations flat on their backs. This time he remained upright, but his back was against the door and he faced the smoke-gray armaglass rear wall of the mat-trans chamber. He felt remarkably clearheaded, a small bonus for which he breathed a sigh of relief. Sometimes even the cleanest of jumps had debilitating effects.

When and if the matter-stream carrier wave modulations could not be synchronized between receiving and transmitting gateway units, the usual result was a severe bout of jump sickness, symptoms of which included minor hemorrhaging, vomiting, excruciating head pain, weakness and hallucinations.

Heaving up on the handle, Kane shouldered the door open. The heavy armaglass portal swung outward slowly, and he guessed it hadn't been opened—or closed—in a very long time. He strained his ears, listening for a tense, breathless tick of time. He heard nothing, so he cautiously eased through the doorway. He wasn't surprised by what he saw, only by the fact that it still looked the same as the last time he had seen it, at least ten years previous. The same vanadium-sheathed walls, the same armaglass, even the same furniture.

Kane stood in a very long room, at least twenty yards in length. The wall on his left was completely covered by armaglass, running the entire length of the room. On the far side of it, a catwalk stretched to a central control complex. Instrument consoles with glass-covered gauges and computer terminals lined the walls. Even at this distance, he could hear the purposeful hum of drive units and banks of computers chittering like startled crickets.

He strode onto the railed catwalk. It overlooked a vast chamber, shaped like a hollow hexagon, and was far larger than looked possible from the outside of the building. A dim glow shone down from the high, flat ceiling, two faint columns of light beaming from twin fixtures, both the size of wag tires. Massive wedge-shaped ribs of metal supported the roof.

Electronic equipment and chassis of machinery rose from plinths and podia, and even after all these years, Kane still had only the broadest idea of their functions and purpose. Overhead lights gleamed on alloyed handrails, glass coverings and the CPUs. Ten chairs rose from the floor before each console.

Crystal-fronted vid screens covered four walls.

Blinding light shone from some of the screens, while others showed only whorls of color. Others displayed exterior views of Redoubt Yankee. The vid network was focused primarily on the Cube and the buildings around it. A black, almost featureless shape, the Cube resembled a gargantuan block of black stone squatting in the center of the circle of dead vegetation.

The massive structure looked very much like a medieval fortress, but with a streamlined architecture. Made of very dark stone, it rose in a complex of pillars and overhanging buttresses. The sheer-walled building loomed nearly two hundred feet above smaller structures like a squared-off mountain peak towering over foothills. Many years before, an explosion had blown out chunks of the facade, but the holes had been repaired.

However, some of the smaller buildings around the Cube had eroded so much they had they fallen completely into ruin. Roofless arches reared from the ground, and a few storage buildings were scattered around the outer perimeter of the walls.

A broad blacktop avenue ran inward toward the Cube. The asphalt had a peculiar ripple pattern to it, and weeds sprouted from splits in the surface. The rippling effect was a characteristic result of earthquakes triggered by nuclear-bomb shock waves.

Lampposts lined the road. Most of them had rusted through and were leaning at forty-five-degree angles. The avenue widened inside the walls, opening into a broad courtyard filled with great blocks of basalt and concrete that had fallen from the buildings. Secondary lanes stretched out in all directions, a spokelike pattern of streets, bike paths and pedestrian walkways.

The entire community served as the seat of Operation Chronos. Code-named Redoubt Yankee, it had been built on one of the Santa Barbara or Channel Islands, disguised as a satellite campus of the University of California. As one of the finest and most secret research establishments in the world, its engineering and computer centers were second to none. Its accomplishments in the field of physics were never matched. The personnel of the installation cracked the so-called cosmic code within the walls of the main building, known as the Cube.

Kane remembered how Brigid described the cosmic code as vernacular for the unified field theory. It referred to the mathematical reconstruction of the first few seconds of the Big Bang, when the universe was a primal monobloc without dimensions of space.

Beyond the perimeter lay the green jungle of Thunder Isle, a savage Eden of the like never before dreamed by any utopian. At one time Kane had considered renaming the isle after Domi, since its discovery derived more from her than anyone else—or rather the apparent death of Domi.

There was something ominous about all of the Western Islands, and this one, named Thunder Isle by its nearest neighbors, the inhabitants of New Edo, was extremely disturbing. According to what they had been told by the then-ruler of New Edo, Lord Takaun, a cyclical phenomenon occurred on the island. He described lightning that seemed to strike up, accompanied by sounds like thunder, even if the weather was clear.

Takaun had no explanation for it, but he knew that on the heels of the phenomenon often came incursions of what the more impressionable New Edoans claimed were demons. Brigid was shown the corpse of one such demon, and she tentatively identified it as a Dryosaurus, a man-sized dinosaur.

She was able to identify other artifacts found on the shores of Thunder Isle—a helmet from the era of the conquistadors, and stone spearhead that resembled a Folsom point, so named for Folsom, New Mexico, the archeological site where the first one was found. It was evidence of a prehistoric culture, many thousands of years old.

According to Takaun, the phenomena had been very sporadic for the past five years, occurring only a few times. Then a new cycle had begun, with a far greater regularity.

When Brigid, Grant and Kane went to Thunder Isle, all of them glimpsed another dinosaur, far larger and more vicious than the Dryosaur. In fact, it killed a group of Magistrates they had been tracking.

Once inside the installation, they found video evidence that Domi hadn't been killed by the implode gren—she had been time-trawled. All of them knew how the technicians of Operation Chronos used the breakthroughs of Lakesh's Project Cerberus to spin off their own innovations and achieve their own successes.

Most of the time-trawling experiments were failures. The living tissue of whatever was trawled forward from the past usually broke down. It wasn't until Lakesh made the first fully functional gateway unit operational that Chronos was able to assemble the trawled subjects in the mat-trans without organic decohesion.

They learned that at the precise microinstant before Domi was swallowed by the full lethal fury of the grenade, she was trawled and then suspended in a noncorporeal matrix. Brigid activated the instruments of the temporal dilator that retrieved the girl, but she had no recollection whatsoever of what had occurred. They themselves saw no one in the installation, but it showed signs of recent habitation.

Only much later did they find out the installation was inhabited by an old enemy, the brilliant but deranged dwarf, Sindri. He himself told them while investigating the installation, he had discovered a special encoded program that was linked to, but separate from, Chronos. It was code-named Parallax Points.

The temporal dilator itself had overloaded and reached critical mass, resulting in a violent meltdown of its energy core. Kane, Grant and Brigid took refuge on nearby New Edo. When the radiation levels in the installation ebbed to nonlethal levels, they returned. No trace of Sindri was ever found, but none of them really believed he had perished. It seemed more likely he had used the facility's mat-trans unit to gate to his space station haven, *Parallax Red,* but that was only speculation, since Sindri had never returned to vex them again.

In the months following the incident on Thunder Isle, Brigid, Bry, Lakesh and several of the Moon base scientists made several visits to the Operation Chronos redoubt, salvaging what could be used. Most of the machinery was damaged beyond any reasonable expectation of repair, but the Parallax Points data was retrieved and put to use, including the protective garments Kane had named shadow suits.

A sudden motion on one of the monitor screens caught Kane's attention and brought his mental meanderings to a halt. He tensed, unconsciously holding his breath as he stared at the image on the screen, trying to identify it. When he did, he began breathing again, but he didn't relax.

He wasn't surprised to see that a squad of Tigers of Heaven, New Edo's soldiery, patrolled the grounds. They were attired in suits of segmented armor made from wafers of metal held together by small, delicate chain. Overlaid with a dark brown lacquer, the interlocking and overlapping plates were trimmed in scarlet and gold. Between flaring shoulder epaulets, war helmets fanned out with sweeping curves of metal. Some resembled wings, others horns. The face guards, wrought of a semitransparent material, presented the inhuman visage of a snarling tiger.

Quivers of arrows dangled from their shoulders, and

longbows, made of lacquered wood, were strapped to
their backs. Each samurai carried two longswords in
black scabbards swinging back from each hip. None
of them carried firearms, but their skill with *katanas*
and the bows was such they didn't really need them—
or at least that had been the case when Shizuka com-
manded the Tigers. New Edo had sustained heavy
losses during the Consolidation War, so the current
generation of samurai might not possess the skills of
their forebears.

But Kane wasn't interested in finding out one way
or the other. He glanced down over the rail of the
catwalk. The shafts of luminescence fell upon a huge
forked pylon made of a burnished metal that projected
up from a concave area in the center of the chamber.
The two horns of the pylon curved up and around,
facing each other. Mounted on the tip of each prong
were blackened shards of what appeared to be quartz
crystals.

Twenty feet tall, a gap of ten feet separated the
forked branches. Extending outward from the base of
the pylon, at ever decreasing angles into the low shadows, was a taut network of fiber-optic filaments. They
disappeared into sleeve sockets that perforated the
plates of dully gleaming alloy sheathing the floor.

Kane strode to the end of the catwalk and swung
out onto a metal-runged ladder that stretched down to
the concave area. He quickly descended and made his
way to the temporal dilator. Many of the floor plates
were buckled, showing bulges and splits. The pylon

itself was canted forward, about ten degrees out of true.

When the pent-up energies of the dilator built to critical mass and were vented, the floor supporting the pylon ruptured, rivets popping loose and the crystal spheres exploding. But fortunately, only the temporal dilator's individual power source melted down, and left the machine itself somewhat intact.

The dilator was composed of a blend of conductive alloys and ceramics, which made it virtually indestructible. Sindri had compared the dilator to a giant electromagnet, creating two magnetic fields, one at right angles to the other. Both of the fields represented one plane of space with a third dimensional field reproduced through sound manipulation.

Kane dropped to one knee beside the base of the dilator, and his fingers explored the support column, seeking out a tiny, nearly invisible latch. After running his hands over and around it, he found the proper prong and depressed it. A section of the pylon sprang open and out, revealing a complexity of circuits and crystal memory cards.

Kane laid out the tool kit and removed first a small flashlight, then an array of tiny metal instruments. He strapped the flashlight around his head, then fit the blade of a tiny screwdriver into the slot of an equally tiny screw on the underpart of a microprocessor panel. He didn't have Brigid Baptiste's gift of perfect and total recall, but he had spent years studying the diagrams of the dilator's molecular imaging scanners.

Quickly but carefully he began removing the data configuration cards.

He knew the purpose of Operation Chronos was to find a way to enter probability gaps between one interval of time and another, using much the same scientific principles and hardware as Project Cerberus. Project Cerberus and Operation Chronos were all aspects of the same mechanism; only the applications of the principle differed. It had occurred to Kane that the entire undertaking might have been code-named the Totality Concept because it encompassed the totality of everything, the entire workings of the universe.

Inasmuch as Cerberus utilized quantum events to reduce organic and inorganic material to digital information for transmission through hyperdimensional space, the temporal dilator was built on the same application to peep into other time lines and even trawl living matter from the past, and perhaps the future.

Although the temporal dilator had been built to access and manipulate the chronon subatomic particle string, Lakesh had postulated that Operation Chronos had triggered a probability wave dysfunction. According to him, the dilator disrupted the chronon structure and created an alternate future scenario for humanity that led up to the nukecaust itself. Kane had never quite been convinced of Lakesh's theories, but over the past twenty years he had come to believe he spoke the truth—even if the scientist no longer subscribed to the same beliefs.

But Kane had gone even further than Lakesh's hypotheses. He knew that time was malleable, a series of events running in a continuous stream from the Big Bang all the way to the future. But for all its malleability, there were limitations—no one could coexist at any point in the past where he or she had already existed. A temporal fault line would then be created, fatally undermining causality.

Kane had spent a good deal of the past two decades looking for evidence of trips back in time that had resulted in the fault lines, and he was convinced he had found the major fault. The crack in the continuum had began on Thunder Isle, on a certain day, decades before.

The first memory card came free of the panel. Kane very gently tucked the flat, rectangular wafer of pressed crystal into a padded pocket of the shadow suit. As he began to insert the screwdriver back into the panel to remove the other three, he sensed rather than heard a presence in the huge chamber. A voice, more of a furious lion's roar than a man's, bellowed, "Are you fused out completely, you stupid bastard?"

The light shining down abruptly dimmed, as if a gargantuan shape blocked its path. Keeping his expression calm and composed, Kane looked up at the sudden shadow. A brown-skinned giant stood wide-legged above him, heavy boots planted like tree trunks on the floor of the catwalk. Thick hands gripped the top rail. He towered six feet four inches tall, his shoulders spread out on either side of a thickly tendoned neck like massive planks. Behind him Kane saw a pair of Tigers of Heaven, bows drawn and arrows nocked, ready to let fly with three-foot-long feathered shafts.

Light gleamed dully from Grant's shaved head. Like Kane, a multitude of scars showed on his face, bare arms and hands. Almost every type of weapon in existence had made those scars. Although he looked too huge and brutish to have many abilities beyond sheer strength, Grant was an exceptionally intelligent and talented man.

Behind the deep-set eyes, fierce, down-sweeping mustache, granite jaw and broken nose lay a genius of tactics, strategies and leadership. He was also the best pilot Kane had ever known, flying with equal skill everything from Deathbirds to the swift and difficult Manta TAVs. It didn't matter what the flying machine was, or whether it was powered by rotors, jets or magnetohydrodynamic air spikes. Grant could pilot it through all weathers like an angel, or a devil.

Like Kane, he had lived a great deal of his life by and in violence. He had been shot, stabbed, battered, beaten, burned, buried and once very nearly suffocated on the surface of the Moon.

All of this flitted through Kane's mind in an instant as Grant's bellow still echoed in the vast chamber, like the vibrations of a gong after it had been struck. No man alive dared to speak to Kane with the unchecked rage Grant directed toward him. Nor would Kane have accepted it from any other man alive except Grant.

Blandly, he said, "Good to see you, too. How're the kids?"

Grant blinked down at him. "Tomei is on New Edo. Kiyomasa is on a trading voyage up along the coast, not that you give a shit. You tripped a silent alarm when you gated in. If I hadn't been here on the island, my Tigers would've cut you up and used what was left of you as chum."

"Tasty," Kane commented, tapping the screwdriver against the palm of his hand. "Is that the standard penalty for trespassing on Thunder Isle?"

"You're out of your fucking mind, you know that?" Grant's voice was no longer the eardrum-compressing roar. Now it sounded like the distant rumble of thunder.

"So you've told me." Kane presented the image of trying to dredge something up from his memory. "Come to think of it, as I recall, that was pretty much the *very* last thing you told me. How long ago was that now?"

Grant gusted out a sigh and pushed himself away from the handrail. "At least ten years, since the first time I caught you dicking around down there. You damn well know what you're doing earns you a mandatory death sentence, don't you?"

Kane returned his attention to the pylon. He raised a shoulder in a negligent shrug. "Yeah, but I figured it was worth the risk this one time."

"As long as you know where you stand." Grant nodded to the two samurai and made a downward gesture with one hand. They obediently relaxed the tension on their bowstrings and unnocked the arrows.

Kane repressed a sigh of relief, despite the fact he knew Grant would not have ordered the samurai to let fly. Grant had been with him through every kind of thick and thin, every variety of horror and joy. They had fought shoulder to shoulder in battles around half the planet, and even off the planet. They had fought everything from Magistrates to Martian transadapts, carnobots and carnosaurs to wily and savage swampies. They had battled against the massed firepower of the baronial armies and the Mongol fanatics of the Tushe Gun—they had made war against nature, natives, professionals, madmen, geniuses and finally, even each other.

Grant had been through all of it covering Kane's back, patching up his wounds and on more than one occasion literally carrying him out of hellzones. Kane knew he was still alive only because of the man, even though he had twice flaunted Grant's death-sentence edict, put into New Edo law twenty years before and grimly enforced. Kane knew of at least three operatives dispatched by the imperator who had been put to death for just setting foot on Thunder Isle, much less actually tampering with the temporal dilator.

Grant spoke again, his voice a hushed, hollow echo. "It wasn't something you can change, Kane. It wasn't a mistake that you can erase. It all really happened."

Kane began removing the second memory card. "I know. I just don't want it to have."

Grant didn't reply. Finally he asked, "Are you hungry? It's about my dinnertime."

Chapter 11

The meal was nutritious but plain—white rice mixed with various steamed vegetables, little cubes of raw fish and garnished with hastily prepared sauces. It was a meal Kane would have disdained twenty years ago, but now he ate it with relish, pleased to treat his palate to anything other than MREs.

Although the food was something less than delicious, the view was magnificent. Kane and Grant sat out on the balcony of the old palace, enjoying the late-afternoon sea breeze wafting in from New Edo's harbor. It stirred a set of wind chimes, adding a tinkling musical accompaniment to the soothing sound of the ocean waves.

Kane was always impressed by the little kingdom, with its cobblestone roads winding up and over a series of gently rolling hills, all green with luxuriant grass. Cattle grazed inside split-rail fences. Cultivated fields made a patchwork pattern over the terrain. Gravel-covered footpaths branched off from the main thoroughfare, leading to modest, single-level homes made primarily of carpentered driftwood, each one with gardened terraces.

There was no litter anywhere, and all the shrubbery

and undergrowth was trimmed neatly back. Some of the hedgerows had been clipped into shapes resembling snails, cranes and dragons.

The fortress of New Edo's daimyo, Lord Grant, dominated the southern side of the island settlement. Built on a spur of land that jutted into the luminous blue waters of the Cific, the small peninsula rose in a flat, broad hill toward its center. There the palace had been raised over three decades earlier.

It was a sprawling structure with many windows, balconies and carved frames. The wide gates were of metal set with suspended gongs. Deep moats surrounded it on three sides, and cliffs formed a boundary on the side that faced the sea. At the top of the walls were parapets and protected positions for archers and blastermen.

The columns supporting the many porches and loggias were made of lengths of thick bamboo, bent into unusual shapes. The curving roof arches and interlocking shingles all seemed to be made of lacquered wood. An inner courtyard held a pool and a fountain shaped in the aspect of intertwined figures.

New Edo was a living testament to the strength of human will, not just to survive, but to transcend any and all hardships. Hacking a little storybook civilization out of the rock of one of the Western Islands was more than just difficult; it had been damn near impossible. Keeping it a thriving society was a series of hardships, but Grant had managed to do it even after the death of Shizuka. But Kane figured that by now much of the day-to-day administrative tedium was left to the couple's children.

Both men sat cross-legged on a tatami mat with a low table between them. Grant wore a dark green kimono, which left his arms bare except for a delicate silver filigreed bracelet around his right wrist. After Kane brought him up to date on the arrival of Tanvirah, the two men ate and drank in silence. However, Kane was very aware of a guard standing silently behind him, leaning against the railing of the gallery that overlooked the lawn leading down to the sea.

The guard was a woman, but she stood in harsh contrast to the serene surroundings. Each segment of her armor was made from strips of lacquered bamboo laced together with chains. A metal *kabuto* war helmet fanned down at the rear of her head and bore a sickle moon at the crest. Her black hair was cut square at her nape. Curved butterfly longswords hung from each hip. Her complexion was like that of honey mixed with butter, a shade darker than he was accustomed to seeing among the average New Edoan.

Grant hadn't made introductions, but Kane could feel the woman's hostility toward him, like an aura of static electricity. He wondered briefly if she was waiting for a signal from her daimyo to cut off the gaijin intruder's head. Kane wasn't surprised by the gender of the guard—even before the nukecaust, the traditional female roles in Japanese society had changed. Women had the right to pursue whatever vocation they wished. Shizuka's own sister had become a geisha, while she had chosen the path of the samurai.

Gusting out a weary sigh, Grant asked, "What am I going to do with you, Kane?"

Kane shrugged. "You know the answer to that as well as I do. Nothing."

"You violated sovereign New Edoan law. Thunder Isle has been forbidden to everybody for over twenty years. I cut you slack once before when you disobeyed me—"

"And now you'll cut my throat for disobeying you?" Kane tried not to sound too scornful. "What happened to live and let live?"

"Kind of a simpleminded philosophy in today's world, isn't it?"

"Great truths often seem simpleminded…even when they're actually profound. Sort of like Domi."

Grant's face creased in a deep frown and he reached out for his cup of sake. "What's she got to do with anything?"

"How long has it been since you even thought about her?" Kane challenged.

"About an hour ago." Grant's voice was muted to a rumble. "I think about her every day…I even think about *you* every day, you self-righteous son of a bitch."

Kane didn't respond. He dropped his gaze to his plate, not wanting to look into the man's eyes. He remembered the discussions he'd had with Grant in the past when the full impact of Domi's death had finally registered. Though the girl had died trying to save Quavell and himself, she had loved Grant. Still, she had probably known more pure enjoyment in her few short years than both he and Grant in their combined lifetimes.

Quietly Kane said, "I didn't go back to Redoubt Yankee because I got bored in Cerberus."

"I didn't think you did." Grant swallowed a mouthful of sake, grimaced and said, "Even if I waive the death penalty, I can't let you take the memory cards back with you. I know what you're trying to do."

He regarded Kane with a dark, level stare. "I know how you feel, I really do. But what you want to accomplish isn't within your power—it isn't within anybody's power. I thought you had accepted that a long time ago. Make the best of your life, of the years you have left. You and Bry are more than welcome to make a life here. Stop fixating on the past."

Kane felt a thickness growing in his chest, and his throat was constricted. He knew his former partner was right, but his dreams always returned to Brigid, Domi and DeFore and even Grant. He had loved them all so very much, and he missed them terribly.

He had realized years before, with more sorrow than surprise, that he would willingly go back to the worst hour of his life, when he lay with his back being flayed open within the Scorpia Prime's torture chamber, if it meant he could share an hour with his comrades who were gone. The time he had spent at the Cerberus redoubt battling the barons had been the happiest, most productive years of his life. He was willing to trade almost anything to live them again.

"Grant," Kane said with all the conviction he could muster, "it's a past that was changed—"

Grant straightened, voicing a groan of exasperation.

"—altered somehow in the past," Kane went on doggedly. "A fault line that has to be repaired. It wasn't supposed to happen this way. I know you're worried that to fix one fracture will create a dozen more, but I know how to do it without making any more temporal ripples."

Between clenched teeth, Grant growled, "We've had this fucking conversation like about what—fifty times before? You don't know *what* will happen. Just when you think you understand time travel, some goddamn X factor pops up and bites you in the ass."

Kane struggled to keep his own temper in check. He didn't want a reprise of the decade-old argument with Grant that had resulted in his virtual banishment from both New Edo and the company of his former partner. "There might be an X factor in all this, but it could be in our favor this time."

"How the hell do you figure that?" Grant demanded.

"Because something has Lakesh and Erica scared to death—so scared they risked their own daughter's life to find out what I'm doing."

Grant scowled, his prominent brow ridges casting his deeply socketed eyes into shadow. "And just what are you doing but singing the same old 'this wasn't supposed to happen' song?''

Kane forced a grin. "I think I'm on the last stanza." His grin vanished as he added, "But more than that…the Nirodha might have figured out the words to the song, too."

AS HE HAD MANY TIMES in the past dozen years, Kane began to justify the actions he had in mind. No one could take this life as a real one if he stopped to think about what had come to pass.

Nearly three decades before, the nine baronies were poised on the brink of civil war, sparked by one of their own, but the internecine strife had its roots thousands of years in the past, beginning with the so-called Archons.

All of the Cerberus warriors had believed the barons were under the sway of the Archon Directorate, a nonhuman race that influenced human affairs for thousands of years. In fact, Lakesh claimed the entirety of human history was intertwined with the activities of the entities called Archons, although they were referred to by many names over many centuries.

The supposed goal of the Directorate and the barons was the unification of the world under their complete control, with all nonessential and nonproductive humans eliminated. Nearly two hundred years after the nukecaust, that objective had almost been achieved. The small population was easier to manipulate. But unification wasn't as easy to maintain as it was to gain.

But eventually all of them in Cerberus had learned that the elaborate back story was all a ruse, bits of truth mixed in with outrageous fiction. The Archon Directorate didn't exist except as a vast cover story, created in the twentieth century and grown larger with each succeeding generation. The only so-called Archon on Earth was Balam, the last survivor of an extinct race that had once shared the planet with humankind. Nor could the Archons be properly described as extraterrestrials, since they had been born on Earth, even if their forebears had not.

Balam finally revealed the truth behind the Directorate and the hybridization program initiated centuries before. He claimed that the Archon Directorate existed only as an appellation and a myth created by the predark government agencies as a control mechanism. Lakesh referred to it as the Oz Effect, wherein a single vulnerable entity created the illusion of being the representative of an all-powerful body.

The nine barons weren't immortal, but they were as close as flesh and blood creatures could come to it. Due to their hybrid metabolisms, their longevities far exceeded those of humans. Barring accidents, illnesses—or assassinations—the barons' life spans could conceivably be measured in centuries. Even the youngest of them was close to a hundred years old.

But the price paid by the barons for their extended life spans was not cheap. They were physically fragile, prone to lethargy and their metabolisms were easy prey to infections, which was one reason they tended to sequester themselves from the ville-bred humans they ruled. Once a year, all the barons traveled to the Dulce facility to have their blood filtered and their autoimmune systems boosted. In severe cases, even damaged organs were replaced from the storage banks of organic material stockpiled there.

All of the hybrids reproduced by a form of cloning and gene splicing, but it hadn't seemed reasonable they would rely completely on the subterranean Dulce facilities. If they didn't have access to a secondary installation, then extinction for the barons was less than a generation away. Or so all the Cerberus exiles fervently hoped, once the Dulce installation was destroyed.

That hope vanished quickly when they learned of the Area 51 complex and the body of legends that had sprung up around alien involvement with the top secret facility. The so-called aliens weren't referred to by name, but they fit the general physical description of Balam's people. If that was indeed the case, Lakesh theorized that the medical facilities that might exist in Area 51 would be of great use to the barons, since they would already be designed for their metabolisms. Baron Cobalt reactivated them, turned them into a processing and treatment center, without having to rebuild from scratch.

It was during Kane's captivity in Area 51 that they learned about a mysterious figure called the imperator. He intended to set himself up as overlord of the villes, with the barons subservient to him. That bit of news was surprising enough, but it quickly turned shocking when they found out that none other than Balam, whom they had thought was gone forever, supported the imperator, who liked to be called Sam.

Sam not only claimed to carry the DNA of Erica van Sloan and Enlil, the last of the Annunaki, but he had also restored Sloan's youth. In order to swing Lakesh to his side, Sam had accomplished the same miracle with him. Only much later did Lakesh realize the imperator's restoration had been something less than miraculous.

None of the Cerberus warriors found the concept of an entity bearing the blended genetic material of three races disturbing. However, the powers he appeared to wield and his autocratic attitude were frightening. Sam hadn't come right out and threatened the lives of those in Cerberus, but he hadn't needed to. The inference that he could do so if they turned down Sam's offer certainly hadn't been subtle.

On the face of it, what Sam offered was exceptionally tempting and even logical. Rather than have Lakesh and his Cerberus exiles continue to wage their uncoordinated guerrilla war on the barons, Sam wanted those resources under his control, where they would be given direction and focus.

By allying with the imperator, Lakesh and his people would be protected, and he would have a voice in the implementation of a new order. There would be no more need to hide, and the Cerberus exiles wouldn't bear the stigma of being outlanders any longer.

Sam's proposal thus made perfect sense—perhaps that was what made all of them so suspicious. And now, decades after the imperator's first appearance, the new free culture he claimed he wanted to build was a reality—and it had the skids under it, sliding down a slippery slope to the lip of a precipice, overlooking the red mists of Hell itself.

In the political backwash of the Nirodha conflict in Asia, and as the standard of living for the population at large dropped off, individual governments fell and the combined military forces of the imperator stepped in. Most of Europe and almost all of Asia came under a worldwide military dictatorship formed by imperial forces.

But the American confederated states hadn't fared much better than the rest of the world. The economy was liable to collapse at any moment. The culture groaned under the weight of countless unskilled unemployables who had to be fed, clothed and housed at the expense of the states. The corrupting influences of state-supplied SQUID implants kept the idle from rioting and committing crimes, true enough, but it also deadened them to truth and individual initiative, blinding them with a cloak of illusory beauty.

No one knew or cared any longer about the difference between freedom and cushioned slavery. Behind the facade of well-being created by the SQUIDs, the culture seethed with indolence and ugliness.

The SQUIDs also kept the population of old and new humans in check by numbing the drive to procreate. It was a cleaner way to exterminate the useless eaters than pogroms and mass executions, for the population would be slashed from millions to mere manageable thousands in less than a decade. And those thousands would be slaves adapted to meet various needs.

The hybrids who now coexisted peacefully with humanity were at risk, even if they were the chosen ones of the imperator. No matter that they were not completely human, they sprang from essentially the same roots as humankind, so they were still a continuation of the race.

The world may not have been as violent and brutal as before, but it was far from being the utopia that Sam had described. It was a comfortable prison, but a prison nonetheless. Kane hated it, and that hatred didn't derive from a sense of dissatisfaction—he knew the world was trapped in a whirlpool of wrongness.

He had contemplated the whirlpool for many, many years, since the apparent destruction of the Nirodha movement. He had tried to decide whether the sense of wrongness was a strictly subjective impression brought about by emotional trauma, or was a true physical distortion of reality.

Finally he reached the conclusion that it was a combination of both—grief and loss had helped him see the distortion. And now that the distortion had been observed and identified, it could be rectified. The plan

Kane had worked out was both direct and clever, although he knew options should be left open for elements of improvisation.

"It has to be done," Kane told Grant flatly. "Someone has to find a solution and call a halt to this insanity. Right?"

"Yes, I know." Grant's deep voice was surprisingly gentle.

Encouraged by Grant's comment, Kane continued, "Sam is like a wizard, a sorcerer with his mind-control techniques through those goddamn SQUIDs. He owns most people. He's accomplished in one generation what the barons tried to do for ninety years...unifying the world under one whip, like a team of dogs. Someone has to save humanity or what's left of it. We have to act for humankind...and even if we die in the attempt, at least the world will survive to judge us."

Grant said nothing. He stared at Kane across the table, not blinking, not moving or even appearing to breathe. Kane felt some of the tension drain away from himself. He was right and he knew Grant was sure of it. Then he saw a tiny glitter of moisture within Grant's deep-set eyes. It took him a few seconds to realize the man's eyes were glistening with tears.

Grant lifted one hand in a gesture. He spoke one word: "Tomei."

Kane caught only a blurred, fragmented glimpse of gleaming metal from behind him, then the edge of the female guard's butterfly sword touched his throat, forcing his head back.

"I'm sorry, Kane." Grant's voice was a hoarse whisper of anguish. "Give me the memory cards without an argument, and I'll arrange for you to get back home safely. But I don't ever want to see you here again."

Chapter 12

"I wouldn't think you'd have me beheaded for trying to save lives," Kane said quietly. "Particularly Shizuka's."

The pressure of the sword blade against his throat increased, and he clenched his teeth, glancing up into the face of the guard. Her lips were compressed in a tight, white line and her dark eyes gleamed with fury. With a cold rush of recognition, he understood why her complexion was so dark.

"I'm sorry, Tomei," he said to her in as measured a tone as he could manage. "I'd forgotten your name. You and your twin brother were only four the last time I saw you."

"I never forgot you, Godfather," she replied, her voice shrill with hatred. "I remember the last time I saw you like it was an hour ago—you and Daddy brought my mother's body back here. She died saving your worthless ass."

For a moment, Tomei's figure faded and was replaced by a vision of an armored Shizuka, standing in the courtyard of Scorpia Prime's stronghold. Monstrous, semihuman Pischacas came at her, and her swords carved them up. They died screaming beneath her whirling blades, voicing either cries of pain or pleas for mercy.

When she finally fell under a massed assault, the surviving goblin-men hooted and jumped up and down on her corpse, performing antics like a crowd watching a sporting event. They cheered when one of the Pischacas held aloft her disembodied head by its long hair.

"Someone I loved more than anyone or anything in the world died that night, too." Kane did his best to keep his voice from quavering with emotion. He didn't want the girl to think he was afraid of dying.

"Hai." Tomei spit out the word. "Your brilliant and beautiful wife who had come to negotiate your release from Scorpia Prime. Both she and my mother died for you. And what have you done to honor their sacrifice? Become an obsessive, delusional madman who does nothing but bring pain to those who once loved him."

Kane cast his eyes from Tomei to Grant. "Is that what you think I am? A madman?"

Grant pressed the heels of his big hands against his forehead as if to keep his skull from breaking apart. He spoke in a guttural growl. "I don't want to talk about this anymore. I'm sick of it, sick of you, sick of your fucking fantasies. Even if you could get those data cards to work in whatever machine you and Bry have cobbled together, you're too goddamn crazy to trust with it. I wouldn't send you to the harbor to bring back a fish, much less send you back in time."

Kane swallowed a surge of sudden fury, and the up-and-down motion of his throat opened a small laceration. The almost weightless crystal cards now felt as heavy as bricks, hidden as they were in a slit pocket of his shadow suit.

Coldly, he said, "I've spent years on this, Grant. *Years.* Do you understand? I've got it all reasoned out. I've traced the primary fault line back to the fracture. *I can change things.* None of what happened these past twenty-seven years need happen, none of those people need die—"

Grant dropped his hands from his head to the table-top with a crash. Dishes and cups jumped and fell clattering to the floor. He snarled, "Turn over the cards, Kane."

"No." Kane bit out the word.

Tomei slid the blade of her sword under his chin and exerted pressure. "Do as my father, the daimyo of New Edo, commands. Ikazuchi Kojima—Thunder Isle—is part of New Edo's sovereign territory. Therefore you are no better than a common thief."

Kane stared directly into the girl's eyes. "You're going to have to kill me, kid."

"Do you think I won't?" she challenged, poising herself for a decapitating stroke. "I would love for you to suffer the same fate as my mother. It would be truly justice."

"I loved your mother," Kane said. "More than that, I respected her and her devotion to *otoko no michi,* the ancient and honorable samurai tradition. She was a fierce warrior, but she wasn't an assassin. Do you think she'd approve of what you're doing now?''

Tomei made a growling sound deep in her throat, a sound Kane recognized. He had heard it issuing from Grant countless times over the past forty years. He hoped it meant the same thing with Tomei as with her father—a noise of frustration when reason won out over angry impulse.

Grant echoed the growl and gestured impatiently. ''That's enough, Tomei.''

She glanced toward him, her eyes widening in surprise. ''Daddy—''

''Do it.''

The girl relaxed some of the tension in her sword arm, but the blade wasn't withdrawn. ''He's a thief! You've executed men for just trespassing on Ikazuchi Kojima. You can't let him—''

''Yes, I can.'' Grant's voice was a weary rumble. ''Do as I say, sweetheart.''

Blinking back angry tears, Tomei whipped the butterfly sword away from Kane's throat and, with an eye-blurring swiftness, resheathed it. Kane gingerly touched the skin at the base of his jaw and examined his index finger with rueful eyes. A spot of blood shone damply against the black fabric.

''I'm glad you're being reasonable,'' Kane said dryly.

Grant rose, slowly coming to his full height like a mountain pushing its way up from the surface of the sea. He extended his right hand toward Kane. "Let's see how reasonable you can be. The cards."

Kane locked eyes with Grant. "Are you getting deaf in your old age? I already said no."

"If you don't turn them over, I'll take them from you...and I won't be gentle about it. You may end up wishing I'd let Tomei cut your throat."

Kane exhaled a long breath through his nostrils. Using the top rail of the balcony as a brace, he got to his feet. "Grant, you're going to have to try to take them from me."

Grant stared at him stolidly, expressionlessly for a long silent moment. Kane met his gaze, but he saw how pain creased his dark, scarred face. Bleakly he realized he had known Grant for nearly half a century and still didn't fully understand him. Even the years they had spent together as Magistrates and then fighting the barons hadn't made them much closer than the first day they had met. He knew why—Grant feared not having any control over events that determined the fates of others.

Like Kane, he remembered how every battle they entered, they lost people they had considered friends. Each death hurt far worse than a bullet glancing off their Magistrate polycarbonate armor. Finally, out of a sense of self-preservation, Grant adopted a pragmatic philosophy: If you don't make friends, you can't lose friends. If you have nothing, you can't suffer losses.

Grant had refused to acknowledge Domi's declarations of love, deliberately dismissing her as something of a caricature of an outlander. He had tried to make the gap in their ages the reason he didn't want to get involved with her, sexually or otherwise. Domi had been patient and understanding for a year, until she grew tired of waiting and the love she had felt for him turned to resentment and then anger.

In truth, Grant had deliberately maintained a distance between him and Domi so if either of them died—or simply went away—the vacuum wouldn't be so difficult to endure. Then he had met Shizuka and fallen deeply in love. Domi had died never knowing how Grant really felt about her. And then Shizuka was ripped ruthlessly from Grant's life, and he was still struggling with the pain of her loss twenty years later.

Kane well remembered his own helplessness and rage when Brigid had been torn from him on the same night Shizuka was killed. Like Grant, the hole her absence left was never filled, but unlike him, the pain it left in its wake strengthened him—he had silently vowed never to let anyone he cared about be taken away from him again, even if he had to warp the laws of science and nature to fulfill that oath.

"Kane," Grant said quietly, an almost pleading note in his voice, "the only reason you've never tried to rule an army or a ville of your own is because you never gave a shit about pushing people around. But if you have the power to change history, you could rule the damn world without giving a single order and nobody would know it. That's too much power in the hands of anybody, including you. That's why I made

Thunder Isle off-limits to the rest of the world. Even Sam is afraid to send people here. Now maybe you've got a foolproof plan—''

"I do," Kane snapped coldly.

"—but you'll never know if it works or not because it's too fucking dangerous to find out!" Grant bared his teeth in a snarl of frustration. "Give me those goddamn cards!"

Kane shifted his weight on his heels, then to the balls of his feet, glancing over toward Tomei to make sure her blades were still sheathed. "No."

Grant blinked, lifted his massive arms as if in a shrug, then he lunged forward, kicking the small table out of his way. He cannonballed into Kane, who whipped out his arms as if embrace him. He locked his arms about Grant's body, trying to pinion him.

Grant rammed the crown of his shaved skull savagely against Kane's forehead, and little multicolored spirals erupted behind his eyes. His grip loosened and Grant broke free of it, snarling and growling in bloodthirsty gratification. The only words Kane understood were "Shizuka *died* for you!"

He slapped both hands around Kane's neck and began to squeeze. Kane jabbed his thumbs into the sides of Grant's neck, seeking out the nerve centers. But all of Grant's tendons and muscles were tense with the fury of his intention to choke Kane into unconsciousness. Kane jabbed three fingers into the man's solar plexus. It was like jabbing a plate of flexible steel. Grant grunted in pain but held on, tightening his thick fingers until Kane's breath blew hoarsely out of his mouth.

Grant applied his thumbs to the blood vessels on his neck. Kane shoved himself away from the gallery, catapulting them both through the wall, taking lathwork and oiled paper squares with them in a loud, clattering crash. They kicked and tore their way through the wreckage as they grappled with each other on wide-braced legs. Tomei shouted shrill words at them, but the men paid her no attention.

They lurched back to the gallery, and Tomei was forced to spring aside to avoid being bowled over. Grant forced Kane's upper body over the top wooden rail. Although tempted, Kane didn't knee him in the groin. He used the heel of his hands to force Grant's head up and back. Grant removed his left hand from around Kane's neck and planted it against his face for further leverage. Kane sank his teeth into the base of the bigger man's thumb.

Grant howled in furious pain. ''You son of a bitch! Cut it out!''

''You cut it out,'' Kane managed to growl around Grant's thumb joint. ''You started it!''

''I'll finish it, too!'' Bellowing, Grant tore his hand loose from Kane's mouth and stumbled backward, still clutching Kane by the throat. The two men staggered drunkenly from one end of the gallery to the other. Kane strained, kicked and fought his way out of Grant's stranglehold.

Grant stiff-armed Kane in the chest, slamming him

back against the railed gallery. He flung himself upon Kane again and seized his throat, squeezing it as if wringing out a towel. Kane didn't have the time to pry the big man's fingers from around his neck. Their combined weight was too much for the wooden railing. With a splintering crack, it gave way and both men plunged to the ground.

The fall was barely fifteen feet. Falling backward with Grant atop him, Kane doubled up his knees and planted his feet against the man's midsection. When he hit the turf on his back, he straightened his legs like steel springs. The soles of his boots pushed solidly against Grant's belly and propelled him up and over.

The man performed a clumsy midair somersault, arms windmilling wildly, the belled sleeves of his kimono flapping like the wings of a crazed bird. He slammed down full length on the ground, the top of his head barely three inches from the crown of Kane's head. The wind left his lungs in an explosive gasp.

Both men elbowed themselves over onto their knees, faces contorted in bare-toothed grimaces. Kane struck first, a swift left jab against the hinge of Grant's prominent jaw. Grant's immediate response was a looping right hook that collided against the side of Kane's head with a sound like a concrete block hitting a block of wood.

For a long moment, the two men crouched on hands and knees, snarling into each other's face as they exchanged a flurry of blows. Then Tomei's shrill cry of ''Enough!'' cut through their grunts of exertion and pain. Kane glanced up just as Tomei somersaulted completely over the broken rail of the gallery like a trained acrobat. She landed beside the two men and came up as though she had steel springs in her legs.

Almost in the same motion, she crossed her arms over her waist and whipped her butterfly swords from their sheathes with semimusical chimes. She placed the flats of both blades against Grant's and Kane's chests, shouting again, "Enough!"

The two men glared at each other, respiration harsh and labored, then they glared up at the girl. "Stay out of this, sweetheart," Grant husked out hoarsely.

"Yeah," Kane agreed in a strained, half-strangulated voice. "This isn't any of your business."

Tomei snorted out a contemptuous laugh. "What isn't my business—watching two old men snap and slap and paw at each other like a couple of bear cubs instead of the trained killers both of you are? If either one of you really wanted to kill the other, one or both of you would already be dead by now."

Tomei removed the sword points from their chests and stepped back. "If I'm wrong, I'll give you the chance to do it right." She jammed the blades point first into the ground and released the hilts. "Have at it."

Grant and Kane stared at the lengths of mirror-bright steel. They shone with the reflected highlights of the setting sun. Kane nodded toward the sword closest to Grant. "Go ahead."

"You first," Grant retorted.

Both remained on their hands and their knees, eyeing each other warily. Then Kane voiced a profanity-salted sigh and struggled to one knee. "It's getting late. I should be getting home."

Grant slowly pushed himself up to his knees. Joints popped audibly and he winced. Lips creased in a small smile, Tomei reached down and helped both men stagger to their feet. A squad of Tigers of Heaven jogged around the corner of the palace, armor and swords clanking. Tomei called to them, waving them away. They hesitated, then slowly withdrew.

Kane turned his head and spit a little jet of blood that had flowed into his mouth from a cut inflicted on his tender cheek lining. Grant dabbed at the blood flowing from his right nostril with the sleeve of his kimono.

Tomei touched his nose gently. "Is it broken?"

Kane uttered a derisive chuckle. "That thing has been broken so many times he wouldn't be able to tell."

"Are you going to give me those memory cards?" Grant demanded in a snuffling, nasal voice.

Kane shook his head. "Uh-uh."

Grant's brow creased and his big hands knotted into fists. Kane declared in a flat, neutral tone, "They're all the hope I have, Grant. My only reason for living, for waking up every day. You have your daughter and your son and New Edo to give you purpose." He patted the left hip of his shadow suit. "This is it for me—this is all I've got. You can kill me to keep me from taking them, if that's the only option you've left yourself. I won't give a damn. I'd much rather be taken out by a friend than a stranger."

Grant groaned in angry exasperation. "I want to believe your motives are as unselfish as you claim."

"All I want," Kane said evenly, sincerely, "is to undo a terrible thing that was done to people who didn't deserve it. That's the simplest way to put my motives. If I eliminate the cause of the terrible thing in the past, then the nature of time will arrange to eliminate the terrible thing from the future."

"You hope," Grant observed sourly.

Kane nodded. "Despite all the calculations I've done, all the studies, all the computer simulations and scenarios I've run, that's really all it gets down to—hope."

Tentatively, Tomei ventured, "And if the Nirodha have actually found an alternate means of temporal manipulation, then Kane may be the world's only chance after all."

Grant folded his heavy arms over his chest. He grunted, "Isn't that a frightening thought?"

Kane frowned at his old friend, trying again to identify the exact, but minuscule, philosophical difference that kept Grant from trusting and joining forces with him. He noticed the subtle change in his bearing at the mention of the Nirodha. With a sense of shock, he understood it was a memory, not a difference of opinion that maintained the wedge between them.

"It's the Nirodha, not me, that have you scared,

isn't it?'' Kane's words, if not his tone, were challenging.

Grant stared at him levelly, then shook his head. ''It's not them so much as your connection to them, Kane. And Lakesh and Erica's connection, too. And now to hear that they sent Tanvirah to you...'' Grant's words trailed off when he saw the expression of incredulity on Kane's face.

''What the hell are you talking about?'' Kane's voice was as sharp as a whipcrack. ''I don't have a connection to the fucking Nirodha—neither do Lakesh and Erica.''

Grant heaved a sigh of soul-deep weariness. ''I always think back to that night when Shizuka and Brigid died.''

''I was there, too'' Kane snarled.

''You were and you weren't.'' Grant's voice was a low rumble.

Kane balled his fists and took a menacing step toward him. ''What the hell do you mean? My back still hurts me in wet weather!''

Grant shook his head again. ''It's been over twenty years...I guess it's time to get this all out in the open. Let's go back inside and I'll tell you.''

Kane felt his stomach turn a cold flip-flop. ''Tell me what?''

Grant's reply was short and brusque. ''What I saw...and what you did, but apparently can't bring yourself to remember.''

Chapter 13

A gibbous moon seemed precariously balanced atop the spired minaret. It thrust up from the center of a huge mass, which in itself rose from a clearing in the Assam jungle. The red sandstone of the ancient walled temple, once a palace dating from the days of the Mo-guls, held a rusty hue like old bloodstains.

The northernmost of the old Indian states, Assam was bracketed on the north and west by the Himalayas and Tibet and by the brooding Naga Hills on the southeast. The land itself was primarily swamps and jungle. The Brahmaputra River slashed through the forested vastness like a great knife. At one time, the region had been considered the premier spot to partake of the royal sport of tiger hunting. At least, that was what Lakesh had claimed.

He also cited local legend that held when the great god Vishnu dismembered the body of Shiva's beloved consort Shakti, Shiva carried the parts away, but her *yoni*, her sexual organ, fell into the jungle. The fortress appropriated by the Nirodha was built on that precise spot. There Shakti worship flourished, which honored women and extolled them to the heavens—in theory, at any rate. A Shakta scriptural text read, ''Whosoever has seen the *yoni* of a woman, let him worship it as he would the feet of a teacher.''

All of the back story Lakesh provided flitted through Grant's mind as he and Shizuka crouched in the shadows and eyed the Nirodha fortress. It had been almost ridiculously easy to breach the security perimeter of Scorpia Prime's stronghold, even if the overland journey from the Goalpara River had been grueling.

Grant, Shizuka and a ten-man contingent of Tigers of Heaven avoided the armed guards easily, the steady booming of drums smothering the rustle of vegetation. They flitted like swallows from tree to tree, not even cracking a twig, in a demonstration of stealth that perhaps only bats could have equaled. They used the ruins of outbuildings as cover. Despite their armor and the swords, the samurai moved almost as silently as their namesakes.

Grant was the only one carrying firearms—a streamlined Steyr AUG autorifle, and a pair of .45-caliber S&W Model 645 double-action handguns. A slender pulse plasma rifle, a so-called Quartz Cremator, was slung over his right shoulder. A dozen grenades were packed into a zippered war bag slung over a shoulder. He had never been able to convince the samurai that guns were just as efficient as blades, their tradition of bushido notwithstanding.

Of course, their almost supernatural skill with *katanas* and the bows was such they didn't really need guns. Even before he had married Shizuka, Grant had offered to supply the Tigers with guns and ammunition from the Cerberus armory, but he had been politely refused.

It wasn't as if the Nirodha sentries carried their own firearms in a way that suggested much expertise or experience. As far as Grant could see, they were all men, and all of them wore simple uniforms consisting of sleeveless jerkins, shorts and turbans, but they were bright red in color. Apparently they had never seriously entertained the concept of camouflage.

Their weapons were streamlined and skeletal, reminding Grant of the spidery SIG-AMTs in use by imperial forces. The faces under the turbans were painted red on the left side and dead white on the other. On the right cheek of each guard, starkly outlined in black, was the silhouette of a scorpion.

Grant and Shizuka examined the building from the shelter of a half-tumbled-down wall. In the sickly lunar glow, they saw how the pillars were carved to represent every conceivable sexual joining of male and female, male and male, female and female.

Lakesh's briefing jacket had footnoted the Nirodha's worship of Shakti and the practice of Tantric rites. Grant didn't quite understand the sect's devotion to the eternal principle of female sexuality, an aspect of the Mother Goddess Devi, the wife of Shiva, but he figured Shizuka did, and that was enough for him. Light glowed between the columns, a flickering, lurid radiance intercut with black, sliding shadows.

Bidding the Tigers to wait for them, Grant and Shizuka slunk into the palace grounds. Both of them were dressed in dark clothing—Grant in a black shadow suit and Shizuka in a partial suit of armor. Her milk-and-roses complexion was blackened by stripes of combat cosmetics, her long black hair bound up at the back of her head.

They entered the fortress through a deserted courtyard full of shadows and overgrown shrubbery. Inside the palace, Grant and Shizuka followed the distant thumping of drums. They made their way silently through vast, empty rooms, up spiraling staircases and along hollow corridors, in and out of dining halls and even storerooms.

The smell of mold and mildew was redolent enough even for Grant's thrice-broken nose to detect. The lack of guards didn't comfort either him or his wife. Instead, they were so suspicious and wary, they tended to overreact to any stimulus.

They heard other musical instruments other than drums—finger cymbals, brass bells and flutes all undercut by wild laughter. The two people rounded a corner and both of them bit back curses of revulsion at the scene that lay below them.

From an inner balustraded gallery, they stared down at the vast central hall serving as the temple of Shakti. The area was illuminated by flaming braziers and lanterns that threw a shimmering veil of color over the naked celebrants. Torches sputtered at equidistant points around the chapel, the wooden columns thrust into buckets of sand. The glow of the torches was dimmed by shifting planes of hot, acrid smoke.

There were at least fifty people scattered around the circular chamber, some lounging on low divans, others indulging themselves from the food on long banquet tables, cramming it into their faces. Many more sprawled on nests of cushions and pillows, their faces slack, their eyes glazed.

The odor of the smoke was familiar. He recognized it as cannabis lupus, known in the Outlands as the werewolf weed. Composed of a mutated form of marijuana and various other herbal narcotics like opium, the werewolf weed stimulated the hindbrain, causing an atavistic regression.

It had been outlawed for many years in America because of its popularity. Its primary attraction was to allow the imbiber to wallow in artificial bestiality for a time. Some bands of Roamers and marauders appreciated the weed's influence before a raid, since it made them fearless and even immune to pain. Grant realized that the blend of the weed grown in India was probably far more potent and addictive than that found in the Outlands.

He caught glimpses of cudgel-wielding Pischacas lumbering about at the edge of the temple, apparently acting as sergeants at arms. He wasn't surprised by their presence, since one of the disadvantages of werewolf weed was that the user could turn on his friends as quickly as an enemy, while under its influence. The fumes stung his eyes and coated his tongue with a foul, sulfurous tang. He breathed shallowly through his mouth, hoping the smoke wouldn't affect him.

Sinuous serving girls slid among the celebrants, allowing themselves to be fondled, caressed and groped. Their tawny, oiled bodies were naked except for jeweled bangles. Grant guessed there were an equal number of men and women in the temple, but as far as he could he see, none of them were engaged in overt sexual activity. Their attention seemed focused on a small stage at one side of the hall. Grant followed their gaze and stiffened. He felt Shizuka tense up beside him.

Kane hung spread-eagled between two of the obscenely carved pillars, his wrists lashed to iron rings sunk deep into the stone. He was naked and his back was a raw, red ruin of slashed and sliced flesh. Blood trickled down the backs of his thighs to his ankles. His head hung limply between his shoulders, and Grant guessed him to be unconscious. He quickly scanned the crowd, looking for any sign of Brigid or Bry.

Suddenly the tempo the drumbeats changed. Grant saw the musicians tucked away in a wedge of shadow. They pounded hide-covered drums with their fists, setting a hypnotic rhythm. Strings and bells and cymbals clashed and whined deafeningly. The musicians shouted words in a singsong chant, but Grant didn't understand them. They didn't sound like any language he had ever heard.

From a brass-bowled brazier near the stage, a cloud of greenish-yellow cloying smoke poured, smelling far worse than the werewolf weed. The opiated stench filled the temple, collecting in a cloud beneath the domed ceiling. Shizuka inhaled a bit of it and nearly succumbed to a coughing fit. Grant felt dizzy for a moment and had to turn away, gulping for fresh air.

When the vapor thinned, a tall female figure stood motionless before Kane on the stage, but the face wasn't human. It required a few seconds of squinting through the veils of sweet smoke and blinking his blurred eyes for Grant to realize the woman wore an elaborate helmet. It was apparently crafted out of burnished silver and fashioned to resemble the body of a great scorpion.

The gleaming mandibles swept over the forehead and formed a mask over the woman's eyes. The fore-claws and pincers curved along the sides of her face, resembling the jaw guards of ancient Roman helmets. The stinger-tipped tail curved up over the ridged crown of the headpiece like a crest.

From the crowd a chant arose, a babble of confusing voices but one word finally became identifiable: "Scor-pay-*ah!* Scor-pay-*ah!* Scor-pay-*ah!*"

Grant exchanged stunned glances with Shizuka. It hadn't occurred to him that Scorpia Prime might be a woman. With her features obscured, he couldn't see much of her face, but a graceful swanlike neck led to voluptuous body draped in a thin, gauzy silk, which only blurred, not obscured her long legs and firm round breasts. Taut nipples pressed against the thin fabric, as if she were in a high state of sexual arousal.

Her body was too perfect. She was like the idealized male image of feminine beauty, rather than a real living woman. For an instant, Grant wondered if a cunningly crafted mannequin had not been placed on the stage under the cover of the smoke, but then he saw Scorpia Prime gesture and he knew she was definitely alive.

In a loud clear voice, Scorpia Prime began speaking. Shizuka hurriedly translated: "The enemies of divine annihilation gather in the darkness. They would continue to ravage Earth by burning away the green from our jungles, turning flower to ash, clean water to poison!"

The assembled horde howled in approval, but Grant sensed a curiously ritualized quality about their reaction, as if they had rehearsed it for many days prior to the ceremony.

"Tonight the forces of annihilation are drawn together!" the woman continued. "Tonight we seal our pact to serve Shiva to bring about the Pralaya, the destruction of the universe. As a scorpion stings itself to death in the hot sun, we shall see to it that humanity does the same! The moment of our triumph is upon us." She gestured to Kane, sagging in his bonds between the pillars. "As we possess him, so do we possess the secret steps to the Tandava, the dance of destruction. He came here to destroy, to prevent us from fulfilling our pact with Shiva. So we will mingle this man's two life forces as a consecration of our pact! Tonight, Shakti strides among us!"

The cymbals clashed again, strings sighed and the drums throbbed. Scorpia Prime began to dance around Kane, moving her hands and arms in ritualistic, intertwining angles and arcs. Steel gleamed in both of her hands. Her thumbs were tipped with curving tips of metal, like claws—or Grant realized bleakly, the stingers of scorpions.

He watched the woman, recalling Lakesh's description of the sacred dances of Shiva, the divine creator and destroyer who haunted graveyards as the lord of ghosts. Scorpia Prime danced the part of one of Shiva's wives, Kali, who feasted on sacrifices of human blood. At that point, the woman swept her right thumb down Kane's torso, the steel spur inflicting a crimson-welling incision from his chest to his pelvis. He didn't so much as jerk in response.

Grant made a motion as if to shoulder his Steyr and start firing at the masked woman, but Shizuka laid a restraining hand on his arm and shook her head urgently. Her face beneath the stripings of combat cosmetics was very pale. She whispered, "Kane is already in so much pain at this point, he can't feel much of anything."

Bleakly, Grant knew she spoke the truth. He couldn't help but wonder at the extent of his friend's numbness, whether he was either suffering from a drug-induced paralysis or simply faking unconsciousness.

Grant could only watch as Scorpia Prime continued to dance around Kane with the consummate grace of

The Gold Eagle Reader Service™ — Here's how it works:

Accepting your 2 free books and mystery gift places you under no obligation to buy anything. You may keep the books and gift and return the shipping statement marked "cancel." If you do not cancel, about a month later we'll send you 6 additional books and bill you just $29.94* — that's a saving of over 10% off the cover price of all 6 books! And there's no extra charge for shipping! You may cancel at any time, but if you choose to continue, every other month we'll send you 6 more books, which you may either purchase at the discount price or return to us and cancel your subscription.
*Terms and prices subject to change without notice. Sales tax applicable in N.Y. Canadian residents will be charged applicable provincial taxes and GST. Credit or debit balances in a customer's account(s) may be offset by any other outstanding balance owed by or to the customer.

If offer card is missing write to: Gold Eagle Reader Service, 3010 Walden Ave., P.O. Box 1867, Buffalo, NY 14240-1867

NO POSTAGE
NECESSARY
IF MAILED
IN THE
UNITED STATES

BUSINESS REPLY MAIL
FIRST-CLASS MAIL   PERMIT NO. 717-003   BUFFALO, NY

POSTAGE WILL BE PAID BY ADDRESSEE

GOLD EAGLE READER SERVICE
3010 WALDEN AVE
PO BOX 1867
BUFFALO NY 14240-9952

GET FREE BOOKS and a FREE GIFT WHEN YOU PLAY THE...

SLOT MACHINE GAME!

Just scratch off the silver box with a coin. Then check below to see the gifts you get!

YES! I have scratched off the silver box. Please send me the 2 free Gold Eagle® books and gift for which I qualify. I understand I am under no obligation to purchase any books, as explained on the back of this card.

366 ADL DRSG   **166 ADL DRSF**

FIRST NAME   LAST NAME

ADDRESS

APT.#   CITY

STATE/PROV.   ZIP/POSTAL CODE

7	7	7	**Worth TWO FREE BOOKS plus a BONUS Mystery Gift!**
🍒	🍒	🍒	**Worth TWO FREE BOOKS!**
♣	♣	♣	**Worth ONE FREE BOOK!**
🔔	🔔	🔔	**TRY AGAIN!**

(MB-01/03)

DETACH AND MAIL CARD TODAY!

an artist, yet with the abandon of a nymph. As Sati, another wife of Shiva, she mimed sacrificing herself to her lord by leaping into imaginary flames. It was the ritual act of suttee, the long-banned custom of Hindu widows joining their husbands in their funeral pyres.

The masked woman then began Shakti's dance of divine lust to the pulsing beat of the drums. In slow motion, Scorpia Prime danced around Kane, embracing him, sliding her arms around him, smearing the blood from the cut she had inflicted all over his body. She assumed a variety of erotic postures to suggest intercourse. Although Kane's head didn't rise, his penis did. Scorpia Prime lowered herself to her knees before him. What followed was almost too sickening for Grant to watch. It was what Lakesh had vaguely referred to as Tantrika rites, the ingestion of the two fluids of life and what Scorpia Prime had called Kane's two life forces.

The drumbeat increased its tempo, and the writhing shadow cast on the wall behind Kane and the kneeling woman was of a multiarmed creature of cosmic lust. All during the act of raw carnality, Kane's eyes didn't so much as flicker, but shudders racked his frame. After a few moments, Scorpia Prime pulled away and majestically rose to her feet. She faced the crowd, the firelight glistening from reddish moisture on her lips. She raised both arms in an imperious gesture and shouted, *"Avatara Shiva!"*

Shizuka breathed a translation in a horrified tone, "Incarnation of Shiva."

The announcement and her performance had its desired effect on the celebrants. The men and woman clutched at each other wildly in a mad variety of sexual joinings. They cried out to Shakti to appear among them. They chanted "Shakti! Shakti!"

The crowd suddenly parted and several of the red-turbaned Nirodha soldiers dragged a woman into the center of the temple. They were laughing, echoing the chant of the celebrants, "Shakti! Shakti!" but they made it sound as if they were delivering a package.

Grant craned to his neck to get a better view of the captive who was being hauled forward. He groaned deep in his throat when he recognized Brigid Baptiste. She was humiliatingly dressed in little more than twists of silk around her breasts and loins. She looked like a prostitute one might find in the street bazaars of Calcutta. Her long red-gold mane of hair hung loose, and it was twined with bright jungle flowers. They had powdered and rouged her cheeks, painted her lips a bright red.

Beneath the harlot's mask they had daubed on her, Grant could read fear and anger in equal measure on her face. Her eyes glinted emerald hard, but they went wide with shock when she saw the spread-eagled and bloody Kane. She struggled to no avail between the turbaned men who pinioned her arms and dragged her toward the stage.

They hauled her up a short set of stone stairs and

brought her face-to-face with Scorpia Prime, who eyed her haughtily. Grant could see Brigid's lips moving, but he couldn't hear what she said. He guessed the fate Scorpia Prime had in mind for her—she was to be the centerpiece of an orgy while she and the helpless and drained Kane watched.

Suddenly, Brigid kicked herself off the floor, using the cultists as braces. Her long legs flashed and bare feet came up and connected solidly against the underside of the Scorpia Prime's jaw, lifting her up on her toes and sending her staggering back against one of the pillars to which Kane was lashed. The woman's scorpion helmet was dislodged and fell from her head, but she managed to catch it.

The Nirodha soldiers instantly tightened their brutal grips, forcing Brigid to her knees. Scorpia Prime held the mask with both hands for a moment, glaring over it in maddened fury before putting it back on.

Brigid met that glare and her delicate features twisted first in astonishment, then a rage that overwhelmed the same emotion imprinted on Scorpia Prime's face. Grant felt the reaction to the woman's unmasking like a forty-pound sledge.

In the couple of seconds before the helmet went back on, he saw how the woman's complexion was the flawless hue of fine honey. Her long, straight hair, swept back from a high forehead and pronounced widow's peak, was caught up in a braid at the back of her head. It was so black as to be blue when the light caught it.

The large, feline-slanted eyes above high, regal cheekbones looked almost the same color as her hair, but glints of violet swam in them. The mark of an aristocrat showed in her sculpted features, with the arch of brows and her thin-bridged nose.

Grant was too numbed to shoulder his rifle, too stunned by the sight of the woman to move, speak or even breathe. He had only seen her a few times in the past, but with a marrow-freezing sensation of horror, he recognized her immediately.

Chapter 14

"Erica?" Kane's voice was a ragged growl of incredulity. "Erica van Sloan?"

Grant nodded only once. "Unless you know another Erica, yeah, that's who I mean."

The two men sat in a room on the far side of the palace from where they had dined. The room opened onto a balcony that overlooked a shoal of craggy rocks and a small bay. The rocks thrust up out of the foaming surf like blunt fangs. They led in an irregular path to the small islet of Thunder Isle.

The chamber, which was on an upper floor of the fortress, served as Grant's office, study and even his trophy room. Light gleamed on upright glass cases holding mementoes of Grant's past. There were knives with old bloodstains on the steel blades, guns of different makes, his Sin Eater and Copperhead from his years as a Mag.

Even Domi's knife, the one with the nine-inch-long wickedly serrated blade that had cut Guana Teague's throat when the Pit boss of Cobaltville was strangling the life from him, was on display. In a case beside it rested her Dectonics Combat Master autopistol, the blue-steel frame oiled and polished.

Reverently spotlighted in a tall display case were two suits of body armor mounted on metal frameworks. One was a suit of samurai armor, standing like a silent sentinel. It was topped by a war helmet that bore twin sweeps of metal, curving out from the sides like dark wings seen edge-on in flight. A sickle moon made of brass served as a crest, positioned between a slender pair of foot-long antlers made of a softly gleaming alloy.

Kane didn't need to be told the armor was Shizuka's, nor did the scabbarded long-bladed *katana* and shorter *tanto* sword resting on pegs inside the case require identification as to their former owner. The blades were almost supernaturally sharp, able to cleave smoothly even through polycarbonate. Shizuka had once attributed the cutting quality to an old technique of laser sharpening the edges to only a few molecules of thickness.

A ceramic jar painted with a stylized tiger rested on a small wooden pedestal at the bottom of the case. Kane knew that within the jar were Shizuka's cremated remains.

Standing beside her samurai armor was the black, close-fitting exoskeleton of a hard-contact Magistrate. Made of molded polycarbonate, it conformed to the biceps, triceps, pectorals and abdomen. The armor was lightweight and had the ability to redistribute kinetic shock resulting from projectile impact. The small, disk-shaped badges of office were emblazoned on the left pectoral.

Grant and Kane sat at a desk and dabbed at their injuries, mainly minor contusions and abrasions, with sponges soaked with water and a healing but strong-smelling unguent.

Too stunned to speak for a moment, Kane stood and went to the balcony, propping his elbows against the top rail. He vacantly gazed out at the harbor. A number of quays and docks were built around a spit of volcanic rock that jutted into the blue waters. A cluster of vessels was tied up there, mainly barges and skiffs, but also a flotilla of larger vessels that had all the characteristics of warships. They were all of a type, riding high above the waterline, consisting of sharp angles, arches and buttresses, with sails made of waxed and oiled paper.

The port was a beehive of activity, with the fishing boats returning with their day's catch. Dusk was creeping up over the sheltered cover, and the orange ball of the sun had already lost its brilliance. Green nets hung from pilings and were spread out over the docks. People wearing a simple ensemble of cotton T-shirts and shorts swarmed all over the waterfront area, laughing and singing as they worked. It was a pretty scene, with a storybook quality, even though Kane retained vivid recollections of repulsing an invasion force of Mags dispatched from Baron Snakefish in those same waters. He remembered how, shortly after the battle, when the tide went out the crescent moon of sandy white beach had been stained red at the waterline.

"Kane?" Grant's voice was both impatient and concerned.

Turning toward him, Kane said, "I don't remember anything like that. All I recall is waking up right as Brigid—" He clamped his lips shut on the rest of his words, unable to put a voice to the memory.

His thought processes moved sluggishly, like half-frozen mud as he strained to dredge up even a fragmented recollection that corresponded to what Grant had just told him of that night.

"You were drugged," Grant replied in a low, even voice, stepping out on the balcony beside him. "And in shock. Besides, even if you could remember, Erica's back was to you when Brigid unmasked her."

The blood pounded in Kane's temples, and he felt like smashing the flimsy door of paper and lathwork with his fists, but he decided he had caused enough damage to Grant's home for one visit. He demanded, "Why didn't you tell me about this then, after we blew the munitions dump?"

"I was in a little bit of shock myself that night," Grant snapped bitterly. "I'd been shot like what, about three times and stabbed twice? And I was positive I saw the Scorpia Prime being burned alive by one of the incend grenades you threw. One of my Tigers found her body, but it was burned beyond recognition...that helmet was welded to her head.

"So when Erica turned up later, alive and without so much as a hank of hair smelling like smoke, I figured I'd made a mistake because of the those damn werewolf weed fumes. I was a little out of it, even before all hell broke loose.''

Kane took a deep, calming breath, trying to control the adrenaline-fueled spasms in his stomach muscles. His mind started to glue the bits and pieces of new information onto the old. With an almost suffocating sense of defeat, he realized that with only a minimal amount of turning and twisting, the pieces all fit together.

Sam, the self-proclaimed imperator who wielded control over the *prana,* the old Sanskrit term that referred to the world soul…

Lakesh and Erica, who had sworn undying allegiance to Sam after he used the *prana* energy to not only restore, but also maintain their youth…

The SQUID implants, which supposedly connected all the new world's citizens with the world soul, and hence to Sam, and thus making them citizens of the adaptive Earth…

The Nirodha's sudden rise from obscurity to ultimate power in the Indian subcontinent, evolving almost overnight from a small sect of fanatics to a well-armed nation within a nation because of their devotion to bringing about the time of Pralaya, the complete destruction of everything except for the world soul…

Brigid's death and Erica's plea that Kane become her consort, choosing Lakesh only after he rejected her…

The rift that developed between him and Grant after the death of Shizuka, leaving her children without a mother, him without a wife and a kingdom without a ruler...

Kane's two-decades-long obsession with understanding the work of Burr and other Operation Chronos scientists, and how it proceeded from the assumption that the nature of time was like an ever rolling river, then learning from Erica how the very existence of time depended on the presence of space...and that if space could be measured, so could chronon strings...

The sudden appearance of Tanvirah at Cerberus, coinciding with a critical juncture of his temporal-manipulation researches, with a tale of how the Nirodha had made similar discoveries, but intended to use them to bring about the time of Pralaya...

Tanvirah's subtle urging that he go to Thunder Isle and the Operation Chronos installation there, pretending that she knew nothing of the hard feelings between him and Grant...

All the arrows pointed in one direction and they pointed so blatantly, Kane wondered if he had been mentally incompetent for the past twenty years, or if he were now suffering from the paranoid delusion to end all delusions.

Although his flesh felt clammy and all the moisture had dried in his mouth, he sounded eerily calm when he said, "We've been duped, Grant. Played for fools since the day Cerberus fell."

Grant grunted in acknowledgment of Kane's declaration, as if he weren't hearing anything he hadn't already suspected. He stared at the bay and the boats bobbing on its surface, without really seeing them. "What do you mean?"

"I mean when Sam and Erica finally realized none of us in Cerberus were going to join them willingly in their war to overthrow the barons, they decided not to give us much option. They purposefully allowed Baron Cobalt to return and take over again."

Grant frowned skeptically, then relaxed with dawning comprehension as the implications of Kane's words sank in. In a hoarse whisper, he said, "There was no way Cobalt could have secretly enlisted the backing of the other barons and managed to grab the reins of power back from Erica without help from some quarter. We always knew that. And you always suspected Sam had something to do with it."

Kane nodded. "That help might have been nothing more than Sam and Erica simply stepping aside and allowing Cobalt to complete his plans. Or Sam could have pretended to negotiate terms with Cobalt, knowing damn well the treacherous son of bitch would crawfish on any promises he made, and turn on him. In that case, Sam would have essentially financed his war of attrition."

Grant vented a heavy sigh. "For the sake of argument, let's believe that's exactly what Sam and Erica did. Are you saying they manufactured the Nirodha movement?"

Kane absently drummed his fingers against the balcony railing. "No, the movement itself was real enough. That checked out. They were just a small rag-ass sect of fanatics, controlling an isolated part of Assam. We've seen it happen before.''

Grant said nothing, knowing what he meant. Despite the global megacull two centuries previous, many concepts survived and even thrived in the new, post-nuke environment. Rituals of sex and a taste for organized religion echoed in one form or another down through the years following the nukecaust.

"However," continued Kane, "the Nirodha received some kind of aid, drew on resources in order to expand their field of operations and sphere of influence and gain new recruits. The practice of Tantric sex worship never died out completely in India…that's a powerful tool and inducement to join up."

"If Sam provided the aid," Grant said, "then there had to have been a payoff of some sort. What could it have been?"

Kane paused, eyes narrowed as he pondered the question. At length he said, "The most obvious objective would be to build a power base in Southeast Asia. Another reason would have been to keep the pot boiling, the shit stirred up."

"What?"

"After the formation of the CCS, we had only a couple of years of relative peace, right?"

Grant nodded reluctantly. "If that. There were Roamer gangs trying to organize and divide up the Outland territories, the Pischaca revolts…and then the Nirodha started their brush wars and exporting their terrorism. A pretty damn busy time…not really peaceful.''

''Maybe too damn busy,'' Kane commented reflectively.

Grant cocked his head at him. ''How so?''

''A society built on war and threats of war is usually too distracted to question itself.''

Grant pursed his lips thoughtfully. Kane paced away from the balcony, crossed the room and then returned to it. He didn't feel as agitated as he appeared, despite the topic of discussion. For the first time in many years, more years than he cared to remember, his point man's sense was awake and alert again. During his Mag days, because of his uncanny ability to sniff danger in the offing, he was always chosen to act as the advance scout, as the point man. When he walked point, Kane felt electrically alive, sharply tuned to every nuance of his surroundings and what he was doing.

He felt alive now, no longer out of sync with the flow or direction of his life. As he and Grant reasoned out a problem that a self-styled genius had concocted to stymie lesser intellects, it was a reminder of an aspect of his years battling the barons he had keenly missed. If only Brigid had been there to round out the triumvirate, to bounce back ideas, possibilities and counterproposals, then the world would be the way it was supposed to be—the three of them, the living incarnation of the Trimurti, contending again with unknowns, facing down a menace, defusing a threat and outwitting death.

"A pattern is forming here," Grant murmured grimly.

Kane nodded in silent agreement. It was a pattern of such long-range, intricate and complex evil, it made his belly twist in knots. "Twenty-seven years of undergoing wars, hardships, strife, loss, both of us growing very old very fast...while Erica, Lakesh and Sam retain their youth...and they stay together while we were driven apart, separated. Everyone and everything that meant anything to either one of us was taken away, while they built the world they wanted. Their adaptive Earth."

"A world of survivors and victims," Grant said dourly. "No different than the one we were born into."

"Survivors survive in different ways," stated Kane. "We did it by being tough but not very conniving. So when being conniving became the prerequisite for surviving, we turned into victims."

Grant chuckled, but there was no real humor in it. "I guess you're right. But that doesn't mean you can change things by tampering with the temporal flow."

"Doesn't it?" Kane fastened a challenging gaze onto Grant's face. "Think about it—time and mind have a way of dealing with things that go wrong. Right at this second, just by discussing what we're discussing, you've joined me in the long process of undoing what has been done. That's the subjective element of quantum physics.''

Grant snorted. "You've been living with Bry for too long."

Kane smiled sourly. "Try to dissuade me from the conviction *that* domestic situation shouldn't be changed by any means necessary, and we'll be rolling around on the grass again."

"Where are you going with this?" Grant asked sternly.

Kane shook his head slowly, his long hair stirred by the breeze coming in off the bay. "I think you know. Everything that has happened to us, to the world from the moment Sam first appeared nearly thirty years ago, was staged. All the events were parts of a plan he— and for all we know, Balam—developed. Maybe even before Sam made his public debut during the baronial council, after we destroyed the Archuleta Mesa facility."

Grant stared at him with open disbelief. "That's stretching things a little, isn't it?"

"What were we taught about strategy back at the Mag academy? It's all about multiple scenarios. When we raided a slaghole, we didn't have just one plan, we had ten. So look at all the evidence."

Kane began ticking off the points on his fingertips. "If Lakesh had joined Sam when they first met, then more than likely Baron Cobalt would have never returned after the siege of his ville. Or if he had, he would have never been able to pull off the coup that he did. We wouldn't have had a Consolidation War, or a Pischaca uprising, since there would have been no reason to breed them. And I doubt we would have had to contend with a Scorpia Prime.''

He paused, inhaled a deep breath then plunged on. ''Brigid, Shizuka, Domi and maybe everybody else we knew would probably still be dead. More than likely, so would we.''

Grant grunted, knuckling his chin contemplatively. ''Because we still would have refused to join the imperator, even though he wanted to overthrow the barons. Eventually, we would have ended up fighting him.''

''Exactly. Baron Cobalt and the others did Sam an enormous tactical favor by destroying Cerberus. That act left us no choice but to join him. It's a pretty fragile chain of coincidence to hang our perceptions of reality on, wouldn't you say?''

''I would. But what about Balam? Lakesh claimed he saw him in Xian, but only once. If he was supporting Sam, mentoring and counseling him, where did he go?''

Kane shrugged. ''Who the hell knows? Who cares? Sam claimed to have Enlil's genetic structure, and Balam had Enlil's—''

''Just like all the other hybrids,'' Grant broke in peevishly. ''That's not particularly significant.''

''Maybe not.''

Kane fell silent. He remembered how Balam was anchored to the hybrid barons through some hyperspatial filaments of their mind energy, akin to the hive mind of certain insect species. Inasmuch as all of the Archon genetic material in the hybrids had derived from Balam, that connection wasn't particularly surprising.

Lakesh had learned that the DNA of Balam's folk was infinitely adaptable, malleable, its segments able to achieve a near seamless sequencing pattern with whatever biological material that was spliced to it. In some ways, it acted like a virus, overwriting other genetic codes, picking and choosing the best human qualities to enhance. Their DNA could be tinkered with to create endless variations; it could be adjusted and fine-tuned.

Even more shocking was Balam's admission that he and his ancient folk were of hybridized human stock themselves, not alien, but alienated.

Kane declared, "Whether Balam was really guiding and counseling Sam way back when isn't very important now."

"What the hell is, then?" Grant snapped impatiently.

In a flat, unemotional voice, Kane intoned, "That we accept once and for all that everything that happened over the past twenty-seven years was all part of a scheme to breed people like me and you out of existence. We're intelligent dinosaurs but dinosaurs nevertheless. If we couldn't be controlled or exploited, then we had to be isolated, like zookeepers used to do with rogue animals.

"Our support systems were taken away from us—our wives, our friends, our beliefs and finally each other. In short, Sam, Erica and Lakesh clipped our talons, pulled our fangs and gelded us."

"Speak for yourself," Grant muttered darkly.

Kane went on as if he hadn't heard. "We also have to accept that none of it was supposed to happen. It was an unnatural twisting of events, of forcing the flow of our lives into directions they weren't meant to go, a distortion of the time line.

"And finally we have to accept that we must take any chance, jump at any opportunity, to make things right again."

Reaching into his pocket, Kane brought out the four memory cards, fanning them in his right hand. The setting sun struck dull glints from their crystalline corners.

Grant regarded the little wafers with suspicious, narrowed eyes. His eyes widened with astonishment when Kane declared blithely, "I can use these to make things right again. I can finally implement my own plan, working backward from *now* to make sure this now, never *is*."

"What?" Grant's voice was a dangerous, threatening rumble.

"It's risky—I won't deny that. I may trigger a transdimensional discontinuity and all of us will be sucked into a temporal cross rip, with our heads in the Triassic Age and our asses stuck in the Renaissance. Or I'll bring into existence a branching probability universe, and nothing will change here and none of us here will be the wiser. But—"

"But," Grant broke in harshly, "you might do nothing more than fuck up a few key events in the past, so that our now is essentially the same as it is at this moment, only worse. Like, I never had children, I never met Shizuka and I'm a blind cripple in the Outlands begging for food from Dregs."

Kane opened his mouth to counter Grant's objection, then he swallowed hard. "I understand. Who knows, maybe I'm under the control of Sam, maybe Erica injected those damn SQUIDs into me twenty years ago and I've been doing the imperator's bidding all along."

"I get the point," Grant growled. "We can fuse ourselves out by counting up all the possibilities."

Kane nodded. "Yes, but that doesn't invalidate your fears."

Grant grinned lopsidedly, placing his hands flat on the top rail of the balcony. "It doesn't validate them, either. All right, you can take the dilator's memory cards. But you still haven't explained to me how you'll get around the double-occupancy paradox. Neither me, you nor Bry can go back to the time before the attack on Cerberus, since we all existed then."

His shoulders stiffened as a sudden notion occurred to him. "You're not planning to send Lakesh's kid, Tanvirah, through, are you?"

Kane smiled wryly. "Nice idea, but no. We'd still have a temporal paradox to try to get around. If I dispatch her back in time and her actions keep our present from coming into being, then she won't have been born and therefore she won't be here for me to send back—''

''Oh, *do* tell me more,'' Grant cut in sarcastically. ''This is so like having Lakesh visit I'm about to cry with the nostalgia of it all.''

Kane didn't blame him for becoming irritated. He remembered how sorry he used to be after asking such questions of Lakesh. They inevitably led to brain-battering concepts better left alone by minds steeped in the elementary ABCs of mathematics and physics.

''So noted,'' Kane said, folding his arms over his chest, clicking the little crystal wafers together in his hand. ''To get back to your question of who to dispatch—for the mission to have any chance of success, it requires someone who was completely out of the chronon stream during all those key years, someone who didn't contribute to the temporal fracture lines, someone who can understand these particular principles of quantum physics in order to initiate the proper sequence of events to change things. Someone who knows us, someone who has a vested interest in this kind of world *not* coming into existence.''

As Kane spoke, Grant's forehead acquired deep creases of consternation and confusion. ''Someone who was completely out of the chronon stream? That would have to be someone who wasn't even born, right?''

Kane shook his head. ''Not necessarily.''

"It can't be someone who died *before* all of this happened, can it? Does that means you're planning to trawl somebody we know from the past like Sindri did to Domi—"

Grant broke off when he saw the almost imperceptible change come over Kane's studious expression. He stared at him silently, wonderingly, mind wheeling with conjecture and wild speculations. A chill hand caressed the base of his spine. His own face contorted in a mask of appalled incredulity.

Pushing himself away from the balcony, Grant took two stumbling steps back, nearly colliding with a display case. He bellowed, "Now, wait just a damn minute!"

Chapter 15

The breeze was light and not particularly cold, even at such a high altitude. It caught Tanvirah's hair and blew it in a delicate tracery over her face, even as it pressed the thin fabric of her robe against the contours of her body.

A half-moon splashed the plateau with an ectoplasmic radiance, small gleams reflecting from the scattering of old metal. Some of it was so corroded, it was impossible to tell its true shape, while other bits were as shiny as if they were freshly minted.

She found herself not quite as distressed as she thought she would be after her communication with Sam, but then she hadn't been able to tell him about Kane's apparent disappearance from the redoubt. She had only discovered he was missing an hour ago, and Bry refused to supply any information about where he had gone.

During the telepathic exchange with the imperator, Tanvirah had expected to be chastised by her half brother for having so little to tell him, but she wasn't surprised when Sam only inquired as to the disposition of Kane and the status of the mission. He was disappointed in her lack of hard intelligence, however.

Tanvirah thought, *I am willing to be questioned. Do you wish a summation of events?*

Unnecessary, came the razor-thin mental response. *I see what transpired in your mind. So you have not learned anything of value from him?*

Tanvirah winced when the Uma stone transmitted the acidic texture of accusation into her mind. *Nothing specific. I am still trying to gain his trust.*

She supplied the image of treating Kane's wound in the shower, accentuating the proximity of his naked body to her own.

I see. The vision of Sam's face in her mind seemed to smile, coldly and mockingly. Behind the smile Tanvirah sensed a dreadful hunger, an equally strong distrust for what it needed to control—human life, human aspirations, human dreams. The imperator would not have admitted to distrust, however. He referred to his objective to control humanity as the Great Plan. She had been a part of it since the day, the very hour, of her birth. She considered it a great honor.

In many ways, her relationship and interaction with Sam was similar to the manner the Trust of the old baronial system was organized, which in and of itself was the last in a long line of secret societies that held and concealed the knowledge of the Archon Directorate from the world. Such societies traced their roots back to ancient Egypt, Babylon, Mesopotamia, Greece and even Sumeria. Throughout humankind's history, secret covenants with the entities known as Archons by kings, princes and even presidents were struck. It was probably the only workable tradition from the barons Sam had retained.

Sam said, *A subtle seduction is taking too long to resolve the problem. I perceive a more direct approach might be necessary.*

Into her mind swelled an image of her thighs gripping Kane, of her hands stroking his sweat-filmed back.

Tanvirah hesitated before replying, *I understand. Good.*

Tanvirah understood that ambition, even the emotionless aspirations of an imperator, had to accept the limitations of reality. It took time to control the wild, mad human beings who infested the planet. It had required decades before the dominion of the imperator could be firmly established on one continent, much less on four. The planet was so vast, and even after several wars, people were so plentiful the task seemed too great to ever be accomplished.

And there were still people scattered throughout the Outlands who refused to become part of the imperial society and therefore had not been subjected to the SQUID implants. There were not a great number of them any longer, nor was it quite the same stigma to be an outlander as it had been a generation earlier.

In baronial days, a person's classification as an outlander was in some ways worse than a death sentence. It was a form of nonexistence. For people who had been born outside the direct influence of the villes, who worked the farms, toiled in the fields or simply roamed from place to place, being an outlander wasn't a punishment; it was simply the way things were. They knew they were reviled by the ville-bred. To be recognized as a person with a right to exist, one had to belong to ville society, even if only in the lowest caste.

Those who weren't chosen to belong, or chose not to, were the outlanders. They were expendable, the free labor force, the cannon fodder, the convenient enemies of order, the useless eaters. Brigid Baptiste, Grant, Kane and all of the exiles in Cerberus were reclassified as outlanders.

Although the advent of the imperator had changed the old caste system, those who didn't submit willingly to his authority were threats to the Great Plan.

The sheer enormity of the Great Plan was enough to intimidate anyone. But Sam's ideals governed his life, and those closest to him—to dominate everyone, control every destructive urge, to eliminate waste, to unify, to establish the law of pitiless logic and cold reason wherever humanity could be found. The only way the species could survive was by domination.

However, the neuronic energy provided by the SQUIDs channeled through the Heart of the World did not allow the imperator to read or directly control minds. It did, however, permit him to give and receive impressions, ideas and visualizations. From these various stimuli, Sam possessed the ability to extrapolate from a handful of known facts and to predict the logical sequence of events. It was truly a talent, not necessarily a learned skill.

To gauge and evaluate and to reach a conclusion that was so probable as to be almost certain, was more than precognition. Tanvirah had often secretly suspected the imperator was accessing a computer program of some sort. He had blended technology to augment his own natural psionic abilities.

Certainly Sam employed molecular technology to maintain his health. The ill, the old and the injured all suffered from misarranged patterns of molecules whether damaged by invading viruses, passing time or genetics. Sam's nanotechnology rearranged cells at a molecular level and set what was wrong aright.

Kane is the only failure I inherited from the reign of the barons, Sam said sadly. *All of them, particularly Baron Cobalt, tried but failed to control him or destroy him.*

Tanvirah knew how deeply Sam was disturbed by Kane, by the very fact he still lived despite forswearing allegiance to him. He was a man who had defeated the barons on numerous occasions and who merited death for all the chaos he had wrought, but who had, incredibly, managed to elude the traps set for him, the snares designed to hold him fast.

He has been lucky, Tanvirah said soothingly.

Luck or something more? An attribute as unusual as his physical prowess. We know the nature of the human mind. We know that the SQUIDs enable my mind to become the mind of the human, old or new, in almost total assimilation. But only of those born in the last twenty or so years.

Kane and his friends were of a very specific mind-set—headstrong, brilliant, even domineering. They filled an important niche before, when the planet was struggling to recover from the nuclear holocaust, but they became obsolete. Nature abhors more than a vacuum, it also abhors and eliminates evolutionary dead ends. I helped nature along, even prodded her, when circumstances required it. I should have devoted more time to neutralizing even the potential for a threat.

You had other things to do, Tanvirah told him. *Implementing the Great Plan was far more important than dealing with a couple of malcontents with deficient comprehension abilities.*

Now you must supply my own deficiencies, Scorpia Prime, Sam replied, deliberately using her royal title. *You must make sure that his foolish tamperings with the quantum field do not impinge on my—our—work. It has reached a critical juncture and will not abide the kind of interference that Kane and Grant were renowned for employing when they were younger.*

There are just two of them, said Tanvirah. *And it appears that the wedge driven between them years ago is still intact. Singly, they can do nothing. Even together, they would only be a nuisance. It would not be like the days when this place, this Cerberus, was a focal point of destructive energy, when the world was full of unbridled savagery, of killing, of torture and hatred.*

Perhaps, said Sam musingly. *Only Kane and Grant remain of those chaotic days. Nature no longer has any use for them, except where and how they may serve others. But as long as one of them exists, they are an energy focus.*

Hesitantly, with trepidation, Tanvirah said, *I do not understand.*

Sam's mind probe carried within it the abrasive texture of condescension. *The universe is a violent maelstrom of energy, of forces that could ravage this world flow just outside our boundaries of perception, but those forces are only destructive when interference is created. And if nothing else, Kane and Grant are creatures of interference. I believe it is ingrained, perhaps even in their DNA. The stronger must survive, and those two men are the ultimate survivors. But they have outsurvived their time. There is no place for them here.*

For the imperator, the words and emotions he had just conveyed were the equivalent of not only baring his soul, but also a lengthy statement of policy. She felt her heartbeat speed up due to the course of action the imperator implied.

They have been controlled for two decades or more, Tanvirah said. *Through personal loss, confusion and manipulation they have posed no threat to you or the Great Plan.*

Plans are brittle, came the cold response, *great or otherwise. And like glass, they can shatter if the proper force is applied in just the right place. There are times when events shoulder aside and ride rough-shod over the most intricately constructed plans. Our work is a very delicate balancing act to bring together powerful forces and events, so they will create what the world needs so desperately.*

The Tandava? she inquired. *The time of Pralaya?* Try as she might, Tandvirah was not able to eliminate a faint touch of sarcasm from her question.

Sam picked up on it. His mental response was so powerful she nearly cried out in pain. *Do you think I will employ excessive force to solve this problem? That it is a demonstration of misplaced and lingering resentment toward those two men who fought with me but not for me?*

Carefully, she replied, *Not at all. I only suggest that to divert resources to neutralizing Kane and Grant might be a waste of potential energy.*

Perhaps so. The response was as sharp as a whip-crack. *But would you not agree that any loss would be minimized against the greater gain?*

Tanvirah recognized the trap. To question him further or to disagree was to betray a weakness. If she challenged him, no matter how diplomatically, then she would be classified as a dreamer, an idealist. She would be denounced as one who could not abide efficiency and applied logic. She would stand with Kane, with Grant, with all those who were the natural enemies of the imperator. Once they had been eliminated, the rest of the populace would be relatively easy to control—or at least that was the common philosophy as espoused by her parents.

She knew Sam was as close to a genuine messiah

as was ever born in the history of the world. She also knew that such messianic claims were usually based on prophecies recorded earlier in history, and there was only one sure way of separating a pretender from a true messiah. The title had to be earned by deed, not by word.

It was a cold and uncompromising way of looking at it, since it ruthlessly stripped away the facade of magic and mystery, and forced whoever claimed the title of messiah to actually bring about prophesied changes.

Sam could do that, and he had been doing so, but only because he brooked no interference from those who didn't share his vision or his lofty goals of a unified world.

Rather than directly address his question, Tanvirah confidently stated, *I follow you, brother, no matter where you lead or what path you direct me to walk.*

The answer satisfied Sam, at least for the time being. *Then gain Kane's confidence. It is unimportant how we do it, but I must know his plans.*

And you shall, Tanvirah responded. *By any means at my disposal.*

And there the communication ended, which was fortunate because the notion of how the means always shaped the ends had crept into the forefront of her mind.

The night breeze suddenly carried with it the rich whiff of burning tobacco, and Tanvirah turned swiftly. She saw Kane standing no more than ten feet away, the tip of a cigar glowing like a red cyclopean eye in the shadows of his face. Chagrined, she realized he had crossed the plateau without a misstep or making a noise. He looked like a shadow, dressed in formfitting black.

"You need to be careful walking out here," he said in a slightly mocking drawl. "One wrong step and all the imperator's soldiers and all the imperator's ass-kissers won't be able to put you back together again."

Tanvirah didn't care for his tone or demeanor. She was disturbed more than angered, however. "I looked for you earlier."

"I just got back a few minutes ago," he replied noncommittally. "Bry told me you were taking an evening constitutional."

Tanvirah nodded. "It's beautiful out here," she said softly. "I've always loved the night. It hides all the dirt and ugliness and suffering, and covers it with mystery and the promise of hope for a new day. My mother and I used to take walks on the walls of High River. All the bright lights of the city, the smells—everything seemed wonderful."

"When it was called Cobaltville," Kane said around the cigar in a corner of his mouth, "all you could smell was the Tartarus Pits, and that sure as hell didn't smell wonderful."

Tanvirah brushed strands of hair from her face and said, "You're a cynical man, Kane. Were you always this way?"

Removing the cigar from his mouth, he blew a

plume of smoke toward the sky. He presented the image of seriously pondering the question. At length he said, "Pretty much, yeah."

"My father has said that those who live the most restricted lives are often the most intolerant. And I suppose there are few lives as restricted as the one you and Bry have been living up here."

Kane blew out another stream of smoke. "I still get around. For example, I just made a trip out to the coast."

"To where?" she inquired, despising how forced and ingenuous her voice sounded.

With a dry chuckle, Kane replied, "Where you wanted me to go—Ikazuchi Kojima."

"Where?" She knew exactly what he meant and she involuntarily hugged herself.

"Thunder Isle."

Tanvirah didn't reply, but she turned slightly away from him, gazing up at the sky. Her profile was sharp against the moonlight, the smooth mounds of her breasts enhanced by the wind-tautened fabric. The long smooth curves of her thighs were parted, and the material of her robe formed a concavity between them.

"Must we talk about that again?" Her voice was breathy, husky. "Let's just enjoy the night and each other's company."

"You're wasting your time, Tanvirah." Kane's voice was a ghostly whisper. "You're certainly beautiful, but I'm not aroused by tools, by walking, talking, performing instruments."

She knew she should have felt rage at his words, but instead she experienced only a wave of sadness so soul deep that she could barely keep a sob from catching at her throat. "No, not you, Kane."

She turned to face him, one hand lifting to press against his chest. "Never you…a man who has been hurt by loss and then adjudges all the world responsible for his pain. You have fire still in you, but not warmth."

He said nothing, but he met her gaze stolidly. With a distant sense of shock, Tanvirah realized he was indeed the ultimate survivor, a creature of the wild, perhaps the most dangerous creature in the world.

She understood why Sam resented him so. Kane was a man who had learned early to live without any protection other than that provided by his own prowess and wits. Unlike Sam, she admired his survivability. A warrior, one not afraid to kill, an explorer, one never afraid to plunge into the unknown, a peacemaker, one compassionate enough to extend the hand of friendship to a defeated enemy. Compared to him, despite his staggering intellect, Sam seemed a petulant, fearful child.

Tanvirah removed her hand from his chest, but she continued to gaze searchingly into Kane's pale eyes. In a flat, uninflected voice he intoned, "Tanvirah, I hope you're not expecting me to break into tears because you've touched my heart and I'm desperate to unburden myself to someone, particularly a woman."

She shook her head in pity. "I'm not expecting anything, Kane…except maybe for you to tell me when I can go home. Since you gated to Thunder Isle, you must have reconfigured the mat-trans for normal use.''

Kane examined the wet end of the cigar before putting it back in his mouth. "True, but Bry is right now reconfiguring it again, back to the spatiotemporal dissociator settings.''

Fear leaped through her, galvanized her. "What? Why?''

"You know why. Your mother, your father and Sam know why—so I can start to undo all of their perfect orchestrations of people, power, governments and more important, *time*.''

She struggled to tamp down her rising terror. "You don't know what you're doing, Kane! You power that thing up without the preset reference conformals and—''

She bit back her words when she saw him angle ironic eyebrows at her. He grinned around the cigar, but it wasn't an expression of amusement as much as one of triumph. "So you do know a bit more about the functioning principles of the dissociator than you let on. Why am I not surprised? But I am surprised that Lakesh would agree to have his daughter act as the imperator's whore to fuck information out of me.''

Tanvirah's lips peeled back in a snarl. She lunged at Kane, swinging her fist at his face. "Bastard!''

Kane only leaned back a bit and easily caught her wrist. Spinning her around, he jerked her arm up between her shoulder blades in a hammerlock, dragging an aspirated cry of pain and frustration from her. "Let me go!"

Kane said casually, "Just a second, kid."

With his free hand he patted her down, and for an instant, Tanvirah wondered if Kane had lost what was left of his mind and was groping her as a way of destroying her dignity. When she felt his hand slide into the pockets of her robe, she began struggling in a panic. "Stop!"

Removing his hand from her right pocket, Kane pushed her away from him and released his grip on her wrist. Tanvirah whirled and saw him twirling the Uma pendant by its silver chain. She snatched at it frantically, but he evaded her reach, allowing it to wrap around his hand with the diamond nestled snugly in his palm.

Shrieking wordlessly, Tanvirah lunged for him, fingers seeking his eyes. Kane planted a hand on her forehead and pushed her away. She sat down heavily on the tarmac with a little "Oof!" of expelled air.

Kane stepped away from her, his face momentarily clouded by a wreath of smoke. He turned his head and spit the stub out of his mouth. "Like your old man said, I only pretend to be stupid. Didn't you think I knew about the Uma stones, how they're used as forms of communication between the SQUID implants and Sam? I was pretty sure you had one on you, since you were acting as his ambassador. Just like I'm sure you've already reported to him. That's why I don't have the luxury of performing further experiments."

Tanvirah started to push herself to her feet, but Kane said sharply, "Stay there, or I'll kick you ass first off the cliff. What did you tell Sam?"

Sullenly, she replied, "Nothing. I had nothing to tell him."

"Let me guess, then." Kane grinned coldly, showing only the edges of his teeth. "You told him how I was half-fused out, tinkering around with my time machine and drooling in my beard, all heartbroken, forlorn and desperate for a cause, an enemy to fight. The story of the Nirodha and the return of the Scorpia Prime was just the thing…offering me another menace to go after and maybe getting a little revenge for the death of Brigid."

Tanvirah didn't reply, but she knew her expression had to have betrayed her feelings, because Kane laughed shortly and contemptuously. "I thought so. And he told you to ease my suffering and in the process find out just exactly what my plans are with the dissociator. After that—did he order you to kill me, or did he hope that would happen if I trespassed on Thunder Isle?"

She blinked up at him in confusion. Neither possibility had occurred to her, but she spit angrily, "You're the strategist—you tell me."

"I'll do better than that." He took a step forward, extending a hand to her. "I'll show you."

Tanvirah recoiled at first, thinking he meant to strike her, then she stared at his hand suspiciously, distrustfully, as if the black-gloved fingers were really venomous serpents. Then she reached up and took it. Kane easily pulled her to her feet. "Show me what?" she demanded.

He marched toward the sec door, striding with a long-legged purposefulness. She hurried to catch up. When they entered the main corridor, she was instantly aware of a high-pitched hum, a distant vibration emanating from the operations center. Her belly turned cold. "What are you doing, Kane?"

Without breaking stride or looking at her, Kane said, "Bry is powering up the dissociator."

He wended his way through the debris in the passageway, and Tanvirah rushed after him, scraping her knees and bumping her elbows. "You can't use it!" she blurted. "You can't change the present in the past—time ripples away from an event horizon and flattens out at the edge, so that'll leave you hanging in a paradox that time itself will have to resolve."

He ignored her. He marched through the operations center and into the antechamber holding the gateway unit. She dogged his heels, still babbling. The door of the jump chamber was sealed, but from within flared a constellation of sparks, blurred and smeared due to the translucent quality of the armaglass. From the elevated platform, a nerve-stinging hum wafted.

Bry sat inside the curve of the crescent-shaped console. He said loudly, "The data cards are uploaded. Retrieval process engaged."

Tanvirah's verbal onslaught of scientific principle clogged in her throat. She swiveled her head so swiftly toward Kane, her neck tendons twinged in pain. "Retrieval process?"

Kane nodded, gesturing to the gateway unit. "You, your parents and Sam were all wrong about my plans. I wasn't trying to build a dissociator to go back in time myself, but to pull someone out of nontime, zero time. For the past twenty-eight years, he's been in the Operation Chronos memory buffer matrix, reduced to digital information. He's been outside space-time for all those years, more or less in a state of nonexistence. It's not too different from a gateway's quincunx effect, which I'm sure your old man has explained to you."

"That's impossible!" Tanvirah exclaimed. "Nobody could exist outside time!"

"You apparently never had Operation Chronos's temporal dilator explained to you," Bry said with a snide snicker. "In certain circumstances, photons—the particles of which light is made—can jump between two points separated by a barrier, and freeze in what appears to be zero time. That's where our subject has been for nearly thirty years. In a holding pattern."

"Who?" Tanvirah shrilled. "Who has been in zero time?"

On the other side of the armaglass walls, great blossoming splashes of color filled the gateway unit. The whine climbed higher in pitch, to such a painful volume everyone covered their ears. All of them stared wide-eyed at the mat-trans.

Faintly at first, as through rolling multicolored clouds, a shape began to materialize, surrounded by an iridescent halo of white mist shot through with corruscating particles of brilliance, like a fireworks display as seen from a vast distance. The multicolored clouds overlapped, and the throbbing vibration continued to climb in scale and pitch, becoming almost painful. Sparks that were more energy than light flashed on the other side of the armaglass slabs.

The air around the gateway unit wavered with a shimmery blur like heat waves rising off sunbaked asphalt. Then a bone-jarring crack of thunder compressed their eardrums, hammered at the marrow of their bones. A deafening, concussive blast cannonaded from within the enclosed jump chamber, then a consecutive series of brutal, overlapping shock waves crashed into the armaglass barrier. The door sprang open as if kicked violently from within.

A terrible shrieking and wailing filled the room, like a hundred steam valves venting simultaneously. The sound tore at their ears even as the display of pyrotechnics stung their eyes.

Kane pulled Tanvirah back as a torrent of dazzling white flame and variegated lightning strokes blazed out of the unit. The room shook as if battered by a heavy surf, pounding relentlessly against their eardrums and bones. Crooked fingers of energy continued to boil and hiss and flare inside the gateway unit, forming a cat's cradle of red crackling threads.

Gushing lines of energy formed a luminous cloud in the center of the cradle and then burst apart in a blizzard of sparks. Amid the glowing plasma splinters, a small body plummeted out of the heart of the cloud and fell heavily to the floor. The body appeared to have been dipped in jet-black dye from the neck down. After a second, Tanvirah realized the figure wore the same kind of formfitting bodysuit as Kane.

The three of them watched in shocked silence as the small figure of a man pushed himself to all fours on trembling arms and shaking legs. Sindri looked around unfocusedly, then lowered his head and vomited.

Chapter 16

Sindri tried to shift position away from the pool of vomit, but in doing so he fell onto his right side, his limbs twitching spasmodically. His eyes were tightly closed and foam flecked his lips, oozing from the corners of his mouth.

"He's seizing!" Bry cried.

Kane went to him instantly, dropping to his knees beside the little man. He lowered his head to his chest, listened and said, "Irregular heartbeat, some arrhythmia."

Kane heaved him up effortlessly and, holding the three-foot-plus man in his arms like a child, rushed out of the operations center. Over his shoulder he barked to Tanvirah, "You've got medical training! Come with me!"

The note of command was so powerful in his voice, Tanvirah didn't realize she had obeyed him until she was halfway out of the control complex. She continued after Kane, her mind spinning with questions, anxieties and outright fears.

"Who is that man?" she demanded loudly, catching up to Kane. "Where did he come from?"

"His name is Sindri," Kane said over his shoulder. "Originally he came from Mars."

"Mars?" she echoed incredulously, scornfully. "You didn't materialize him from Mars!"

Kane entered the infirmary and laid the little man on the nearest examination bed. She glanced around the big room, noting its orderliness as Kane said tersely, "I pulled him from the Operation Chronos memory buffer, where subjects who had been trawled from the past were stored as digital patterns. He jumped into the temporal dilator almost thirty years ago, and he's been locked in zero time ever since. Give me a hand here."

Tanvirah moved to the bedside, looking down at the man who resembled a child lying in his parents' bed. Although he appeared to be only three and a half feet tall, his perfect proportions confused her sense of perspective for a moment. Unlike other dwarves she had seen, his legs weren't stumpy or his arms too long, or his head too big, but she couldn't help notice the impressive size of the bulge outlined by the tight black fabric at the juncture of his thighs.

His dark blond hair was swept back from an unusually high forehead and tied in a ponytail at his nape. He was ashen, with a mixture of bile and saliva dripping from the corners of his mouth, but he was still one of the most handsome men she had ever seen.

Kane opened Sindri's bodysuit by releasing a seal on the right side and roughly peeling it down over his torso, revealing a broad chest with a downlike covering of hair. Kane turned, took a bag from a shelf and removed a stethoscope. He listened to Sindri's heart, took his pulse and examined his eyes, moving from one task to the other with a grim, brisk efficiency.

"We've got auricular fibrillation," Kane announced.

"Do you have any supplies of digitalis or guanidine?" Tanvirah asked. "Or a defibrillator?"

Shaking his head, Kane reached into the medical bag again. "No, but I prepared for this a long time ago."

He removed a hypodermic syringe with a frighteningly long needle. It was filled with a faintly amber liquid. Tanvirah grimaced. "What is that?"

"Adrenalin," he said, then jammed the needle into Sindri's chest. "Hold him down."

Tanvirah did as he said. There was a faint crunch of gristle as the needle penetrated the chest cavity. Sindri didn't react to the sensation, but when Kane emptied the syringe's contents into his heart, he gave out a loud, gargling cry and tried to jackknife up from the bed. His legs kicked madly as if he were running in place. His back arched as if he had received a kick between the shoulder blades.

Then the little man fell back onto the bed. Tanvirah released him, looking down into his sweat-sheened face. "I don't think he's breathing," she said worriedly.

"The little pissant is breathing, all right," Kane said

roughly, removing the hypodermic. A little pinpoint of blood shone on his skin.

Sindri's chest rose and fell. His hands and feet stirred, and then the stirrings became movement. Finally, his eyes, which had been tightly closed, fluttered and opened. They were glassy but a clear, clean azure. He looked around vacantly, his mouth open. His eyes held no recognition of the man or woman leaning over him. From his open mouth came a wordless gargle, either a plea or an inquiry.

"Welcome back to the world," Kane said to him. "It's not any richer for having you back in it, but maybe you'll be able to change that."

Sindri's blue eyes contained a dim, conscious spark, but they were still glazed and unfocused. His lips writhed, and reedy sounds neither Tanvirah nor Kane could identify whispered out.

Kane slapped Sindri across the face, once, twice, three times. They weren't gentle, attention-getting taps. The infirmary echoed with the loud smack of his gloved hand striking flesh. Sindri's head rolled and wobbled on his neck. Between clenched teeth, Kane grated, "Get it together, goddamn you. You're not going to be brain damaged after all the trouble and time I've spent retrieving your slagging ass. *Get it together!*"

Tanvirah reached across Sindri to grab Kane's hand, to keep him from striking the little man again. "Stop it! He'll either come around on his own, or he won't! Hitting him like that will only—*ooh!*"

Kane gaped at Tanvirah as she bounded away from the bed. She let loose with a stream of profanity, hastily closing her robe over her half-exposed breasts.

"The little pervert grabbed me!" she shouted in outrage.

Kane couldn't help it. He laughed uproariously as all the tension drained out of him. He leaned over Sindri, hands on either side of the small man's shoulders. The dwarf blinked up at him blearily, a crooked grin creasing his lips. In a hoarse, scratchy whisper, he asked, "Did I dream those boobs? I hope not...."

Kane decided not to answer that particular question. "Do you know who you are?"

A glint of the man's old characteristic arrogance showed in his eyes. "Of course I do. But I don't know who the hell you are."

"Take a good guess, Sindri."

Sindri squinted up at him, his forehead wrinkling in concentration. His eyes flicked back and forth. Then his face became a slack mask of shock, and in a dumbfounded tone he said, "It can't be."

Kane chuckled. "Oh, but I assure you, it be. It very much be. You thought you'd escaped from me, didn't you? It took me damn near thirty years, but I have you again."

While Sindri stared at him in disbelief, Kane swiftly applied the bed's restraining straps to the man's ankles and wrists. By the time he had recovered somewhat from his astonishment, he was securely affixed to the bed.

Finally Sindri asked, "Mr. Kane?"

"The same."

"Good God, what happened to you?"

In a nonchalant tone, Kane replied, "About three decades of hard living, Sindri, which you were fortunate enough to miss out on. But I'll guarantee if you don't cooperate with me, I'll make your next thirty days a hell of a lot worse than the thirty years I went through."

Kane walked toward the adjacent laboratory. "I'll get you some water."

Tanvirah stared at Sindri who stared back, then she joined Kane in the laboratory. He stood at a sink, filling a pitcher with water from a faucet. "Who is that man?" she demanded.

"You mean your father never told you about Sindri?"

She shook her head.

A smirk lifted the corner of his mouth. "I guess I shouldn't be surprised. He was the only other man in the world who was able to figure out the workings of the mat-trans units and overcome all of Lakesh's security settings."

Impatiently, Tanvirah declared, "That doesn't answer my question!"

Kane turned off the faucet. In a distant voice, he said, "Have you ever heard the old saying about hate being as strong a bond as love?"

"No," she snapped.

As if he hadn't heard, Kane said, "There's a bond

of hate between me and the little man in there. The hate he feels toward me made him the most vicious enemy I ever faced, and that's saying something. But as sick as it sounds, that hate links us in an intimate way. I'm putting all of my faith and dreams and aspirations of the last twenty-eight years into his little baby hands."

Tanvirah frowned, nibbled nervously on her underlip, and then said quietly, "Tell me about him."

KANE RARELY ENGAGED in any nostalgia about his enemies, even the ones he had come to respect. Before the Consolidation War, he, Grant and Brigid had collided with, rebounded from, were captured by, almost killed by but finally defeated adversaries with the most deadly ambitions and equally lethal weapons. The war had thinned out most of the self-styled conquerors.

Although the majority of them had either died at his or Grant's hands, or through their own machinations, Sindri was one of the exceptions. He had apparently perished twice, and after the second encounter, Kane didn't figure it was reasonable to think they'd ever contend with him again. But Sindri delighted in unpredictability. The fact he existed at all was due to unpredictability and the often cruel whims of nature.

Thirty years before, while exploring an anomaly in the Cerberus network of functioning gateway units, Lakesh, Brigid and Kane visited Redoubt Papa near Washington Hole.

They found the body of a strange, stunted troll-like

man, and returned with it to Cerberus. After a post-mortem, the troll was found not to be a mutant or a hybrid, but a human being modified to live in an environment with a rarefied atmosphere and low gravity.

After a bit of investigation and a process of elimination, Lakesh traced the quantum conduit used by the transadapt to jump into Redoubt Papa, to a point in outer space—a predark space station on the far side of the Moon, known as *Parallax Red*.

Kane, Grant and Brigid gated to it, finding the station functional, if not exactly comfortable. It was populated by the group of stunted people known as transadapts, and led by an ingenious gnome of a man calling himself Sindri, after the master forger of the troll race in Norse mythology.

Sindri impressed them all with his wit, his charm, his probing intellect and his affected manner. They were particularly impressed by the startling story he told about *Parallax Red* and its connection to a human colony on Mars.

They later encountered Sindri on Thunder Isle, where he had commandeered the Operation Chronos facility. There his experiments with the temporal dilator had saved Domi's life. But unfortunately, he had also brought through Megaera and her group of fanatics, as well reconstituting a homicidal maniac from nineteenth-century England, whose pattern had been held in the matrix.

When the dilator reached critical mass, Kane had assumed Sindri had gated back to *Parallax Red*. He always figured the little man with the space-station-sized ego would return to vex him and his friends again with some other destructive scheme. After the passage of many years with no sign of him, Kane began to suspect Sindri had met an altogether different fate—unable to use the mat-trans unit to escape the installation, he had instead used the machinery to digitize himself, so his energy pattern was stored in the dilator's memory buffer.

As far as Sindri's perceptions were concerned, he had made the rash decision to expose himself to the dilator's chronon radiation less than a minute before. As far as Kane was concerned, Sindri had managed to duck out on thirty years of war, terror and hardship.

He looked forward to giving the little man a crash course in history. He expected Sindri to extend himself to change it—even if it meant killing him.

Especially if it meant killing him.

Chapter 17

Kane knew Sindri wouldn't take long to orient himself to his new circumstances and start scheming how he could affect them to serve himself. He was a true survivor and exceptionally adaptable. Moreover, the little man saw his purpose in life as an integral part of the flow of the universe, so the very idea he couldn't be involved in it was inconceivable. He also believed his very existence served as a force for social change, and therefore that made him pretty much a law unto himself.

In the past, Sindri's vision of himself had brought him into conflict with Kane and his friends. They tried to impose a degree of order on chaos; therefore he was chosen by fate to be an agent of anarchy. He never would have admitted such a thing, however. He would have referred to it as working to achieve a state of equilibrium. Now Kane intended to persuade him that the universe was seriously unbalanced, and only he could set it right again—and that meant doing what Kane told him to do.

Due to the method by which he was retrieved from the pattern buffer matrix, Sindri was physically weak and his mental faculties less than razor keen. By using the dissociator rather than the temporal dilator to snatch Sindri from zero time, Kane had circumvented hundreds of built-in security and safety protocols.

Bry had warned him on more than one occasion that by jury-rigging the dissociator's hardware to accommodate the dilator's software and then to engage the gateway's energy-to-matter conversion process might initiate an irreparable breach in the quantum field. That was the worst-case scenario. The best case was that Sindri might reconstitute as three feet worth of shapeless protoplasm and powdered calcium. Kane had never doubted for a second it was worth the risk. As far as he was concerned, if the worst and best cases occurred, it was a win-win.

However, judging by Sindri's lassitude, the latter outcome might have only been narrowly avoided. After a few minutes of lying quietly in restraints and drinking the water from a cup held by Tanvirah—who kept her face averted from his hungry eyes—Sindri finally felt confident enough to start making demands.

"Mr. Kane," he said in his sonorous, lilting voice, "are you not going to introduce me to my dusky female attendant?"

Kane, sitting on a stool at the foot of the bed said, "Tanvirah, this is Sindri."

Sindri smiled up at her ingenuously. "Tanvirah? A lovely name, evoking imagery of sultry jungles and the palace of King Solomon." He paused, his smile broadening, and he quoted, "'And when the queen of Sheba had seen all Solomon's wisdom, there was no more spirit in her.' How is your spirit faring, gorgeous?"

With a stony expression and tone of voice as hard as flint, Tanvirah shot back, "'My father hath chastised you with whips, but I will chastise you with scorpions.'"

She swept Kane with a quick glare, then veiled her dark eyes with her lashes. If she hoped Kane would outwardly display a sign that he found her quote significant, she was disappointed. He pretended not to have heard her.

However, Sindri's blue eyes widened with genuine surprise, then he laughed loudly. "Mr. Kane, regardless of all your other faults—and they are legion—your taste in female companionship is always without peer. Like Miss Brigid and Captain Shizuka with whom I was briefly acquainted, Tanvirah is equally witty, knowledgeable and beautiful to a fault."

Kane quoted quietly, "'King Solomon loved many strange women.'"

Tanvirah swung her head toward him, eyes glinting briefly with suspicion. Sindri regarded Kane with a mixture of surprise and resentment. "Despite the three decades of hard living you alluded to, you evidently found time to further your education."

Kane shrugged. "Not a hell of a lot to do up here on long winter nights, except to read."

Sindri eyed Tanvirah slyly. "I think with such a companion I could come up with a pastime far more entertaining than memorizing the Bible."

Tanvirah's lips worked as if she were going to spit at the little man bound to the bed. Then she speared Kane with a stare of pure venom, spun on her heel and flounced away. Sindri uttered an exaggerated groan of disappointment.

He called, "Come back, little Sheba, don't be so sensitive. I was complimenting you!"

Turning pleading eyes toward Kane, he said, "Please smooth things over…tell her I meant no offense to a gracious and lovely hostess."

"She's just a guest, Sindri, like you. She's only been here since this morning. But, if not for her, you might not be lying there right now able to play the minilech."

Sindri's brows knitted at the bridge of his nose. "What do you mean?"

"I mean she more or less inspired me to move on a plan I've had in the works for many years."

"What plan is that?"

"To retrieve you from the temporal dilator's memory buffer."

Sindri smirked contemptuously. "Are you telling me her soulful eyes melted your heart as to my incorporeal plight?"

Kane stood up from the stool, shaking his head. "I'm telling you the exact opposite. I think the imperator has a way of monitoring what I was doing with my own version of the dilator and somehow figured out what I had in mind."

Sindri glowered at him. "Who the hell is the imperator?"

Kane chuckled dryly. "Somebody who by all rights should be your role model. But right now, if he finds out I've hooked and landed you from zero time, he'll be wanting to fillet you alive."

Blowing out an exasperated sigh, Sindri fixed his eyes on the ceiling and strained briefly against the canvas straps holding him to the bed. In a very calm but aggrieved tone of voice, he said, "Mr. Kane, in any enterprise there is a point where a wise man accepts his limitations."

"Meaning?"

"Meaning I have no idea of who or what you're speaking. Therefore I see no profit in continuing to verbally spar with you or flirt with the girls. You definitely have me at a disadvantage in just about every way conceivable. I can't even be sure if you are *you*."

Kane nodded graciously. "I'm impressed, Sindri. You reached that conclusion in half the time I expected you to. So we can talk now without either one of us resorting to threats or boasts or bullshit?"

Sindri removed his gaze from the ceiling and gave Kane a slow, speculative stare. "I'm the one who's impressed, Mr. Kane. You are displaying a degree of mental acuity and depth of emotion I didn't think was possible for you. That's why I harbor a bit of doubt as to your actual identity."

Kane frowned at him. The old smugness, the old superiority was creeping back into Sindri's tone and manner, and it made him impatient. In a cold, almost menacing half whisper, Kane said, "It really is me, Sindri and it really is you...two old friends reunited at last."

Sindri's handsome face registered apprehension at the grim, almost fatalistic note underscoring Kane's voice, but he said nothing.

"You and I are going to have a long talk, Sindri. At the end of it, I'm going to present you with a proposal. Depending on your answer, this very well may be your last measurable hour on Earth. Your own zero hour so to speak. So—" he began unbuckling the restraints, enjoying Sindri's startled expression "—I'll arrange it so you'll spend that last hour as a free man...or at least as free as you can be on the imperator's adaptive Earth."

USING CLEAR, CONCISE language, without trying to dramatize or minimize, Kane related everything that had happened in the world and to him since he and Sindri had last seen each other.

Kane told him about the rise of Sam and the so-called Imperator War, which had actually happened a few months before he and his friends encountered Sindri on Thunder Isle.

He told him about how Baron Cobalt, thought dead for many months, had secretly enlisted the aid of several disaffected members of the baronial oligarchy. Since they were autocratic by birth and treacherous by nature, they formed a covert alliance to break the influence of the imperator.

The war that followed, the Consolidation War, lasted for nearly five years. Early on, the barons scored a string of impressive victories, occupying several villes with troopers conscripted and recruited from the slums of the fortress cities and Outland pestholes.

Atrocities became commonplace, wherever baronial armies marched or encamped. However, Baron Cobalt's policy of merciless cruelty boomeranged against him. Instead of breaking the spirit of the conquered outlanders, it only fired resistance, particularly when people knew there was a viable alternative to baronial rule. Many of the hybrids who shared the Archon-derived DNA of the barons joined imperial forces, although most of them made very poor soldiers, due to their physical fragility.

To offset this deficiency, Sam saw to the creation of genetically engineered warriors, the Pischacas. They augmented the imperial armies. Part of Kane's duties was to go into the Outlands and recruit people there, if not making them official soldiers in Sam's armed forces, at least convincing them to become guerrilla fighters. The ones who refused to take sides were neutralized.

Over the course of the war, the entire system of baronial rule withered from within and without. More and more Outland territories split away from the direct influence of the barons. By the time the imperator claimed those territories, the baronies lacked the former strength in unity that had once enabled them to hold firm against all threats.

The end, when it came, was swift. All the surviving barons were killed, either in battle or executed. The Consolidated Confederation of States was formed shortly thereafter. Victory, although absolute, was not celebrated for very long, due to the revolts of the Pischacas. They were created to wage war against baronial forces. With those forces defeated, they turned on their creators.

Shortly after the worst of that threat was ended, the Nirodha movement extended its claws across the seas to latch on to like-minded fanatics in America.

As a method of insuring that menaces from within the body politic would be minimized, Sam ordered that every citizen of the CCS would be required to have SQUID implants. During the last several years of the Consolidation War, the implants were mandatory for new recruits. Now, even infants born within the direct sphere of influence of the CCS cities were implanted with the devices.

By the time Sam instituted this policy, the Consolidated Confederacy of States was completely entrenched as the form of government, far more securely rooted than the god-king system practiced by the barons. With every citizen now linked by the neuronic energy of the SQUIDs, old and new humans alike lived in harmony. Sam announced his intention to build a new world—an adaptive Earth, as he called it. He described it as a world where everyone had an important niche to fill. Therefore, they would be able to adapt to any changes or new set of circumstances that might arise, confident they could deal with it efficiently.

Now, twenty years after the fact, the citizenry of the CCS were so accustomed to obeying the edicts of imperial law, that any question, much less opposition, was unthinkable. From babyhood, they were indoctrinated to serve the universal good of imperial law.

It was a world of peace, of modern cities that were connected by monorail tunnels, where hellzones had been remade into Eden-like parks. The ruins of nuke-scarred cities were torn down and playgrounds were built in their place. Human and hybrids, once bitter enemies, each perceived the other much like the Cro-Magnon had looked at the Neanderthal. Now they coexisted, even married. They had adapted.

Sam envisioned transforming Earth into a garden of beauty and knowledge, but only if the planet's inhabitants could adapt to his vision....

SINDRI RUBBED his forehead and said ruefully, "Sounds ideal."

"Too ideal," Kane replied.

Sindri frowned at him. "Nothing can be too ideal."

"It can when you make everything so easy for a human that he loses his instincts, his independence. His ability to effect change on his own."

"This whole story...it's not easy to accept."

"Think how I feel," Kane countered. "And I lived it."

Sitting on the edge of the bed, his legs dangling, Sindri regarded Kane with a lopsided grin. "In all my dreams of punishing you, Mr. Kane, what you just told me of your suffering makes them seem like petty little resentments."

"Good," Kane retorted gruffly. "Then you don't have any reason to waste time trying to get revenge on me for past defeats. And we can move on."

Sindri cocked his head at a quizzical angle. "Move on to what?"

"To start undoing the events I just described. To make sure they never come to pass."

Sindri's eyes widened. "And how do you figure to do that? With the temporal dilator at the Operation Chronos facility?"

Kane shook his head. "No, that's wrecked. Brigid caused it to hit critical mass, remember?"

Sindri snorted. "Of course I do. To me, it happened only an hour or so ago. You let me go in the hopes I could disengage the chain reaction. I was able to, just barely. However, I knew there would be a venting of energies, of the subatomic particle stream. So I jumped into the memory buffer matrix to save myself."

Kane nodded. "It took me a while, but I figured out that's what you did."

Sindri made a spitting sound of derision. "'A while'? It took you over twenty years." When he saw

Kane's eyes glint hard with anger, Sindri amended his statement by saying, "But I'm grateful nevertheless."

"You should be," Kane stated. "Because now you'll have a chance to actually contribute something worthwhile to the world, rather than take from it."

Sindri crossed his right leg over the other and cupped the knee. "Beyond the fact you've threatened to kill me if I don't cooperate, why shouldn't I try to introduce myself to this imperator of yours and hook up with him, strike an alliance? From what you've told me, it sounds like he and I have similar attitudes...particularly in regards to you."

Kane folded his arms over his chest and smiled without humor. "Because he would see your attitude as a threat to his own. There's room for only one imperator, and he'd definitely think you'd be trying to steal his crown. And of course, you would."

Sindri nodded agreeably. "True enough."

"Besides," Kane continued, "even if you escaped from this place, it's not like the wild old days when you had free rein to try and carve out your own little piece of empire someplace. Your helper monkeys, the transadapts, are most likely all dead by now, since you told me their life spans were around thirty years. And the few who might survive either on Mars or *Parallax Red* would barely remember you. They sure as hell wouldn't obey you. So there goes any potential followers."

The frown tugging at Sindri's mouth deepened as Kane continued to talk. "About the only halfway organized bunch that you could maybe persuade to follow you would be the Pischacas…but in my opinion, they'd be having you for lunch before you finished your first recruitment speech."

Kane grinned bleakly. "Yeah, it'll be pretty damn hard to reestablish yourself as a messiah, a conqueror or simply as a plain old criminal mastermind on the imperator's adaptive Earth. He's just about got a monopoly on all your old vocations."

Sindri sighed mournfully. "I see your point, Mr. Kane. What's your proposition?"

"It's pretty simple, actually." Kane paused, took a breath and stated, "I've built a machine called a spatiotemporal dissociator—"

Sindri's eyebrows crawled up his high forehead. "*You* built?"

Kane paid no attention to the interruption. "It's linked to the autosequencers of the mat-trans gateway unit here. With the data cards I took from the temporal dilator, we can transmit a channel through the quantum stream and focus an injection point in a particular time and place…in this case, the time is twenty-seven years ago. The place is here, Redoubt Cerberus and our gateway unit."

Sindri's lips pursed as he considered Kane's words. "I thought old Lakesh had set up a security lock on the system."

"He had. You overcame it before. You can do it again."

"True," Sindri conceded. "But what kind of tests

have you conducted? How do you know this will work?"

Bluntly Kane answered, "I really don't know if it'll work at all. We only attempted one test about a week ago. We tried to send an old coin through, but we weren't successful."

"Did the coin come back whole?"

"Actually, no," replied Kane breezily. "It reassembled as its constituent parts, like little metal and alloy particles."

Sindri's face paled by several shades. "Then how the hell do you—?"

Kane raised a preemptory hand. "I'm not done. I have a vague recollection of a particular day twenty-seven years ago, when an unauthorized carrier wave activated the gateway. It lasted only a minute and nobody could figure it out. Bry and Lakesh just wrote it off as some sort of electromagnetic interference, a glitch in the network."

"How do you know that's not exactly what it was?" Sindri demanded hotly.

Kane chuckled a little self-consciously. "I don't. But inasmuch as you're the only man I know who has been out of the time stream for the required twenty-seven plus years, that makes you the only man perfectly suited to find out if the dissociator works or not."

Sindri shook his head in disgust. "Lucky me."

"You've been given a singular honor, Sindri. You can finally undertake an action that might justify your existence…and the best part of it is, you'll also be doing it for a selfish reason. If you survive the trip, you'll be back in your own time period, free from the memory buffer and able to implement your own dreams of empire again. We'll be back at each other's throats just like nothing ever happened. Brigid will be alive for you to try to seduce, you can attempt to take Thunder Isle away from New Edo once more, or even try to conquer a barony for your very own.''

Sindri waved away Kane's words impatiently. "You make me sound like some kind of sadistic little boy.''

Kane shrugged. "If the diaper fits—''

Rage glittered in Sindri's blue eyes, but he managed to keep his temper in check. "Assuming I live through the trip, how do I convince the you in the past that the you in the future sent me back? How can I affect a change or keep the you of twenty-seven years ago from killing me on the spot?''

"I've got that covered,'' Kane replied, turning toward the door. "I've had years to think about this. Wait here and I'll show you.''

"Send Tanvirah in here to keep me company,'' Sindri called after him.

"You two wouldn't have anything to talk about,'' Kane said over his shoulder. "She's a little out of your league.''

"But not yours?'' Sindri's tone was challenging "I can tell her about the time I tricked you into helping me steal the Aurora spy plane. That might impress her.''

Kane ignored him. He stepped out into the corridor, wondering as he knew he would, if he hadn't made a grievous error in retrieving Sindri. As brilliant as the little man was, he was also as untrustworthy as he was ingenious—as his parting shot about the Aurora reminded him. However, he could only hope that Sindri would swallow down his ego-fueled hatred and make common cause with him.

He went to his quarters, the same ones he had been assigned by Lakesh nearly thirty years before. They hadn't changed much, except for the computer terminal and desk he'd brought in some years ago. He sat in front of it, making sure the little vid cam was connected.

From a padded sleeve envelope he withdrew a small compact disc and inserted it into the port. He touched the drop-down window's Play option. Pixels sparkled on the monitor screen, and a head-and-shoulders image of himself appeared, appearing to stare into his own eyes.

''I've just gotten back from Thunder Isle,'' he heard himself say. ''I already turned the data cards over to Bry, and we'll be making the retrieval attempt shortly. Before we do, I need to locate Tanvirah because I don't trust her to be out of my sight when we power up the dissociator—''

Kane stopped the play and fast-forwarded the CD until the screen glowed blue and blank. After making the proper adjustments with the vid cam, a real-time image of his head and shoulders appeared on the computer's monitor screen. He used the mouse to click the record icon.

"It worked," he announced. "Sindri came through alive and whole and apparently as nasty as he was when I—you—last saw him. I've already briefed him on what Bry and I hope to accomplish by injecting him into your time period. He's agreed to it, but then I haven't given him many options."

He paused to smile, but he knew it would look forced. "I hope this works, but if it does, I won't know it. I won't be here to think about it. But if it does work, do me and yourself a favor, even though you won't like hearing this…" He took a deep breath, then declared in a rush, "The next time you're alone with Brigid, stop acting like an idiot and tell her how you—"

A distant sound like a wet paper bag bursting suddenly echoed down the passageway and into his quarters. Kane paused the recording, his nape hair tingling. The noise was vaguely familiar, but he couldn't immediately identify it. Pieces of the redoubt's roof still came down occasionally, so he attributed it to that at first.

He listened for a count of five for another sound. When one was not forthcoming, Kane ejected the CD, slipped it into the padded sleeve envelope and went out into the corridor. The fact that the sound was not repeated did not comfort him. He experienced the opposite emotion, so he hurried on to the operations center, carrying the CD.

Even as he entered the central control complex, Kane sensed something was terribly wrong. Quietly, his flesh crawling at the oppressive silence that filled the room, he went forward through the big, vault-walled room and into the anteroom, breathing shallowly.

Bry lay sprawled facedown on the floor underneath the dissociator's control console, blood oozing in a dark pool around his head. His wheelchair was pushed into a corner, canted up on its left wheel. Above the chair, smeared on the wall was spread a great slurry of blood and brain matter amid a scattering of bone chips.

Heart trip-hammering within his chest, he knelt beside Bry, pressing his fingers against the side of his neck as he did so, knowing in advance he was wasting the effort. Only a moist, pulsing cavity occupied the back of Bry's skull, and he recognized the kind of weapon that had made the ghastly wound. From the way the blood was still spreading and had yet to begin to congeal, he knew whatever had happened hadn't been that long ago, perhaps only a matter of a minute.

Suddenly, he sensed a presence in the room and he came to his feet in a rush, knee joints popping. Tanvirah stepped out from behind the mat-trans unit. "He tried to stop me. I didn't want to kill him."

Gripped in her slender right hand was a pistol that looked as if it were made from brushed aluminum. It held the general configuration of a revolver, but instead of a cylinder, a small round ammo drum fit into the place where there was normally a trigger guard. There wasn't a trigger, just a curving switch inset into the grip.

The barrel was unusually long, nearly ten inches in length. A unit of energy inside the grip moved a piston that propelled the explosive projectile made of tungsten carbide. The handgun had been in use on the Manitius Moon Base, part of the matériel salvaged from there and stored in the armory. It possessed almost no recoil to speak of.

Kane didn't raise his hands, noting Tanvirah had put her bodysuit back on even though the front still gaped open. In an unruffled, uninflected voice he asked, "He tried to stop you from doing what?"

Tanvirah patted the pocket of her garment and Kane heard faint clicks. "I have the data cards. I'm taking them with me."

"To where?"

"To High River first. Then to my brother, to Sam." Her tone was matter-of-fact, businesslike. "I'm sorry I must do this, but I can't allow you to send Sindri back in time."

"Actually," Kane said, "Sam can't allow it. He's controlling you, don't you realize that?"

Her knuckles whitened on the firing switch as she gestured with the pistol's long barrel. Tightly, she said, "I don't want to have to kill you, too. You were a great man once. Now, remove the dissociator's power cables from the gateway. I can reset it myself.''

''I'm sure you can. Your old man taught you well.''

Tanvirah's lips compressed. ''No more talk. Just do it, or I'll kill you and do it myself.''

Kane shuffled forward, surreptitiously placing the CD on the console on his way to the elevated gateway platform. He began unscrewing the coaxial couplings from their sleeve sockets. Tanvirah watched him alertly. He removed them in silence, not even looking at the woman.

''Tanvirah,'' he said as he tugged on the last wire. ''I doubt you'll believe me, but I'm not crazy.''

''I know you're not,'' she replied darkly. ''Just selfish beyond belief. You want what you want and to hell with the rest of humanity.''

Kane worked the length of cable loose and straightened with a weary sigh. He used his foot to close up the cover plate. ''Tanvirah, if I could only—''

He gave the cable a jerk and whiplashed it across the intervening yards between him and the dark-haired girl. He had accurately gauged the length he would need. The metal-collared end of the cable struck the back of her right hand with a loud, meaty impact. Crying out in shock and pain, Tanvirah's fingers opened and the pistol clattered to the floor at her feet.

She stumbled backward, nursing her injured hand. Kane bounded forward to scoop up the pistol, but her leg flashed up, the foot catching him solidly on the jaw and knocking him backward. He would have fallen if he hadn't grabbed the edge of the console.

Kane was shaken by the force of the kick, half-stunned. The salty tang of blood filled his mouth as Tanvirah went into a series of graceful, sliding dance-type steps. She moved her arms and hands in intricate motions, and her expression became one of calm, masklike beauty.

Kane pushed himself away from the console, recognizing the fluid, formal grace of the movements. A fragmented memory of the Scorpia Prime's sinuous dance flitted through his mind. A cold sick anger filled him, and recklessly he bounded toward her. Tanvirah whirled on the ball of one foot. The other sprang up and out and glanced off Kane's right ribs.

Despite the protection offered by his shadow suit, the ax-inflicted wound flared with a burst of agony. Clutching at himself and gagging, he backed away. He found Tanvirah's expression of serene detachment chilling. Her dark eyes were wide and seemed to give off a luminous, malignant light. She almost appeared to be in an altered state of consciousness; with her SQUID implants, that was a very real possibility.

Kane realized that Tanvirah was as determined to kill him as any opponent he'd ever met, and she was probably a good deal more capable than a lot of them. He moved toward her, kicking his right leg in a long arc, intending to catch her on the chin with the toe of his boot.

Almost negligently, yet with blinding speed, Tanvirah shifted laterally to the left. Kane did his best to shadow her fluid movements, filling the air around her with a flurry of closed-fist karate blows. The punches she couldn't duck or dodge she blocked, her arms as graceful and swift as snakes, but feeling as hard muscled as oak.

Angry and frustrated, Kane put all of his upper-body strength into an uppercut. His fist missed the underside of her jaw by a fraction as Tanvirah's body abruptly doubled like an eel. She bent backward at the waist, her spine seeming to be as flexible as rubber. She somersaulted backward a good four feet and turned to snatch up the pistol. She was in the process of firing it when Kane leaped forward and stab-kicked at her hand. His foot struck the long barrel and wrenched it from her fingers.

The explosive tungsten-carbide pellet crashed into the generator with a whomp of impact and a shower of white sparks. A cloud of greasy black smoke belled out and up.

Even as the pistol hit the floor, Tanvirah was lunging to the counterattack. Kane shunted aside a crescent kick, but couldn't fend off the edge of the flattened hand slashing into the side of his neck. Pain streaked up and down his spine like needles of fire, and the room grew blurred at the edges. Fighting unconsciousness, he staggered to the right, shifted position in a feint and then reached for her. His hands closed on empty air as Tanvirah danced gracefully out of reach, kicking with her left leg at his kneecap as she retreated.

Her timing was a shade off, allowing Kane to sidestep and latch on to her ankle. He pulled upward, intending to dump her onto her back. To his astonishment, Tanvirah sprang into the air as he pulled, almost as if she and Kane were partners practicing an acrobatic trick. Holding her body almost perfectly perpendicular to his, she hugged herself and pirouetted clockwise in midair, twisting out of Kane's grip. At the same instant, she used the torque of her spin to kick with her right foot, the heel catching Kane in the chest and driving him backward against the console. She performed a somersault and came up on both feet, facing him.

At that point, kneading his sternum and gasping for air, Kane realized he had better not take any more chances with Tanvirah. She was one of the most skilled and deadly opponents he'd ever faced in unarmed combat—or at least he couldn't think of anyone with superior abilities at the moment.

Tanvirah sidled toward the gateway chamber, and Kane moved to cut her off. He launched a roundhouse kick in the same split second she did. The calves of their legs collided, but since he was stronger, he knocked her off balance. She stumbled but didn't fall. By the time she recovered her footing, he was inside her defenses.

As he clutched a handful of her bodysuit, she tried to jack her knee into his groin, but he managed to turn aside so the blow landed on his thigh. Kane closed both hands around her shoulders, intending to out-muscle her, since he knew he had the advantage in strength.

She knew it, too. Teeth bared, Tanvirah tried to butt him under the chin with the crown of her head, but Kane contorted his body, avoiding the blow. He wrestled her around and applied a full nelson, bearing down, trying to force her to her knees.

Tanvirah bunched the muscles in her legs and sprang upward, planting the soles of her feet against the armaglass walls of the mat-trans chamber and kicking rearward. Both of them stumbled backward, and Kane felt his grip loosen. In the split second it required for him to bear down with the full nelson again, Tanvirah flung her arms straight up over her head, relaxed, bent her knees, wriggled her hips and slipped down between his arms.

Kane knew what her next maneuver would be, but his mind and his reflexes didn't work in tandem. As he expected, Tanvirah knocked his legs out from under him with a scything arm sweep. Kane fell heavily, the rear of his head striking the edge of the console. Even as he heard the crack of bone hitting metal, little multicolored pinwheels exploded behind his eyes.

Kane wasn't aware of losing consciousness completely. He had a vague recollection of falling, then a sound like a gale-force wind was filling his head. He levered himself up by his elbows and squinted at the bright flares bursting on the other side of the armaglass walls. The hurricane howl climbed in pitch as the device cycled through its dematerialization process.

Then the electronic wail from the jump chamber faded, dropping down into silence. The bursts of energy behind the brown-hued translucent slabs disappeared. Clamping his jaws on a groan, Kane slowly dragged himself to his feet. The back of his head hurt abominably. He touched it and felt a lump, but his fingers came away dry. He glanced toward Bry's corpse and hissed, "Shit."

Sindri chose that instant to stroll in. He glanced around the smoky, gore-soaked room without a flicker of emotion and inquired mildly, "She was out of *whose* league again?"

Chapter 18

While Kane tended to Bry's body, Sindri sauntered around the mat-trans unit, pursing and unpursing his lips in thought. The slit pockets of his shadow suit were too shallow to allow him to put his hands in them, so he clasped his hands behind his back.

"Where is this High River place she told you she was going?" Sindri asked, nudging the elevated platform with a foot.

Kane rolled Bry over, dragging him away from the pool of dark blood. The wound on his forehead was small, but the pellet had broken through the skull bone as if it were old plaster. Bry's eyes were partially open and even through the blood masking his face, Kane saw a slight smile touching his lips. It was a smile of peace.

"Colorado," he answered absently. "On the site where Cobaltville used to be."

Sindri nodded and stepped up onto the platform, jiggling the wedge-shaped door handle of the unit. "I presume some security measures would have been taken to keep us from pursuing her via the mat-trans."

With thumb and forefinger, Kane closed Bry's eyes. "I would imagine so...but even if there weren't, if we followed her through we'd be gating into a nest of blasters. Soldiers would be waiting for us.''

Sindri cast him an annoyed look over his shoulder. "So your whole plan is screwed, right? You can't send me back without those data cards?''

Kane stood. "Not through the dissociator, no.''

"The dilator?''

Kane shook his head. "No. It's inoperable.''

"Then what—?''

"I'll explain later," Kane broke in sternly. "Give me a hand with Bry's body.''

Sindri sniffed diffidently. "I'm not an undertaker.''

Kane stared at him in silence for a couple of seconds, then he crossed the room in two swift strides. Sindri saw the look on his face and tried to jump down from the platform, but Kane caught him. He latched his hands around Sindri's neck and heaved him from the floor, slamming his back against an armaglass slab. He held him at eye level.

"You'll by God need an undertaker if you don't do as I say," Kane spit between clenched teeth. "I'm not in the mood for your above-it-all horseshit, pissant.''

Sindri's feet kicked impotently as he clutched at Kane's wrists and glared at him with pure, unadulterated azure fury. "You don't dare kill me, Mr. Kane. You need me to bring Bry back to life…to bring back all your friends to life.''

Kane pressed his thumbs against Sindri's larynx, evoking from him an aspirated cry of pain. "I won't kill you," Kane growled. "But there's nothing in the manual that says you can't travel through time with dislocated arms and legs and even a skull fracture.''

He shook him for emphasis, bouncing the back of his head off the gateway's wall. "Do you understand me?"

Mouth working, Sindri gasped for air around his protruding tongue and he nodded as best he could. "I understand," he managed to husk out.

Kane relaxed the pressure around the little man's neck and lowered him to the floor rather than drop him. Picking up the CD from the top of the console and pocketing it, he turned toward the door. "Come with me."

Adopting a demeanor of wounded dignity, Sindri followed Kane out of the operations center and back to the infirmary. From a storage closet on the far side of the laboratory, Kane pulled down a folded plastic body bag and a number of thickly napped towels. These he shoved into Sindri's arms.

The two men returned to the anteroom. Sindri, his mobile mouth twisting in disgust, helped Kane wrestle Bry's corpse into the body bag. The scrawny man weighed not much more than a suit of clothes, and Sindri knew Kane could have done the insertion by himself.

After Bry was snugged within the zippered cocoon, Kane and Sindri began swabbing up the blood and wiping down the wall, cleaning it of viscera. After a few minutes of hand-and-knees mopping, Sindri exclaimed peevishly, "Throttle me again if you want,

Mr. Kane, but in my opinion we're wasting precious time. And I'm not making a pun."

"Not in my opinion," Kane replied flatly. "And in this place, my opinion is the only one that matters."

Sindri's body stiffened with barely repressed anger. "Have the last three decades of hardship and deprivation addled your memory? You ought to remember that I can be pushed only so far."

Kane's face—what Sindri could see of it through the black, silver-stippled beard and long, forward-falling hair—was a mask of bemusement. He continued to work but quietly he said, "Donald Bry was an obsessive-compulsive pain in the ass. But when all was said and done, he remained a friend to me when most did not. We'll be going after Tanvirah, but I won't leave the man to lie like this, as if he's no more important than a squirrel run down by a wag. We're going to clean up in here and give him a proper burial. Then we'll be about our business."

Sindri sighed. "All right. But how can we be about our business? Colorado is a long way from here."

"Just wait and see."

After the mop-up was completed to Kane's satisfaction, he and Sindri carried Bry's bagged body out of the operations center and the redoubt altogether. The air was still surprisingly mild, even at hard on midnight. Sindri appeared a little startled by the warm breeze, then disconcerted when he glanced up at the vast, star-speckled canopy of the sky overhead.

As Sindri had been born in an enclosed, artificial

environment, and after spending most of his life in specially built habitats on Mars and then *Parallax Red,* Kane figured the little man had a touch of agoraphobia, a fear of open spaces. However, he didn't complain as he gripped the body bag by its strap, lugging his burden at an oblique angle across the plateau.

At the edge, where the tarmac disappeared into grass and shrubs, they struggled up a slope to a row of grave markers. At the far end, a pair of graves gaped open. They were partially obscured by tangles of scrub brush with high mounds of dirt between them. The headstone of the one on the end read Donald Bry. The inscription on the one beside it was even more succinct. It bore only a single word: Kane.

"I can see you were prepared for this eventuality," Sindri remarked dryly. "Or was this the work of Bry?"

"I dug them both," Kane said with a studied indifference. "I figured if I went first, the best Bry could manage was to haul me up here and dump me. Since he preceded me—"

Kane shrugged and slid Bry's body into the waiting hole. Sindri watched him do it in silence, alert for any sign of tears. There was none. From beneath a clump of bushes, Kane pulled out a canvas-wrapped bundle. He tossed aside the flaps and removed a pair of T-handled spades. Tossing the shorter one to Sindri, he said, "Let's cover him up."

As they dug into the mounds of earth, breaking

through the dried outer crust, Sindri asked, "Was Bry born a cripple?"

"No," Kane replied, dumping a spadeful of dirt onto the body bag. "Over twenty years ago he and Brigid tried to rescue me from an enemy stronghold in India by trading tech for my freedom. Bry came along with her more or less as a Trojan horse, a geek who was supposed to explain and demonstrate the instruments."

Sindri grunted, jamming the blade of his tool deep into the soil and levering it up. "Apparently his masquerade wasn't successful."

"It was to a point," Kane said. "During the negotiations for my release, he planted incendiaries all around the place. But—"

Kane's words trailed off, and he began spading up and dumping the dirt with a sudden fierce vigor.

"But what?" pressed Sindri. "What happened to him and to Miss Brigid?"

Kane hesitated a moment then declared flatly, "Brigid was killed. So was Grant's wife, Shizuka. We cremated their bodies there. Grant kept Shizuka's ashes, I scattered Brigid's here. We all thought Bry was dead, too, consumed by the fires. He was seriously hurt, but he was alive. He crawled off into the jungle where he was found and nursed by locals. A year later I came to the place as a sort of memorial, and that's how I found him again."

Sindri nodded and said softly, "I'm sorry about Miss Brigid."

Kane glanced at the small man across the open grave and realized he was trying to extend sympathy, the little of which he was capable. Kane was once more reminded that even the darkest of hearts harbored a glimmer of light. As it was, Kane never had been able to dredge up much genuine hatred for Sindri. Brigid had once referred to him as a warped little man with ambitions enough to challenge God. He was certainly that, but he had also proved he operated on his own skewed code of honor.

Also, and Kane had never admitted it to anyone, he had always felt a grudging admiration for the little madman, and he was never sure why. He was just as crazy as some of the enemies he had killed and even more fixated on carving out a personal empire as others, but the one characteristic that separated Sindri from that kind was his ability to entertain. The man possessed a childlike enthusiasm for wreaking havoc, and Kane had always related to that, as ashamed as he was of it now.

By working in tandem, the two men filled the grave within a few minutes. After tamping down and smoothing the dirt, they stood on either side of it, leaning on the spade handles and panting. Sindri gestured toward the headstone bearing Kane's name. "Who is there to bury you now, Mr. Kane?"

Kane chuckled, a harsh, bitter sound without mirth. "I charge you with that responsibility, if the situation arises."

Sindri matched his chuckle, but added a sinister rattlesnake rasp of his very own. He nodded graciously. "I accept that responsibility if you grant me one codicil—that I have your permission to piss on your grave after I've laid you to rest."

Kane imitated his nod. "Permission granted."

He placed the spades back within the canvas square, rewrapped it and shoved the bundle back beneath the bundle. Then he started climbing up to the ridgeline. "Follow me."

With a mystified expression on his face, Sindri did so. At the top of the slope, Kane walked a more or less straight route for a score of yards, then down the face of the incline. He marched through closely growing trees following a faint path that Sindri wouldn't have noticed as such if he hadn't been following Kane. After they had walked some hundred yards from the burial ground, Kane came to a halt.

At first glance, they stood in a small, bowl-shaped clearing, with a tall tangle of bushes, shrubs and foliage making up the inner curve. Sindri's eyes picked out shorn saplings and tree stumps protruding only a few inches above the ground.

"Why are we here?" he demanded.

Kane gestured. "To go about our business."

Sindri followed the taller man's gesture and saw only the snarl of overgrowth. Kane stepped to it, thrust his arms into the tangled vines and leaves and pulled. He lifted away a large section of a carefully camouflaged shelter made of cross-braced tree limbs interlaced with grasses, weeds and shrubs. The forepart came away in three large pieces. Inside he saw the outline of a tall, streamlined shape, which at first glance was unrecognizable in the darkness.

Kane tugged away camouflage netting, and Sindri saw a metal-sheathed object that reminded him of the general shape and configuration of a flattened javelin head, not much more than a wedge with wings. Stepping closer, he asked, "What the hell is it, Mr. Kane?"

"It's a Transatmospheric Vehicle," Kane replied, pulling away more of the screen of shrubbery. "We found several of them on a Moon base nearly thirty years ago and flew them down. This is the only one remaining. We called them Manta ships."

Sindri's eyes passed over the ship's contours, seeing that the resemblance to seagoing manta rays was more than superficial, particularly with its pair of extended, curving wings. He judged the wingspan at around twenty meters and the fuselage at fifteen. A short tail assembly was tipped by an ace-of-spades-shaped rudder.

The hull's composition appeared to be a burnished bronze alloy. Covering almost the entire surface were intricate geometric designs, deeply inscribed into the metal itself. There were interlocking swirling glyphs, the cup-and-spiral symbols, even the elaborate cuneiform markings. The hull was smooth, with barely perceptible seams where the metal plates joined.

The craft had no external apparatus at all, no ailerons, no fins, no airfoils. The cockpit was almost invisible, little more than an elongated symmetrical oval hump in the exact center of the sleek topside fuselage.

"This TAV doesn't look like Terran manufacture or design," Sindri said skeptically. "Not like the sub-orbital X-planes the Air Force was designing before the nukecaust, or the Aurora stealth plane. Those markings look like Sumerian."

Checking out the landing gear, Kane replied casually, "That's because they are Sumerian. We never knew for sure, but these craft were more than likely created by the Annunaki."

Sindri's eyes widened in astonishment. "The Annunaki? Do you know how old that would make that crate, then?"

Kane answered, "Only approximately. The metallurgical analysis Bry performed on the hull suggested it's a minimum of ten thousand years old. It could be twice as old. But don't worry—being stored on the Moon for all those millennia kept it in perfect working order."

"How in God's name did you get to the Moon?" Sindri's voice hit a high note of incredulous challenge.

Kane said dismissively, "It's not really important. I'll tell you about it when we have more time."

Sindri made a spitting sound of derision. "Pun intended?"

Kane came out from beneath the Manta and clambered up a wing to the fuselage. "Actually, no."

Sindri gave the machine a long, distrustful stare. "What powers that thing?"

Kane found the canopy latch and popped it open. "Two different kinds of engines—a ramjet and solid-fuel pulse detonation air spikes."

Sindri nodded in understanding. "So working together, they enable it to fly in a vacuum and in an atmosphere?"

"Exactly."

"The maximum cruise speed should be around Mach 20."

"More like Mach 25, on a good day." Kane extended a hand downward. "Come aboard."

Sindri started forward, then hesitated. "There's enough room?"

"I installed a secondary jump seat a few years back. Anyone else would be cramped, but you should have plenty of leg room."

Sindri flushed in irritation, but he took Kane's hand and allowed himself to be hoisted up onto the hull and the cockpit. As Sindri strapped himself in, Kane slid into the pilot's chair. He directed Sindri to put on a radio headset.

A bronze-colored helmet with a full-face visor was attached to the headrest of the pilot's chair. A pair of tubes stretched from the rear to an oxygen tank at the back of the seat. The helmet and chair were of one piece, a self-contained unit.

The instrument panel was almost dismaying in its simplicity. The controls consisted primarily of a joystick, altimeter and fuel gauges. All the labeling was in English.

When Kane slipped the helmet on over his head, he heard the whine of an internal power source juicing up immediately. The interior curve of the helmet's visor swarmed with a squall of glowing pixels. When they cleared a nanosecond later, he had CGI icons of sensor scopes, range finders and various indicators.

At the same time the helmet automatically extended a lining and seal around the base of his neck. As he strapped himself into the chair, he heard a hiss of static and asked, "Can you read me, Sindri?"

"Loud and clear."

"I'm powering us up."

"Don't I get a helmet or an oxygen mask or something?" The little man's voice was plaintive yet peevish.

"You won't be needing an oxygen mask," Kane replied. "My goal is speed and stealth not altitude."

"What about a helmet?"

"You won't need one of those, either. At the speed we'll be traveling, if we crash, the impact will kill you instantly. A helmet might prolong your agony by a second or two."

"Safety first." Sindri's voice was heavy with sneering sarcasm. "As always."

Kane was glad the visor concealed the grin that had crossed his face at Sindri's discomfort. He closed and latched the canopy, then pulled the joystick lever back slightly. He rotated it and pushed it forward. It caught and clicked into position.

The hull began to vibrate around them, in tandem

with an electronic whine that steadily climbed in scale. The CGI inventory of all the dials, switches, gauges and fire controls flashed across the helmet's visor. Each one showed green. Then on HUD inside of his helmet glowed the words: VTOL Launch System Enabled.

The cockpit resonated with a high-pitched whine as Kane engaged the vectored-thrust ramjets. The Manta began to rise straight up with a steady grace, and Kane withdrew the tripodal landing gear. Fine clouds of dust puffed up all around. Kane nudged the control and increased the speed of the lift.

The humming drone changed in pitch as with a stomach-sinking swiftness the TAV lifted upward as smoothly as if it were a needle being drawn by a celestial magnet. Kane's helmet HUD displays offered different vantage points of the ascent, and his eyes flicked from one to another. He watched as the burying ground and the plateau quickly receded. The mountain peaks that contained the Cerberus redoubt shrank into gray cones. The Manta made a wide, slow, circling turn that gave Kane time to double-check all engine and flight instruments. The precision-tuned machine operated flawlessly.

Sindri remained silent in the jump seat behind him during the maneuvers, either too enthralled by the experience or too terrified to speak. Grinning within his helmet, Kane engaged the pulse detonation wave engines and the Manta hurtled across the sky like an artillery shell exploding from the barrel of a cannon.

The trailing sonic boom slammed its thunderclap behind the Manta, and Kane felt the concussion running through the hull of the ship.

Sindri yelped in astonishment as he was slammed back against his seat. Kane couldn't help but laugh.

Chapter 19

The Manta followed an NOE course, nap of the earth, skimming above and flattening the treetops beneath the fury of its passage. Kane flew with unerring precision from Montana and into Colorado by cutting across southern Wyoming.

Kane didn't want to fly too high, nor did he want to fly too slowly. He compromised with a general altitude of 150 feet and 300 miles per hour. He kept to the wilderness areas, skirting mesas and mountains, forests and waterfalls, basins and plateaus. The LARC subsystem, the low-altitude ride control, fed him turbulence data. The controls automatically dampened the effects of turbulent air pockets by the deflection of two small fins extending down from beneath the cockpit area.

When the Manta entered Colorado's Canyon Lands, Kane increased the altitude. The TAV wended its way around the Grand Mesa and skimmed the Book Plateau until it reached the Gunnison National Monument, a rugged wilderness of gorges and cloud-scraping pinnacles of rock. Once past it, they would be in the official Outland territories of High River, but Kane didn't relax.

He was not surprised when his ears started buzzing. He recognized the sound as the radar lock-on warning, piped from the forward sensor array into his helmet. Glancing out of the starboard side, he glimpsed a brief flash of distant silver. It was high and moving as fast as the Manta. It grew larger until he caught the reflective glint of moonlight on the silver backswept wings.

Seeming to float in the air between his eyes and the visor, a column of numbers appeared, glowing red against the pale bronze. When he focused on a distant object, the visor magnified it and provided a readout as to distance and dimension. Now he focused on the aircraft soaring in from the direction of High River. Kane had expected an airborne welcoming committee.

The aircraft looked like one of the supersonic Dragonflies that had seen brief action toward the end of the Consolidation War. As he recalled, they were good for high-altitude recon work, or bombing runs, but not so suited for low infighting or fast, tight maneuvering.

However, the Dragonflies were equipped with a murderous array of firepower, including a complement of short-range-attack minirockets and a 30 mm Vulcan cannon. For inflicting destruction at a safe remove, the aircraft had slung beneath its scanard outrigger fins six homing cruise missiles for use against moving ground targets, like armored divisions or supply convoys.

The Manta was at one thousand feet. He shoved the joystick forward and pushed the TAV toward the rocky ground. The Dragonfly followed, for a moment flying at a wing-to-wing level, although separated by several hundred yards. Still, it was close enough for Kane's helmet sensors to allow him to see the red triple-elongated triangles insignia on the delta wings. Then the craft rose above and ahead of him, sweeping into a screaming, high-speed curve. If he had been trained properly, the pilot would try to maneuver behind him.

Kane reduced his altitude even further, until the Manta skimmed barely a hundred feet above the stone-littered plateau floor. He watched the Dragonfly complete its turn and disappear briefly from his line of sight behind a cliff.

Kane yanked back on the stick and fed the ramjet thrusters full power. The acceleration slammed him against his chair and dragged a short, breathless cry of pain from Sindri.

The Manta whipped over on its port-side wing in a steep bank just above the rushing earth. A second later, a stream of tracers blazed through the darkness like phosphorescent threads and exploded against the ground.

Sindri, oblivious to the situation until the moment of acceleration, cried out wordlessly in shock, then demanded, ''What the hell is going on? Who is shooting at us?''

Kane hooked a thumb to starboard. ''See for yourself.''

The Dragonfly flashed by the Manta, and Kane caught a blurred glimpse of a helmeted head with a grimacing face below a dark visor.

Kane leveled off the TAV. On his new course, he headed toward the gaping jaws of the Black Canyon. Beyond it rose the peaks of a low mountain range, the Sangre De Cristo, he thought it might be. The mountains were four or five miles away, just about perfect for his next tactic. Keeping the Manta low, he maintained watch on the CGI signature representing the angry Dragonfly.

He could easily imagine the kind thoughts—and profanity—going through the pilot's head. No doubt he had been scrambled out of a warm bed to fly a recon with orders to destroy the Manta on sight. Kane was sure the orders made no allowance for failure.

The pilot seemed relatively skilled, at least in high-altitude and substratospheric flights. But the ground had to have seemed frighteningly close, and maneuvering at such high speeds would make him nervous. Kane decided to stress him out even more. Sideslipping the Manta to port, he guided the machine into the Black Canyon.

Sindri groaned in sick terror, "Oh, my God."

Flying through the Black Canyon was like trying to thread a needle with a runaway locomotive. The sheer rock walls grew closer and more threatening with every maneuver. Treacherous downdrafts buffeted the Manta perilously close to the foaming rapids of the Gunnison River, which gushed through the ramparts of stone. Kane's hands were constantly busy with the pitch, tab and trim controls.

He gazed at the computer-generated image of the

landscape on the HUD. Data scrolled down the side of the display, reviewing and assessing primary areas of danger beyond his line of vision. Each boulder, outcropping and curve in the canyon showed in detail.

At the beginning of the flight some thirty minutes before, Sindri had yipped and crowed with delight at the precision flying. Kane remembered the little man's jubilation thirty years before when he put the Aurora through its paces. Now he was having a difficult time keeping the yips of delight from turning to bleats of terror, as the walls of the gorge whipped by in a blur.

Suddenly a fireball bloomed port side, barely two yards above the Manta's wing. The aircraft shuddered from the rolling concussion. Kane felt the shock from the fuselage traveling through his body.

"What the fuck was that?" Sindri screamed.

"A rocket with a low-impact warhead," he answered calmly. "He's trying to shake us up."

Kane swerved the Manta around an outthrusting shelf of rock. As he completed the maneuver, the ship lurched sideways as a piece of the canyon wall exploded in a flaming, flaring shower of rock chips. The fragments rattled noisily against the fuselage.

Sindri shouted, "Dammit, why don't we defend ourselves?"

"Because we aren't armed," Kane replied, unruffled.

Sindri's response, if he had one, was lost in the shrill keening of wind as Kane pushed the Manta into a steep dive, down toward the foaming surface of the river. The ship skimmed over the top, sucking up plumes of water in its wake. A column of water erupted off to their right as another minirocket detonated in the riverbed. The Manta was splashed and jarred by the shock waves, but Kane kept it steady.

The canyon's winding and twisting course became worse instead of better. It was a helter-skelter jumble of outcroppings, detritus and scatterings of house-sized boulders. It looked as if this particular part of the gorge had been the playground of gargantuan children, and they had left the place as it was after particularly protracted temper tantrums. The only good aspect was that the terrain was far too confusing and obstructive for the Dragonfly to try launching another attack. The pilot gained as much altitude as possible and hung back.

After five or so minutes of the nerve-jangling flight, the canyon walls receded and the gorge widened out into a valley. Instantly, Kane heeled the Manta over, working it into a flat spin. It was a dangerous maneuver so close to the ground, but he had calculated the risks. The range was still too long for the Dragonfly's minirockets, but Kane figured the pilot would remedy that very quickly.

The HUD showed the Dragonfly banking and diving in pursuit, shortening the distance between them very swiftly just as Kane had predicted. Because the pilot had been trained in the techniques of high-altitude, maximum-power approaches, but was too nervous to cut in his throttle so close to the ground.

He was a skilled air jockey, nevertheless. He performed a smooth barrel roll to shorten a pass that would have carried him miles away and made a roaring return for another strafing pass. But the fast decreasing altitude made him back off after launching only one rocket. It went wide, doing nothing more than coating the Manta's hull with dust.

Still, the pilot had his orders and apparently a set of stainless-steel testicles. Even as the Manta skimmed swiftly above the ground, casting a shadow ahead and below it almost identical to its seagoing namesake, the Dragonfly prepared for a final effort.

It rose up on an arc, then soared down at a forty-five-degree angle, its cannon thudding, a tongue of flame dancing from the barrel. Kane saw the fountains and divots of dirt and rock explode as the rounds hammered a cross-stitch pattern into the terrain.

A minirocket exploded on the right, a brilliant red-yellow spout of fire. The control stick fought his hands as the sudden concussion made the TAV shudder. Clods of turf and shrapnel rattled briefly against the hull's undercarriage. He banked the craft a few degrees to starboard, but maintained the altitude.

The mountains came toward them rapidly. Both aircraft were well below the summits. Kane saw no vegetation to speak of on the higher slopes, just a litter of stone. Under the cold moonlight, the range looked menacing and the deep dark valleys between them filled with forest weren't much more inviting.

He pushed the control stick forward, and the Manta surged ahead, its speed increasing to 500 miles per hour. The Dragonfly buzzed in pursuit, its own velocity building. Kane kept a careful watch on the HUD readings, which clocked the enemy ship's rising speed levels. He knew that in order to catch them now, the pilot would have to kick in the afterburners.

Kane slowed the Manta at the precise instant the Dragonfly's afterburner spit blue flame. It soared overhead, like a projectile loosed from a slingshot, heading directly toward the mountains. The peaks were very close, and Kane held the TAV's nose toward the nearest one.

"What the hell are you doing?" Sindri screamed.

Kane didn't answer, watching as the Dragonfly's pilot struggled to reduce his craft's speed as it closed in on the mountain range. The sheer, deeply fissured rocky peak swelled in his visor, and according to the measurements scrolling madly within the helmet, a collision was unavoidable. The conical mass loomed up over them like a thundercloud.

Sindri began shrieking and kicking the back of his seat. "Veer off! We'll crash! Veer off!"

Kane ignored him. Sindri's cries reached a peak of hysteria, then he lapsed into a hypnotized silence. A red square of light suddenly appeared on Kane's HUD, superimposed over a small, grid-enclosed digital simulation of the mountain and the Dragonfly. Simultaneously, the warning chime sounded. Then the icon representing the Dragonfly seemed to be sucked into the CGI mountaintop.

Instantly, Kane pulled back on the control column and the TAV swept into a steep climb, the pulse detonation jets roaring. The Manta skimmed across the crest of the peak with only a few feet between it and the TAV's undercarriage. A shaved sliver of a second later, he was blinded by a hell-hued blossom of light as the Dragonfly's fuel tank ruptured, ignited and exploded. Tongues of flame ballooned in all directions.

Bouncing pieces of metal rang reverberating chimes on the Manta's hull. Fragments of the aircraft, pinwheeling at incredible velocities, smashed into the TAV's fuselage, actually scoring it.

Kane swung the Manta around and headed back away from the mountains. As he recrossed the peak, he saw a great ball of flame marking the crash point of the Dragonfly. It had collided with the mountain less than fifty feet below the summit. The wind of the TAV's passage tore enough holes in the pall of smoke so he could see the burning, blackened hulk of the Dragonfly.

The Plexiglas canopy was too flame scorched to discern movement behind it. Sparks corkscrewed into the air. The impact and explosion started a small avalanche, and pieces of wreckage tumbled down along the mountainside.

Sindri's headset accurately conveyed his relieved sigh. "Mr. Kane…I can't believe you managed to accomplish the miracle you just did."

"Neither can I," retorted Kane. "I thought my miracle-making days were behind me. But before you put too much faith in me, we still have to make it to High River in one piece."

Chapter 20

The Manta soared over the irrigated greenness of cultivated fields and over the silvery windings of the Kanab River, a tributary of the Colorado.

Kane looked down at the clean, well-lit city spread below. High River was built on the bluffs overlooking the waterway, on the foundation of Cobaltville, which in turn had been built on the foundation of Vista ville, once the domain of Baron Alferd Nelson. He was now a very long time moldering in an unmarked grave, but even after the city became Cobaltville, the streets still seemed haunted by the memories of his bloody deeds.

The walls rose fifty feet high and at each intersecting corner, a watchtower protruded. At one time the towers had housed Vulcan-Phalanx gun emplacements, but those had been removed years before.

The walls themselves had been rebuilt in the years since the Consolidation War. The old stone was sheathed in a blue-gray alloy. In its flat expanse were faint, swirling patterns, but no seams or cracks. The construction technology that had refurbished the walls and changed Cobaltville to High River was far beyond what had been in use, even before the nukecaust.

There were no longer any checkpoints on the road

leading up to the city's gate, no "dragon's-teeth" obstacles, no armed patrols. But, as in the old baronial days, powerful spotlights still washed the immediate area outside the walls, leaving nothing hidden from their glare. One of the official reasons for fortifying the baronies was a century-old fear—or paranoid delusion—of a foreign invasion from other nuke-scarred nations. It had never happened, and Kane had always wondered how the barons figured any country could mount a large enough army to establish anything other than a remote beachhead.

Inside the walls still stretched the complex of spired Enclaves. Each of the four towers was joined to the others by pedestrian bridges. Few of the windows in the towers showed any light, so there was little to indicate that the interconnecting network of stone columns, enclosed walkways, shops and promenades was where thousands of people made their homes.

The dark and noisome streets of the Tartarus Pits no longer crisscrossed at the base of the Enclaves. The ville baronial society had been strictly class and caste based, and the design of the villes themselves reflected the cultural demarcation—the higher a citizen's standing in society, the higher he or she might live in the Enclaves.

The lowest level of the ville castes were the servant classes, who lived in abject squalor. The population of this class was ruthlessly controlled. Those lower levels were known in the ville vernacular as the Tartarus Pits, named after the abyss below Hell where Zeus confined the Titans. But the seething melting pots of cheap labor and crime had long ago been rehabilitated and merged with the rest of the community.

However, the Enclaves still formed a latticework of intersected circles, all connected to the center of the circle, from which arose the tower known in baronial days as the Administrative Monolith. The massive, round column of white stone jutted three hundred feet into the sky, standing proud and haughty, but now a symbol of consolidation.

It was from this structure that the city of High Tower took its name, since all other monoliths in all the other former baronies had been either demolished during the war, or torn down afterward. The only reason this particular one still existed was out of deference to the wishes of the imperial mother, Erica van Sloan.

As Kane piloted the Manta in a wide, low-altitude circuit around the city, Sindri commented, "Looks peaceful enough."

Kane said, "Wait."

As if his one-word response were a cue, circular hatches opened up all over the walls, dilating like the lenses of cameras. From the hatches rose disk-shaped lifts, depositing uniformed troopers at various points on the parapets. They swarmed out and took up position in well-ordered drills. At a quick count, Kane estimated there were perhaps twenty of them.

Their boots, coveralls and helmets were midnight-blue, with facings of bright scarlet. They brandished streamlined rifles with barrels like truncated cones. Power cables trailed from the stocks to bulky power units attached to their belts.

All the troopers were slender of build and so blank of expression they might have been mistaken for mannequins in military dress. The faces under the polycarbonate helmets were of human shape and features, but all of them were identical as to complexion and expression—paper pale with a strange waxy sheen. Their eyes beneath the overhang of their headgear barely blinked, and their small mouths did not so much as twitch.

"What the hell are they?" Sindri asked.

"Soldiers of the CCS," Kane answered in a sardonic drawl. "Generation 2.5, I'd guess. Frightening spectacle, aren't they?"

Sindri snorted. "Are they droids or something?"

"Something. A hybrid of hybrids is the best way to describe them. They're synthetic, not necessarily artificial. All their parts are organic, except for the SQUID implants, which more or less program them like droids."

Tower-mounted searchlights tracked the TAV, white funnels of incandescence sweeping up and across the ramparts of the city walls. Two of them struck the Manta and stayed there. Despite the tinted canopy and Kane's visored helmet, the light was blinding. But the light activated the electrochemical polymer of the canopy and it immediately polarized, cutting off at least half of the lights' candlepower.

As the Manta made another pass, the troopers lifted their rifles and triggered them almost in unison. Neither Kane nor Sindri saw or heard anything but brief flashes of light. However, both men felt the Manta shudder beneath multiple impacts before Kane whisked the craft up and out of range.

"What kind of weapons are those?" Sindri demanded. "Lasers? Tasers? Phasers?"

"None of the above," replied Kane. "They're called ASPs—Accelerated Streams of Protons—something Sam developed."

Sindri grunted in grudging admiration. "Very inventive. The weapons accelerate protons to great speeds and discharge them as bolts of plasma. They must pack more kinetic and thermal power than a laser."

"Exactly."

With a snide chuckle, Sindri asked, "Then perhaps you will be good enough to explain exactly how an unarmed aircraft will be able to land without being protoned to pieces."

Kane matched his chuckle. It sounded hollow and false within the confines of his helmet. "One thing I learned about the Mantas—they don't always need weapons to be deadly. With the right pilot at the controls, they *become* weapons."

Before Sindri could request clarification, Kane twisted the control stick and the TAV surged upward, almost standing the ship on its tail. He made an almost vertical bank, and the Manta plunged directly toward the surface of the wall. The cockpit resonated with the high-pitched whine of stressed engines and the slipstream of air sliding around them.

The soldiers raced back and forth, putting the ASP rifles to their shoulders again. Light flared from the barrels, and the TAV's fuselage shook from jarring blows.

Static discharges crackled inside the cockpit, crawling and leaping from one piece of electronics to another. Sindri howled in pain and clawed the radio headset away from his face. Kane ignored him, waggling the Manta's wings, tilting the craft up from side to side. He steepened the angle of the dive to gather momentum. The searchlights still tracked across the empty sky, swinging to and fro.

At the very last instant, Kane pulled back on the control stick and the Manta leveled off, roaring above the raised lip of parapet by scant inches. Troopers dropped flat as the undercarriage skimmed over their helmeted heads, but a few of the massed soldiers weren't so fast or so lucky. The wings of the TAV scythed into them, breaking them in the middle or crushing their skulls. They were swatted off the walls like red-and-blue bugs.

The violent downdraft of the Manta's booming passage buffeted a few others, slamming the soldiers up and over the edge of the wall. At least four of the uniformed troopers were sucked up in the wake of the ship and dragged behind it for several hundred feet before their bodies lost momentum and plummeted into the streets of the city.

The facade of the white tower swelled in the TAV's view port, and Kane kicked the Manta into a tight orbit around it, as if the huge structure were a maypole. He retraced his course back to the wall. The few remaining troopers fired their rifles at the ship, halos of white energy dancing around the barrels.

Engaging the vectored thrust ramjets, Kane dropped the Manta straight down and gracefully brought it to rest on the extended tripodal landing gear right in the center of the parapet.

"Now what?" snarled Sindri. "The soldiers have guns and we have shit!"

"You didn't listen to me very closely, did you?" Kane touched the controls and changed the angle of the ramjet vents.

Five-yard-long tongues of blue flame licked out from the apertures and touched the soldiers approaching the ship from the rear and to the sides. Instantly their uniforms burst into flame, and they became capering scarecrows made of fire.

Kane touched the controls again, and concussive bursts of superheated gas battered the burning men, driving them back with drunken, reeling steps. They vanished over the edge of the wall, either hurling themselves to safety or to their deaths. Kane didn't know which and at the moment didn't give a damn. He cut power to the engines.

In a voice breathless with awed tension, Sindri said, "You're a cold-blooded bastard, Mr. Kane."

"That's quite the compliment coming from you," Kane shot back, removing his helmet. "Or was it a compliment?"

Sindri shrugged. "I'm not sure."

Kane unsealed the canopy and slid it back. He and Sindri climbed out and down. The odor of scorched flesh and heated metal hung heavy in the air and Sindri wrinkled his nose at it. "Now what?"

Kane gestured to the nearest corner tower. "We can get to the street level through there."

"And do what?" Sindri demanded in angry frustration. "Get shot at some more, arrested, killed? You don't even have a gun! When I knew you before, you were always loaded down with enough firepower to take out half of the Cydonia colony!"

Kane waved a negligent hand through the air and started toward the corner tower. "We got this far without guns, didn't we? Besides, I lost my faith in musketry a long time ago."

"And when was that?" Sindri hadn't moved. "Around the time you moved out of the playpen?"

"Around the time Brigid was killed." Kane's voice held no particular inflection.

Sindri sighed with a soul-deep, put-upon weariness and hurried after Kane. "Where are we going? To see the imperator?"

Kane shook his head. "No, he sees nobody, not no way, not no how. Besides, he doesn't hang out here."

Sindri scowled. "Whoever hangs out here has tried to kill us twice!"

Kane nodded genially. "Very true. But now that we're here, I'm betting that Lakesh won't want us dead until he's had the chance to talk to us."

"What are you basing that bet on?"

"I think Tanvirah reported only to her mother about me bringing you out of zero time. Erica was the one who gave the orders to have us intercepted and shot down...not to mention killed if we tried to land. But by now, Lakesh has seen the vid of the two of us—" Kane saluted the air in the direction of the tower and the small spy-eye atop its spire "—and he'll give us safe passage. At least so we can be questioned. He'll be sending an escort."

Sindri shook his head in exasperation. "It would be nice if you had informed me of your wagers, plans and hopes before we embarked."

Kane smiled. "That would spoil the spontaneity."

The men had walked a little over half the distance to the tower when a lift disk hatch irised open directly in their path. It didn't disgorge more troopers. Instead a SPIDE rested on the platform.

Sindri stiffened, mouth dropping open in astonishment. "What the hell is that thing?"

"The escort I mentioned," Kane replied calmly. "It's called a SPIDE."

"A SPIDE?" Sindri echoed, sounding on the verge of panic.

"A SPIDE," Kane confirmed. "It's an unmanned drone, based on the old hover tank designs."

The SPIDE's bulbous metal body was about the size of a small wag. A dome-shaped turret-head dominated the top of it, with six glassy eyes that looked very much like convex crystal lenses. On each side of the body protruded four jointed rods ending in bifurcated steel claws. Alternating between the legs were long, flexible tentacles. The entire body was mounted on a circular base about ten feet in diameter.

The SPIDE didn't produce a clatter of treads or rumble of wheels or even the growl of an engine. All they heard was a faint throb. Kane heard Sindri's breath coming in quick pants, and he didn't blame the little man one bit.

"They ride on a cushion of air provided by huge turbine fans," Kane continued. "So we can't really outrun it."

Sindri swallowed hard. "Another invention of this Sammy the imperator?"

"Actually, no. They were put in use by the barons as siege engines. Several of the original versions were kept in the Anthill. You might recall seeing a couple of them in the same place the Aurora was stored."

Sindri's brow wrinkled as he tried to match the machines in his memory with the device that stood before him now. "It doesn't look like the same things I remember," he muttered.

"Sam improved on them."

Even though Kane knew the SPIDE was only a remote-controlled automaton, not a demon, the machine still wasn't exactly a sight to soothe the nerves. He eyed the mechanoid, noting the design differences between this model and the ones used during the Consolidation War. Sindri shifted his feet, as if he intended to return to the Manta.

"Don't run," Kane sidemouthed to Sindri.

Instead of a reply, he heard Sindri suck in his breath with a hiss. There was a faint whirring sound and the SPIDE extended its tentacles. They snaked along the surface of the wall toward them.

Sindri watched the metal serpents slink closer and closer. He shouted a curse as his courage deserted him, and he did the exact opposite of Kane's warning—he turned and ran, dashing back toward the Manta. Before he had crossed more than five feet, an eardrum-compressing hoot blasted from the SPIDE. Its glassy eyes flashed. A gust of compressed air heaved it several feet from the surface of the lift platform, and with a whine of turbofans it glided after him. The four legs provided extra support while both of its tentacles shot out after the little man.

Kane threw himself to one side, barely avoiding being struck by one tentacle as it lashed out and whipped around Sindri's knees. He was jerked off his feet and lifted into the air. The SPIDE dangled him upside down. He yelled in fright, arms flailing as he pried at the flexible metal conduit entrapping his legs.

Kane leaped after the machine, jumping onto its back, his feet skidding and seeking purchase on the slippery alloyed surface. He crawled toward its head, hoping to deactivate the sensor array in the turret. He barely made it halfway. With a whir, the head swiveled to face him, and Kane experienced a shuddery instant of staring into the crystal eyes and sensing outrage.

Then the other tentacle coiled up and slid over him like a noose, cinching tight around his waist. Kane struggled as he felt it raise him above the surface of the SPIDE. He tried to fit his fingers between the tentacle and his body—but the world dissolved around him in a blaze of blue flame and a torrent of pain.

Chapter 21

Kane dreamed in fragments, but none of the fragments made any sense. A humid cloak of darkness swathed most of his mind in sweaty, ebony folds. Only infrequently came brief flares of light and cogent thought.

The wavering lights took on the appearance of faces, faces that somehow resembled his mother, his father and other people he knew, but couldn't name all at the same time. He had an inchoate awareness that he had promised to do something for that face, but he couldn't remember what.

He knew he was dreaming, just as he knew it was pointless to try to remember what kind of promises he had made to dream faces. He doubted he would remember the dream or the faces in the light of day. There were far too many dreams to recall over a lifetime of them. Aloofly, he wondered just how many dreams he might have experienced over a span of decades. Daydreams didn't count, for they allowed the dreamer to possess at least a modicum of control, and most of his daydreams had been pleasant.

No one except the incurably psychotic would daydream a nightmare when more pleasing fantasies of power and sex and simple happiness were but a thought away. So Kane realized he was in the throes of a nightmare, simply because he wasn't enjoying himself. Time seemed to hang motionless, even while his mind raced onward like a runaway war wag with the pedal bolted down hard to the metal. He was aware of nothing but a void surrounding him.

Then with the kind of abruptness that happens only in dreams, the void ended against a huge iron-braced door. It loomed up before him, but he didn't slow his mad flight. Right before he thought to crash headlong into it, the door opened directly into a long, broad hall that grew indistinct in the murky distance. Kane raced along the corridor, not allowing himself a moment to clear the confusion from his thoughts. The corridor walls were lined by flickering torches in metal sconces. The floor, walls and ceiling were of stone, cut into huge square blocks. The walls on either side of him were covered with brightly colored friezes, portraying men and women he thought he recognized.

The images flickered and changed whenever Kane tried to focus his eyes on them. As he plummeted past, it almost seemed that the women in the friezes bore Tanvirah's face or hair or eyes. The women smiled as their bodies were fondled by various male partners, some of them with handsome, finely chiseled features and others who looked more like animals.

Sweet William stepped out from the frieze, oozing slime from every knobby wart, ridiculously clad in the open red jacket of one of Lord Strongbow's dragoons and nothing more. The Pischacas greeted him with outstretched talons and foam-flecked fangs. Kane flashed through him as if the goblin-man were no more substantial than a shadow.

Voices spoke, a man's deep rumbling tones and another woman's, a childish piping. It took Kane a long time to visualize the people who belonged to the voices. At first, he tried to outrun the voices, to leave them behind in the void, but they followed him. Not calling him, but simply talking as if he were privy to long-forgotten conversations.

"You're breaking old, ingrained habits and acting out of character...that can be deadly."

Grant...

"You brought all this up. Curiosity always has its price, you know."

Brigid...

"I mean if you keep on pretending you're too professional for Brigid, she'll find somebody who doesn't think he is."

Domi...

Grant...Brigid...Domi...the names echoed in the hollow halls of his memory. There were other voices, other names he knew he should remember, faces he knew he had seen somewhere.

He tried to call out into the dreamscape surrounding his racing body, but he could force out no sound. The only noise he could hear was inside his chest, the oxygen within his lungs echoing heavily with the dull thump of a multitude of air sacs expanding open and slamming shut. With each new opening-and-closing sound, he felt his lungs constrict.

Kane kept flying, feeling his heart clenching and unclenching painfully inside his chest. He dashed through a series of empty chambers, lit by a ghostly, illusive illumination. The long corridor abruptly ended in utter, impenetrable blackness, like a sepia sea. Kane couldn't stop himself and he plunged into it.

All around the darkness was filled with stars. His vision blurred, and he wondered to himself which would kill him first—his heart bursting or soaring into the heart of a star. He managed to twist his neck and look down and around. There was no horizon, no land, no Earth, only stars, and he realized he was surrounded by an inky black curtain dusted with a million grains of diamond-dusted starlight.

The stars were everywhere at once as he plunged through them. All around him suns burned with a pure, clean radiance. The clouds of nebula glowed silver against the primal black. Constellations wheeled and glittered. He could feel the movement of the universe pulsing against him, hear the songs sung by the stars.

Somehow, he realized he was floating through a point in nonspace and time from which all spaces and times were accessible. He also knew a single consciousness was responsible for that accessibility, and it was unnatural.

Almost as soon as the notion registered in his mind, he saw a pair of crimson stars smoldering among the millions of constellations. They glittered before him, glowing like malignant eyes. They drew Kane forward as if his consciousness were made of metal filings and the eyes were magnets.

He tried to stop, to slow down, to change direction. Instead, he plummeted toward hell-eyes, all control gone. The crimson radiance grew brighter, more vivid, and around the crimson stars formed a face.

It was a man's face, undeniably human, yet with alien, hellishly glowing red eyes. The high-boned face was very pale, with sharp cheekbones and a jutting chin. His ears were very small and delicately shaped, nestled close to the hairless skull. His inhumanly large, curved eyes had no pupils, only obsidian irises with a bare hint of white at the corners. The eyes were less organs of vision than apertures leading to the fathomless ends of the universe.

Then the flesh seemed to melt away, revealing a gleaming metallic mask of burnished silver, made even more ghastly by the red eyes burning in sunken sockets. Delicate inlays of circuitry coated his fleshless skull. Small white teeth grinned in a mirthless leer.

The grinning naked skull floated in the sepia sea, a gleaming silver in which sparks of livid red flame danced within the shadowed sockets.

A sudden riot of images exploded in his mind. They were only wheeling pieces, splinters of fire and blood and the gulfs of deep space. He felt a crazed tumble of emotions, all different but all simultaneous—anger, stark terror and a grief so deep it seemed his heart would shrivel.

He felt a sickening sensation as all stability and sanity crumbled, then he careened through scenes of carnage, of blood and fire.

Monstrous pillars of flame roared above the skyline of cities. Men, women and children fled, howling like souls in Hell.

He saw rows of red things strapped to tables, living human beings in the process of dissection. He glimpsed white bones and blood and strips of flesh laid back for the inspection and removal of internal organs.

He stared at a world, at many worlds in torment, of skies across which curtains of black smoke scudded, of blistering shock waves wrenching mountains from their beds, flattening cities, monuments and all the works of humankind.

A voice seemed to whisper to him, not from far away, but from everywhere. It was a voice he had heard before, just like the apocalyptic images his mind swam through were frighteningly familiar.

The voice said, "I penetrate all the barriers between casements, going back into the past, infiltrating the highest corridors of power, so that when the proper historical moment arrives to strike, the world changes. Forever."

Kane struggled not to scream in horrified realization, as recollections of the warning from so many years before flooded into his mind. "You will know my presence in your own casement soon enough. By then, I hope you will have resigned yourself to what cannot be changed. Do not fight anymore. There is no use in it.''

Kane was no stranger to fear. He had lived with it daily, and it was an emotion he long ago had learned to bottle, to contain. Now it escaped and spread through him like a virus, consuming him with terror, horror and panic. He set his teeth on the scream rising from his throat.

The death's-head leered at him and the jaws of the skull opened. A peal of hideous laughter poured from the yawning jaws. Kane plunged toward that gaping maw, determined not to give voice to his surge of terror.

KANE FELT an insistent, jiggling pressure, as though he were riding on the back of a wag as it jounced over a bumpy road. He tried to roll with it, but he couldn't seem to move. Finally he realized a hard object was prodding his right shoulder.

He didn't open his eyes, but tried to decode his surroundings and circumstances with his other senses. Warmth surrounded him and the ennui it evoked kept him from responding to the pressure. His nostrils filled with a rich floral odor.

''Kane.'' It was a woman's voice, one he had heard before, but not in a very long time. She sounded worried, impatient.

With his eyes still shut, he managed to reach up and his fingers closed on something that felt like a wrist covered by a satiny fabric. His eyelids lifted. The lighting was muted, diffused, and the world looked strange. Shadowy figures moved, wavered back and forth.

"Kane..." the voice said again, this time underscored by a note of relief.

The woman who leaned over him seemed grotesque at first, impossibly deformed as if stretched by some monstrous torture device. Then Kane realized the impression was one created by his poor vision and artifice. The woman's pants hugging her long, lithe legs were cut high at the waist and fell over stilt-heeled boots that gave the illusion of great height. Her waist was tightly cinched by a red sash and the narrow shoulders of her black tunic were lifted by tapered pads.

The fabric was tailored to conform to the thrust of her full breasts. Emblazoned on the left breast was a familiar symbol. A thick-walled pyramid was worked in red thread, enclosing, and partially bisected by, three elongated but reversed triangles. Small disks topped each one, lending them a resemblance to round-hilted daggers.

Kane squinted up at her, trying to pierce the fog that seemed to float over his eyes, and see her face. At the same time, he realized he lay in an uncomfortable bed, covered from the neck down by a thick quilt. He was surprised not only by the bed, but also by the fact he was alive so he could wake up, the bed's discomfort notwithstanding. His thought processes moved ponderously, like half-frozen mud, but he realized the SPIDE had rendered him unconscious with a jolt of voltage, rather than frying him like a slab of bacon.

He didn't feel particularly grateful for the machine's restraint. The back of his head ached fiercely, and his skin prickled painfully, as if he were suffering a body-wide sunburn. He started to sit up, but pain hit the back of his head like a club and the bed spun. A wave of nausea churned in his belly, and he lay down again, closing his eyes tightly.

Erica van Sloan said softly, "Don't move too quickly...you're still recuperating."

Kane nodded as if he understood, even though he didn't. "Is it really you, Erica?"

"You know it is, Kane. It's been many, many years. When Tanvirah told me that you would be coming after her, I didn't know what to feel. I apologize for the reception. I didn't authorize the airborne attack or the soldiers' assault."

"But the SPIDE was your idea?"

"Yes." The flat, almost dead intonation of her voice caused the hairs on his nape to tingle. She sounded old and weak and helpless.

"How long have I been out?" He was disturbed by how raw his voice sounded in his ears.

"Around fourteen hours."

He opened his eyes a slit, and his sense of perspective slowly returned, in a piecemeal fashion. He slowly looked around, gauging his surroundings, feeling a distant sense of familiarity with them, despite the fact the room was small with cheap furnishings—a narrow bed not much better than a cot, a cabinet and small table on which was placed a framed photograph. He squinted at it, trying to identify the three people it featured. Then he realized it was a pic of himself standing between his father and mother. He hadn't seen the photograph in many, many years, or the people in it.

He looked at the image of the cocky, eager kid he used to be. He was smiling in the picture. His father and mother weren't. His dad had the same dark hair and high-planed features as he did, but he looked brooding and unhappy. His mother's somber expression spoke of the same emotion.

Kane's mother had vanished from his life right after he entered the Magistrate Division training academy. Her disappearance wasn't unusual. Though matrimony and child producing were considered the supreme social responsibility by the barons, it was also considered only a temporary arrangement.

Children were a necessity for the continuation of society, but only those passing stringent tests were allowed to bear them. Genetics and social standing were the most important criteria. Generally, a man and a woman were bound together for a term of time stipulated in a contract.

Once the child entered a training regimen of one of the ville divisions, the parents were required to separate, particularly in the case of male children recruited by the Magistrates. So his mother had removed herself. She had probably realized there was a limit to the pointlessness she could endure of being a parent in absentia.

Kane had never really known, but he had often wondered if the entire purpose of her life had been to give birth to him. After he entered the Division, her duties discharged, the rest of her life had to have been one long, total anticlimax.

As for his father, the last sight of him was impressed indelibly and eternally in Kane's mind. He knew even if some horrible accident wiped his memory clean of everything else in his life, he would never forget his visit to Nightmare Alley in the Archuleta Mesa installation.

As the center for advanced and ongoing genetic experiments, Nightmare Alley was well named. It was horrible, unbelievable, insane. There he, Brigid and Grant had found Kane's father, suspended in cryonic stasis, his body now supplying its superior genetic material for later hybridization. His father's fate remained unknown, even after the incendiaries they had touched off during their first incursion had wreaked wide devastation. The odds that his father had survived were exceptionally remote, but Kane was by nature a percentage player and even a one percent chance provided a feeble ray of hope.

However, the devastation caused by the crash of the Aurora a year later was certainly more widespread, and even if his father's cryostasis canister had come through the incendiary explosions intact, the last wave of destruction more than likely engulfed it, as it had the rest of the installation.

Trying to clear a dry-as-dust throat, Kane croaked, "I'm in Cobaltville, aren't I? In my old flat?"

Erica pushed a flexible straw between his lips. As he gratefully drew in a mouthful of cool water, she said, "You're in High River in the Enclaves, yes. They were restored many years ago as a way to honor you, if you ever decided to join us. Like a memorial for the services you rendered to the cause of unity before, during and after the war."

Kane nearly choked on the water as the absurdity of her statement sunk in. All four-room apartments in the residential Enclaves were essentially interchangeable. Conformity, standardization, whatever the euphemism, the flats were about as homelike as a cell block.

None of the doors on any Enclave level had locks. It was a carryover from the Program of Unification, when the Council of Front Royal had decided that privacy bred conspiracy. The council had further decreed that since everyone had the same possessions as everyone else, there was no need to steal, especially among the elite. The desire for privacy was viewed not just as gauche, but as an expression of deviant thinking.

He recalled his few paltry personal possessions from those days. He had owned absolutely nothing anyone would want. Most of his property had been inherited from his grandfather and father, including the photograph. Since the apartment was more or less the Kane ancestral home, it should have been filled with relics of earlier generations.

It wasn't. There were a couple of lamps, a chair, a table, a sofa, the futon in the bedroom, a few antique books wrapped in plastic, a couple of ancient muzzle loaders confiscated from 'Farer traders nearly sixty years ago.

Wincing against the pain in his head, he mumbled around the straw, "This must be the ugliest and most boring museum display in the entire history of the world."

Erica didn't laugh. She sat on the edge of the bed and held the cup of water with one hand while stroking his forehead with the other. "The pain will soon pass. Once you heal, you won't even have a scar."

Still swallowing water, Kane squinted up at her, finally able to see her face clearly. The mirrored lenses of the sunglasses covering her eyes gave her the expressionless stare of an insect. Her black hair hung loose around her shoulders, pushed back behind her ears. It looked lusterless, almost like a cheap wig.

Spitting out the straw, he echoed uneasily, "Scar?"

"From the surgery," she replied matter-of-factly. She touched the back of her head. "You now have a SQUID in your brain, just like everybody else. Welcome to the CCS. Welcome to the adaptive Earth."

Chapter 22

Heart pounding frantically within his chest, seeming to hammer against his rib cage as if trying to escape, Kane levered himself upright.

His temples throbbed with the effort. He noted he was naked except for a pair of briefs.

His fingers explored the occipital region of his cranium, and they touched a scabrous lump at the vertex point. A sharp needle of pain stabbed through his skull from back to front and made his eyes water.

"Why?" he demanded hoarsely, flatly.

Erica smiled, but it looked mechanical. "I'd like to say it's so you won't be so hard to get along with." The smile vanished. "But in reality it was done so you'll understand how being linked with Sam, with the Heart of the World, is not quite the form of cyberslavery you think it is. You'll adapt in time."

"Was this done to Sindri?" he demanded.

"Not yet," Erica answered. "As the authorities of High River, Lakesh and I are still trying to decide how much of a contribution he might make, how adaptive he would be." She paused and added with a wan smile, "Besides, he's been telling us the most interesting stories about what you've been up to with my spatiotemporal dissociator.''

Struggling with his fury, trying to restrain himself from striking her, Kane saw his distorted reflection in her glasses. His face looked different somehow, but he couldn't instantly identify the changes. Then with a surge of shock, he realized all the gray was gone from his beard and hair and the fine lines around his eyes had been replaced by firmer flesh.

Snarling, he raked the glasses from her face. She didn't move or even react, except to smile at him sadly. He had half expected to see red eyes bright with the fires of Hell, but did not. The fury rising in him was choked off, replaced by a sick horror when he looked into her blind eyes.

The violet glints were covered by a milky sheen. They were old eyes, eyes that had seen too much and given up trying to make sense of the visions. He noted the deeply etched creases of weariness at their corners, the half-moons of puffy flesh beneath them, the seams and lines she had tried to bury beneath coatings of cosmetics.

"Not much to look at nowadays, am I?" Her voice was a rustling sigh of regret.

Still angry, Kane put a hand around the graceful column of her throat, seeing the wattles sagging beneath her chin. "Sam has let you grow old, but he makes me younger?"

"Sam sees himself as a teacher," she murmured. "He teaches lessons in humility and obedience."

''Did you need such a lesson?''

Erica tried to shrug. ''Perhaps I did. Perhaps not. I'm no longer strong enough to know. It's been a hard life, Kane, damn hard.''

She caressed his wrist with a long-fingered, delicate hand. It, at least, bore no signs of aging. ''Sam has already begun the lessons with you.''

''How did he do this to me?'' Kane demanded. ''He didn't touch me like he did you and Lakesh all those years ago. Is the implant the secret?''

She nodded and Kane removed his hand from her throat, pulling away from his touch. ''Nanotechnology is,'' she replied softly. ''It took me years to learn the true source of my son's powers. They are not organic—they're not psionic.''

Kane edged off the bed. ''I never really thought they were.'' He placed his feet on the floor and stood, swaying, unnerved by how rubber kneed and light-headed he felt. ''Can you get me some clothes?''

Erica gestured to the cabinet across the room. ''Look there.''

Kane followed her hand wave and opened the doors. He snorted, then removed a pearl-gray, high-collared bodysuit. He recognized it as the old day-duty uniform of the Magistrates. It smelled slightly musty, but it was the only article of clothing inside. He knew asking about his shadow suit would garner only evasive answers, particularly if he asked questions about the data cards and the CD.

As he pulled on the bodysuit, Kane said, ''I remember how DeFore found nanites in Lakesh's blood a long time ago. They had attacked his cellular structure, as I recall.''

Erica nodded. ''The simplest medical applications of nanomachines didn't involve repair, but selective destruction. Cancers were only one example. Infectious diseases provide another. The nanites were programmed to recognize and destroy the dangerous replicators, whether they were bacteria, cancer cells or viruses.''

Kane tugged up the collar, feeling his strength and equilibrium return. ''So Sam's nanites performed selective destruction on the genes of DNA cells, removing the part that spells *aging?*''

''Something like that,'' Erica admitted. ''Or in my case right now, removing the part that spells *youth.*''

Kane faced her, eyebrows knitting in a frown. ''Where in the hell did the nanites come from in the first place? Did Sam make them or find them?''

She shrugged, groping on the bed for her sunglasses. ''I really don't know. I never found out, even after all these years. But Sam has to have access to a huge database somewhere. Repairing damaged or cross-linked molecules is one thing—identifying them is another.''

Kane reached around her and picked up the glasses from the quilt and handed them to her. ''What would be the most efficient way of doing that?''

Slipping the sunglasses back on over her eyes, Erica answered, ''Faced with a damaged protein, a cell-repair machine will first have to identify it by examining short amino acid sequences, then look up its correct structure in a database. The machine will then compare the protein to this blueprint, one amino acid at a time.''

As Kane pulled on the ankle-length boots, Erica provided him with a swift overview of the function of the nanomachines and how they had restored her and Lakesh's youth and maintained it for so long.

She told him how repair nanites stimulated the heart to grow fresh muscle by resetting cellular control mechanisms. The list continued through problem after problem, physical ailment after physical ailment, until Kane grew impatient.

''I get the picture, Erica,'' he stated tersely. ''What about the damn SQUID in my brain?''

She hesitated before answering, ''That's a little different...a lot more complicated. I could tell you what I designed them to do over two hundred years ago, but Sam has twisted their operating principles into a totally different direction.''

''I figured.'' He put his hands on his hips, finding it strangely comfortable to be wearing the gray uniform of a Mag again. He watched Erica slowly rise from the bed, saw the stir and lift of her breasts beneath the glossy fabric of her tunic. Her figure appeared to be the same as he remembered it, despite the changes in her face and demeanor. He tried, but failed, to reconcile the tired, saddened woman standing

before him with the fragmented memories of the wild
and imperious Scorpia Prime.

"Take me to Lakesh and Sindri," he said curtly.

"That's why I'm here." Erica started toward the
door, moving uncertainly at first, reaching out for the
frame. Kane took her by the elbow to guide her, but
with a short laugh, she pulled free. "Thank you, but
I don't really need your help."

He gazed at her in momentary confusion. "But your
eyes—"

"Still work." She tapped the lenses of her sunglasses. "With the help from the nanites in my system.
The microprocessors in the frames hook up with them
and generate a weak electromagnetic field that stimu-
lates my optic nerves. The glasses give me photomul-
tiplier vision, gathering all available light. Another setting gives me infrared."

"Nice," Kane grunted. "Better than your own
eyes."

"More efficient," she said bitterly. "Not necessarily better."

They left his flat and entered the main promenade.
The wide, curving passageway was thronged with
movement, with people heading to and from their duty
stations in the Administrative Monolith. Erica and
Kane skirted a knot of black-and-red clad functionaries
milling around the sweeping curve of the promenade,
officials, clerks, bright of eye, brisk of manner and
neatly dressed. They made him feel that his drab gray

bodysuit was distinctly out of step with the current fashion, which of course it was.

But then as he and Erica moved along, he noticed the heads of men and women turning toward him, eyes widening with recognition, and he heard his name whispered. If nothing else, I've got fame, he reflected sourly. I'm a legend.

Kane told himself his legendary status sprang less from his exploits than from being the only man to refuse an authority's position in the CCS, in the imperator's adaptive Earth, but he knew that wasn't true.

A number of the people who stared at him and the imperial mother were small and compact, with delicately featured faces that seemed to be primarily brow, cheekbone and chin. Their craniums were large, but not inhumanly so. Their heads bore wisps of thin, fine hair. The eyes beneath delicately arched supraorbital ridges were big and slanted, but white could be detected around the irises. Their steps were graceful, almost mincing, their hands long and slender. Several of the men wore Magistrate black and had plastic tube-shaped holsters strapped to their thighs.

Kane experienced an instant of shuddery dread when he saw the holsters. One part of his mind knew the infrasound batons, which converted electrical current to sound waves by a maser, weren't very precise weapons and were very limited in range, as well. But he had been on the receiving end of the wands too often to dismiss them as unthreatening.

As he and Erica reached the elevator bank, a tiny

hybrid female, pretty and crisp in a white bodysuit, despite her large cranium and oversized eyes, gave him a startled look of appraisal, then of recognition. Kane felt his heart clench in his chest due to her resemblance to Quavell. Like her, the female's huge blue eyes were startlingly clear and calm.

Kane found himself unable to hold her gaze and he heaved a sigh of relief as the doors to the lift slid shut on the staring eyes. He could only assume that the hybrid woman had been one of the many ordered to participate in the breeding experiment over a quarter of a century before. Since the hybrids aged very slowly, she could very well look the same now as she had all those years ago. She was probably disturbed by how old Kane appeared, despite the lack of gray in his hair.

To his irritation, Erica van Sloan had observed the silent exchange and smiled wryly. "There are many of her kind serving in High River, Kane. You know they can never forget anything." She paused and added, "And I have a few memories of my own that have never grown stale with the passage of time."

Kane only grunted.

The lift disk upon which they stood shot upward. In less than half a minute, the disk hissed to a pneumatic stop and the door opened automatically. Erica and Kane strode quickly down the ramp and onto the uppermost level of the Monolith. It had once served as Baron Cobalt's suite, the Olympian seat from which all strings of power in the ville extended.

The foyer was as magnificent as Kane remembered it. Glittering light cast from many crystal chandeliers flooded every corner of the entrance hall.

At the far end of the foyer loomed huge ivory-and-gold-inlaid double doors. They were open and the two people strode through them. Kane recalled how on his first visit to the level, on the night he was inducted into the Trust, only a deep, primal dark lay on the far side of the doors.

At one time, the baron's level was the only one in the Monolith without windows, but the deficit had been remedied since Cobaltville became High River. Round portals containing beautiful stained glass illuminated almost every wall in every room, giving it a cathedral-like feel. Erica and Kane trod on colorful disks of light cast by the sunlight flooding the tower.

One room led to another, through a wide, low arch. Another room lay beyond, and another, all illuminated by the lovely, multihued circles of light. In the fifth and final room, Kane and Erica van Sloan stopped.

Kane barely managed to keep the surprise he felt from showing on his face. A shaft of sunshine from a skylight fell onto three people in the center of the chamber. A young slender man wearing a white turban and Sindri faced each other over a chessboard, with Tanvirah looking on disinterestedly.

"Here we are," Erica announced listlessly.

The man in the turban sat straight up in his chair. When he turned his unlined, clean-shaven face toward them and grinned, Kane was too stunned to do more than gape in openmouthed silence.

"Friend Kane!" the man exclaimed in a familiar singsong cadence, his voice vibrant with the strength of youth. "Oh, my dear friend!"

THE TURBANED MAN PUSHED his chair back from the chessboard and crossed the room in a rush, catching Kane up in a crushing embrace. If not for the fact of the man's blue eyes, startlingly bright in the deep olive of his face, Kane would not have believed him to be Mohandas Lakesh Singh. The last time he had seen the man, some twenty-three years before, he had looked to be in early middle age, a few years older than Kane himself. The temples of his thick, jet-black hair had held some gray threads, and his complexion had shown a few creases from either age or stress; he certainly had a stockpile of both.

Of course, his appearance had been an astonishing improvement over the first time Kane had met him. Then he was a wizened cadaver of a man, his only halfway youthful feature being a pair of blue eyes. Kane recalled how in the year before the nukecaust, Lakesh had been diagnosed with incipient glaucoma. The advance of the disease had been halted during his century and a half in cryostasis, but it had returned with a double vengeance upon his revival. The eye transplant was only the first of many reconstructive surgeries he underwent, first in the Anthill, then in the Dulce installation.

After his brown eyes were replaced with blue ones and his leaky old heart exchanged for a sound new one, his lungs were changed out, his arthritic knee joints were removed and traded with polyethylene. But by the time all the surgeries were completed, Lakesh had changed from a robust, youthful-looking man to a liver-spotted scarecrow. His glossy jet-black hair became a thin gray patina of ash that barely covered his head. The prolonged stasis process had killed the follicles of his facial hair, and he could never regrow the mustache he had once taken so much pride in.

His once clear, olive complexion had become leathery, crisscrossed with a network of deep seams and creases that bespoke the anguish of keeping two centuries' worth of secrets. For a long time, Lakesh could take consolation only in the fact that although he looked very old indeed, he was far older than he looked.

But now, he could have passed for a man in his early twenties, more like Tanvirah's contemporary than her father. It was almost as if Erica had aged in direct proportion to the years Lakesh had shed, in the time since Kane had last seen them both.

As Lakesh hugged him, crooning endearments in Hindu, Kane caught Sindri's eye. The little man still wore his shadow suit. Surreptitiously he pointed to Lakesh, then placed his index finger against his temple and inscribed a counterclockwise circle, the immemorial signal of mental derangement.

Carefully, Kane disengaged himself from Lakesh,

patting his shoulder. The man seemed sincerely over-joyed to see him, if the tears glimmering in his eyes were any indication. They rolled down his cheeks as he clutched at Kane's arms, as if to assure himself the man was indeed real.

"It's all right, old man," Kane told him quietly, falling back into his habitual form of address. "It's really me."

"Unfortunately." Tanvirah's voice was sharp and icy. "Get away from the general, Dad."

Sindri's eyes widened in mock astonishment. "General?" he echoed with a heavy, ironic emphasis on the word. "General of what? Confusion?"

Kane ignored both Sindri and Tanvirah. She wore a duplicate of Erica's black-and-red ensemble, but with a plunging neckline. It revealed not only a goodly amount of cleavage, but also a silver medallion in the shape of a scorpion. Her hair was coiffed and glossy, but the look she directed toward Kane was pure venom.

"Scorpia Prime, I presume," he drawled casually. "Is the title a generational thing, or is it only a masquerade when it suits the imperator? Or is it a matter of what silly slut fits the crown, rather than the other way around?"

Tanvirah merely smiled at him enigmatically. She toyed idly with the data cards in her hands, shuffling them back and forth between her fingers. Kane stared at her stolidly, and she stared back, beautiful, formidable and dangerous. He realized she hated him, not so much because he had tricked her, but because he had rejected her, and like Kali, like Shakti, her pride demanded a redress. He had ruined any possible chance of winning her over as either a friend, lover or ally.

Tanvirah's melted-chocolate eyes seethed with a challenge, silently daring him to reclaim the cards in her hands. He knew that in order to take them from her, he would have to kill her outright.

Kane forced a lazy smile to his lips. "What are we doing up here, Lakesh? Is it recreation hour?"

Beaming in delight, Lakesh announced, "Making you one of us!"

Kane matched the wide grin with a goofy one of his one. In the same enthusiastic tone, he replied, "Over my stinky corpse, old man!"

The grin on Lakesh's face faltered, and he gazed into Kane's eyes as if trying to ascertain his degree of sincerity. Tanvirah said coldly, "I told him those would be your sentiments. But it doesn't really matter. The issue of your death or life is no longer up to you. It's up to Sam."

Lakesh turned away and returned to the chessboard as if he had forgotten all about Kane. "Friend Sindri, I'll have you checkmated in two more moves."

Sindri groaned and said, "I've told you and told you…the game is over. I beat you thirty minutes ago."

Kane shot a quizzical glance at Erica. She murmured, "The nanites can regenerate fresh brain tissue, but sometimes you lose skills and short-term memories. If a unique neural pattern was truly obliterated, then cell-repair machines could no more restore them than art conservators could restore a burned tapestry from its ash.''

Kane inquired, ''So physically Lakesh is younger than he's ever been, but mentally he's senile?''

Tanvirah said defensively, ''Certain tasks are beyond the abilities of nanomachines or the SQUID implants. Maintaining mental health is almost impossible if the cause isn't biochemical or neurological. If the mental impairment is due to extensive emotional or mental stress—'' She lifted a shoulder in a shrug, her breasts rippling in the deep V of her tunic. ''A machine might be able to repair a computer's hardware while neither understanding nor changing its software.''

''The question begs to be asked, then,'' Sindri said. ''Why bother improving his hardware—returning him to the physical condition of a youth—while allowing his software to completely degenerate?''

Kane stroked his beard. ''Very good question. Why start shaving years off my hardware when my software won't feel anything approximating gratitude?''

Erica said softly, sadly, ''It's not gratitude the imperator wants. He wants you to be in good health for the ordeal yet to come.''

Kane felt a chill hand stroke the buttons of his spine. ''What kind of ordeal?''

Tanvirah eased around the table where Lakesh and Sindri sat, provocatively clicking the cards together, setting up an unnerving castanet-like rhythm. "Sam wants to know your plans regarding a space-and-time penetration."

"He could always ask."

Tanvirah smiled at him lazily. "He intends to...his way."

"When you were recuperating from the implant surgery, did you dream?" Erica asked.

Kane glanced toward her, startled. "As a matter of fact I did. Rather vividly."

"Did you experience visions of stars, of galaxies?"

Kane's brow furrowed, and reflexively his hand went to touch the back of his head. He checked the movement. "If I did, is that significant?"

Tanvirah nodded. In a silky-soft tone she said, "It is indeed. That means your neuronic energy is now linked to Sam. You are part of the Great Plan, whether you like it or not."

"What the hell is that?" he demanded.

He received no response. Kane glared first at Tanvirah, then at Erica and finally back to Lakesh. The man sat staring at the chessboard, chin supported by a hand, poking at the pieces, pushing a pawn to one square and a rook to another.

"Lakesh!" Kane said loudly.

The turbaned man didn't glance at him. In a sharper, sterner voice, Kane repeated, "Lakesh! I'm talking to you, old man!"

Lakesh swiveled his head toward him, blinking his

blue eyes as if he had just been awakened from a nap. "Friend Kane? Is that you?"

"Yes. It's me. Lakesh, tell me about the Great Plan."

Lakesh smiled impishly. "I'm the only one who figured it out. For a long time, I thought the imperator was just another false messiah working to make ancient prophecies about the end of time come true."

"And he's not?" Sindri inquired.

"Oh, no," Lakesh replied. "He's actually doing it."

"How?" Kane snapped, moving closer.

Lakesh's smile widened, then it froze on his face. "He's building a window that will reach into the past or the future, and inject matter into the present or place it throughout the chronon stream whenever and wherever he wants."

"What kind of matter?" Sindri demanded.

Lakesh pinched the air between thumb and forefinger. "He will start small, targeting nations united in mutual dependency, then move on to those that are self-sufficient. The nations of the past that are barriers to unity. He'll break the barriers by the introduction of plague."

"Plague?" Kane repeated in a husky horrified whisper.

"A mutated virus," Lakesh went on. "It will decimate population centers and empires, monarchies and democracies. Didn't like the outcome of World War II? Well, what difference would it make to an America laid low by an incurable and virulently toxic pathogen? Unhappy about how Emperor Constantine converted to Christianity? Hey, presto! One sprinkle of virus and you'll have a superpagan Roman emperor coming in to take his place.''

Kane said slowly, "Killing off half the planet with a plague virus doesn't seem a very effective way to implement unity.''

"Think about it, friend Kane." Lakesh's mouth was creased in a smile, but his eyes shone with tears. "The survivors will be struck down by an enervating weakness. Resentments and jealousies between nations that were once allies will be exacerbated, since none of them can extend aid to the other. They will look for a savior. And one will be there with his nanotechnology treatments.''

"Sam?" Kane's voice was barely audible.

Lakesh nodded. "By the time Sam is done, he will not only have everyone in this time period neuronically linked by the SQUIDs, he'll have accomplished it throughout the past. Everyone who was ever born, or who will ever *be* born will be his servant. No one will know it, because after the temporal manipulation ripples fade, the whole of humanity's history will have always and ever been determined by Sam.''

Sindri stared at Lakesh in goggle-eyed shock. The man met that stare with a sweet smile, then returned his attention to the chessboard. Tanvirah continued to click the data cards together in her hands.

Finally Sindri turned to Kane and intoned flatly, "I

can only think of three things to say…. Oh. My. *God.*"

Lakesh made a swift but elaborate motion over the chessboard. With a flourish like a conjurer, he placed a white knight on a center black square and favored Kane with a sly smile.

Chapter 23

The Moon floated within a silvery aura behind the top of the vast pyramid, its glow varnishing the beautiful snow-covered valley below. A keen, cold wind raised swirls of snow up toward the star-speckled night sky.

Kane had never forgotten his first sight of the Xian pyramid, nearly three decades before. It was as vivid in his memory now as if he were seeing it for the first time. He, Sindri and Tanvirah stood shivering at its base. They could only see a small portion of its staggering proportions.

The gargantuan structure was composed of countless fitted blocks of stone, the top quarried perfectly flat. Moonlight played along its painted facade, lending an air of otherworldly majesty to the huge monolith. Even in the uncertain light, they could see how the immense structure was painted black on the north side, blue-gray on the east, red on the south and white on the west.

In predark days, archaeologists had theorized the Great Pyramid of China was part of the tomb complex of Emperor Shih Hunag Ti. The purpose of the pyramid or tomb was never known, though Taoist tradition attributed its construction to a very powerful race called the Celestials—which Kane had assumed to be Balam's people, the First Folk. Whoever was responsible for its building, one thing was certain: the pyramid of Xian was a cardinal point in the world grid harmonics, a network of pyramids built at key places around the world to tap Earth's natural geomantic energies.

Sindri eyed the immense structure and said only, "I've seen bigger."

Kane knew he was referring to the mile-high pyramid on Mars and so didn't dispute him. Tanvirah looked to be on the verge of it, when an armed sentry appeared from the square-cut doorway. He was a small Asiatic man in the black-and-red uniform of the CCS, wielding an old-fashioned SIG-AMT autorifle. A black truncheon was attached to his belt. Two small metal prongs gleamed at its tip, and Kane guessed the instrument was a smaller version of the Shocksticks once used by the Magistrate Divisions. In a flat alto voice, the sentry announced, "The imperator wishes you to join him."

The man stepped aside with a deferential nod as Tanvirah swept past him into the pyramid. Kane and Sindri followed her, aware of the trooper bringing up the rear. She stalked purposefully down the passageway, taking long-legged strides, adopting a hip-swinging swagger. Her self-confidence reminded Kane of Erica's former arrogance, but he didn't feel impressed, only saddened.

Less than thirty minutes ago at High River, Erica

had informed Kane that Sam wished to see him, Sindri and Tanvirah in Xian immediately. Tanvirah had led the two men to the gateway unit on Level A of the Administrative Monolith. They hadn't been given a choice.

But right before they entered the jump chamber, Erica slipped the compact disc into Kane's palm and brushed her lips lightly over his cheek. She breathed into his ear, "Good luck...and I hope this makes up for some of things I've done to you...and caused to be done."

Sindri tugged at Kane's sleeve, indicating he should slow down. He whispered, "Why are we doing this again? We could have just taken the data cards from that snooty bitch and escaped."

"Taken them from her, maybe," Kane replied in the same low tone. "But I probably would have had to kill her."

Sindri bared his teeth in a grimace. "No great loss."

Kane let the comment pass. "But we wouldn't have been able to escape. The gateway in the Monolith is a direct unit-to-unit lock—from there to here."

Sindri began, "Now that we are here—"

"Shut up, you sawed-off bit of nothing," Tanvirah snapped over her shoulder. "We'll soon be with the imperator, and if you don't show respect to him, none will be shown to you."

Sindri glared at her, but decided the threat implicit in her words was enough to prevent him from responding with an insult of his own.

The passageway subtly changed. The floor became smoother and the square-cut blocks of stone on the walls gave way to smooth, seamless expanses. They glittered dully with inestimable flecks of all colors, providing a soft light. The ceiling rounded overhead like an arch, winding gently in an ever widening curve. The floor, gleaming like oiled slate, gave a solid footing.

The corridor opened onto a railed balcony that ran around a vast circular chamber, more than two hundred feet across. All around the balcony were arrayed consoles, conduits, displays, switchboards and computer terminals. In the center of the chamber, some fifty feet below, lay what appeared to be a pit or a pool. Kane couldn't be sure what lay in the pool, but he knew what was supposed to.

"The Heart of the Earth," he murmured.

"Not exactly," said a soft voice from a set of control consoles. "I've expanded it since you were last here…it might be more accurate to call it the Heart of Creation."

A tall figure in a white linen suit stepped out into the light. Kane hadn't seen Sam in many years, and even though he had changed in the interim, he still didn't look right. He was tall and thin, so exceptionally lean he looked like a poster child for anorexia. His hollowed-out cheeks stressed his high, jutting cheekbones. He had no facial hair to speak of, not even eyebrows.

A white turban covered the top and sides of his

head, so even if he had any, Kane would not have been able see it. The light glinted from the blue diamond brooch pinned at the turban's forefront. The slight slant of his golden eyes beneath prominent supraorbital ridges gave his pale, narrow face a slightly feline cast.

As always, his hands were his strangest physical attribute, inhumanly long and slender, but the backs and palms were crackled and crisscrossed with a network of deep lines, like those of a very old man. Glistening between the exceedingly long fingers was a faint pattern of what appeared to be scales. Judging by his smooth, unlined face, Sam looked to be no more than twenty.

Tanvirah ducked her head and handed the data cards to Sam, who took them with a detachment bordering on disinterest. "Kane," he said mildly. His eyes flicked over Sindri. "And guest. When Tanvirah conveyed to me the use to which you put the spatiotemporal dissociator, I must admit to being astounded. Out of all the possible combinations that I assessed you might attempt with the device, the possibility of pulling a subject from zero time completely eluded me."

"Thanks," Sindri said snidely. He hooked his thumb toward Kane. "But it was his idea, so blame him, not me."

Sam's mouth turned down at the corners. "I had no intention of complimenting or blaming you."

"Whatever," retorted Sindri. "But you sure look sad about something, your imperialness."

Tapping the edges of the data cards against his chin, Sam said, "Stop needling me, short pants."

Kane, Tanvirah and Sindri all reacted with various degrees of surprise to Sam's sudden lapse from formality. His posture even became more relaxed. "Of course I'm sad. For all intents and purposes you cease to exist today, Sindri."

Kane tried to fix the position of the guard out of the corners of his eyes, but he was unable to locate him. He resisted the impulse to turn and look, fearing that would tip off Sam and Tanvirah as to what was flitting through his mind.

"Great," Sindri said with icy sarcasm. "Thanks a lot, Kane. You pull me out of my nice, comfortable zero time, just so this hat-challenged asshole can kill me."

"Kill you?" Sam looked disturbed, even vaguely insulted. "Not at all. True, your blood, skin and bone will be removed and reduced to their basic constituent elements, but your brain will remain. I'll make use of its electromagnetic energy. It's all a matter of maximizing potential."

He waved extravagantly to the machines and the pool below the walkway. "Just like I've done here."

Kane carefully walked toward the railing. "I thought your Heart of the World was a nexus point, a convergence of geomantic energy."

He looked down over the rail and instantly slapped his hands around the metal bar, as a surge of vertigo assailed him. In a serene tone, Sam said, "That's exactly what it is…spirit of the Earth Mother, the Gaia force. Or if you care to be more scientific, it is the essential building block of the universe, the primal monobloc of creation.''

Kane pushed himself away, turning toward Sam. Sindri and Tanvirah stared at him in puzzlement. He husked out, ''My God, Sam…what have you done?''

Sam smiled almost shyly. ''The universe was formed by an explosion of gases, plasma and matter known as the Big Bang. A collection of those proto-energies exists here in a temporal pocket, a ripple in the quantum field. All I did was expand the ripple.''

Tanvirah and Sindri eyed him curiously and then joined Kane at the railing of the balcony. Sam contin-ued, ''The Heart contains the energies released in the first picoseconds following the Big Bang, channeling the matrix of protoparticles that swirled through the universe before physical, relativistic laws fully stabi-lized. It exists slightly out of phase with this dimen-sion, with our space-time.''

Kane, Sindri and Tanvirah looked down and felt as if invisible forces were tugging at them, as though waves of energy flowed around their bodies. And for what felt like hours they simply stared, their minds numb with amazement, shocked into silent paralysis.

They were looking into what seemed like outer space itself. They looked down and outward, and what they saw was a sphere of dense black dotted with bril-liantly gleaming pinpoints of intense light. They saw a slow swirl of white vaporous dust, forming a long, sweeping curve that dissected the main half of the black mass, cutting through the center.

The black mass was not solid. It gave the impression of being utterly empty, and yet sprinkled with myriad infinitesimal number of tiny sparks, shining and glowing within it. There was the effect of motion, as if each spark was moving and as if the central spiral mass was slowly revolving, each glittering facet of it alive and fighting against the eye-hurting blackness— which Kane finally realized was not so much blackness as deep emptiness, a total lack of existence.

Looking into it, they had the impression of gazing down into infinite depths of being, about to fall outward into unending space. The glittering points of light pained their eyes and tantalized them at the same time. They wanted to look away and they were afraid that if they did, they would miss something wonderful. It was an entrancing masterpiece, but it was also subtly terrifying.

After a couple of minutes of staring with unblinking eyes, Kane wrenched his gaze away, looking toward Sam, who smiled at him genially. "What is it?" he demanded. "A Singularity?"

"No," Sam replied calmly. "Nothing so prosaic as a black hole."

"It's like looking into the universe," Tanvirah murmured in a stunned voice. "A miniature universe next door to our own."

Sam's smile widened. "It's like looking into the universe because it *is*, for all intents and purposes, the universe. It's the microcosm, a slice view of the universe compressed and condensed. We're looking at it through a dimensional window.''

Sindri whirled, brows knitting at the bridge of his nose. "That's impossible!''

"No,'' Sam said smoothly, "it's an aperture into our universe, a portal through which all places and times are accessible. Come over here and see for yourself.''

Tanvirah and Kane turned toward the grouped banks of instruments—they recognized telescopes and spectroscopes tied into monitor screens. Also, there were several machines they weren't familiar with at all.

Sam walked over to the nearest telescope, adjusted it on its tripod, then flicked a knob on a monitor screen. The image showed a field of stars, shining hard and bright. He turned the dials and the view shifted steadily. Suddenly a bright object sprang into view. It was a star, a brilliant burning disk of white, with the flaring arms of its corona shimmering around it.

"Is that our sun?'' Sindri asked in a hushed voice.

"Sol,'' said the imperator with a trace of smugness. "We are looking at it from a dimension outside the space-time continuum.''

Kane found himself almost too paralyzed to speak, but he managed to ask, "What uses will you put it to?''

Sam shrugged as if the question were almost irrelevant. "This was an idea that arose from a conjunction of two laws of physics. The first has to do with the changes in the mass of a particle as it approaches the speed of light. Many predark physicists determined that a moving object gained mass and lengthened in the direction of infinity as it approached the speed of light. Theoretically, at the speed of light, a particle would be of infinite mass and infinite length.

"In my work with the Heart of the World, I determined this was indeed so. Definite measurements of particles that had been accelerated close to that speed showed a strong and rapidly rising increase in their mass—so much so that it seemed as if it would always be impossible to supply enough energy to bring the particle finally to its ultimate speed."

He paused as if waiting to be interrupted. When no one spoke, he continued, "The other factor that occurred to me was at first immaterial. This is almost the opposite end of the research spectrum. The idea of absolute zero in temperature. It is known that the temperature of an object is the product of the relative speed of its molecules. As a body heats up, its molecules are farther apart from each other and move faster. As it loses heat, they slow down and approach each other.

"At absolute zero, the molecules would lose all motion and come to a dead stop. Such a stop would presumably cause all the molecules to come together to form one mass without internal motion. This, too, seemed an unattainable outcome. Experiments had produced temperatures of only fractions above absolute, but again the final zero could not be attained.

"It was my idea to combine both operations. To attempt to have a particle of matter reach both the speed of light and absolute zero simultaneously. It was a challenge, but I had plenty of time. I also had a hunch—one of those queer inspirations that come out of nowhere sometimes, when you are consumed by a difficult problem—that by combining the molecular speed-up with ultra-low-temperature physics I might solve both. The addition of mass to a particle brought near absolute zero might be the extra factor. And vice versa."

Sam gestured to the pool beneath the balcony. "For as you see, there is this interesting quality about the speed of light and the absolute zero of temperature—both are apparent boundaries of our universe. Both are part of the restraining walls of our particular continuum."

"What happened?" Kane asked, dreading the answer.

"The result of the experiment," Sam replied calmly, "the achievement of bringing a particle of matter to infinite mass and infinite length at absolute zero was the creation of a state of existence that could not possibly exist in our universe. Do you understand that? Our universe cannot contain something of infinite length and mass, nor could a particle at absolute zero remain fixed in our perceptions of space or time. Therefore, the Heart of the World became a true independent space-time unit, free from the constraints of our continuum, yet still connected.''

He eyed Kane intently. ''Now do you understand why I was concerned with your own temporal manipulations? I feared your blundering might cause chronon ripples that could impact negatively on my own ambitions.''

''What do you mean by ambitions, exactly?'' Sindri asked skeptically.

''Exactly?'' Sam chuckled patronizingly. ''That would be difficult to describe. However, the entire principle of causality, that causes precede effects, would be toppled. There will be no more temporal paradoxes to contend with.''

He nodded toward the computers. ''I can enter the proper coordinates of a particular point in space, or even time, and inject whatever elements I choose from here. And now the Great Plan is no longer a plan, but has become the sole reality.''

Tanvirah gazed at Sam with something akin to adoration in her eyes. ''That means you are truly the master of the universe, a god. No, not just *a* god...but...God!''

There was dead silence on the platform for a long, tense tick of time. It was broken by Sindri sticking out his tongue and voicing a loud, very wet and very rude raspberry.

Chapter 24

"Give me a fucking break," Sindri snarled. He put his hands over his belly and mimed an attack of nausea. "How much of this ass-kissing frenzy are we expected to tolerate before we puke ourselves to death?"

"How dare you!" Teeth peeled back over her clenched teeth, Tanvirah made a motion to kick Sindri in the head. He scuttled out of range, standing between a computer console and Kane.

The smile Sam bestowed upon Sindri was so condescending, so insipid, that for an instant Kane wrestled with the insane urge to wipe it off his face with his fist. But despite the smile, Kane could tell Sindri's sarcasm had penetrated the imperator's carapace of self-assurance. He began clicking the data cards in his hands nervously.

In a soft, gentle voice, as if addressing a cranky child, Sam said, "Even taking into account my half sister's penchant for the theatric—partly due to her upbringing by Lakesh, and partly due to her devotion to me—you still can't deny my accomplishment deserves more of an acknowledgment than you have given it."

"The accomplishment, perhaps," Sindri shot back.

"But the opinion that it elevates your status from some kind of hybrid mutie to a deity…no, I don't think so."

A faint flicker of anger glinted in Sam's eyes, like a distant flash of heat lightning. The clicking of the memory cards increased in rhythm. "You are in no position to judge me, little man. What are you but a genetically engineered monstrosity, created to serve as a beast of burden?

"Oh, yes…I know all about you, and your own petty ambitions to conquer and rule. But you never rose much above a common criminal. You haven't done a fraction of the things I've done. I've laid the groundwork for humanity's salvation, I've seen to the creation of a new life-form—"

"Life-form?" Sindri broke in with a jeering laugh. "Mr. Kane told me about the Pischacas. In the predark days, the poor and underprivileged served as cannon fodder. All you did was artificially *raise* cannon fodder. That doesn't meet my criteria of a new life-form."

Tanvirah made a hissing, spitting sound of fury and started toward Sindri. Sam restrained her and turned slightly toward the guard standing just outside the balcony. Instantly the uniformed man stepped forward, hefting his SIG-AMT rifle.

Sam drew in a deep, calming breath through his delicate nostrils. "By the time the Great Plan has been fully implemented," he intoned, "there will never be a need for cannon fodder again."

"Why?" Kane demanded. "Because *everybody*

will be cannon fodder? Those that survive the plague, that is?''

Sam's golden eyes narrowed to suspicious slits, and Tanvirah murmured, ''Dad told him.''

''Oh.'' Sam shook his turbaned head with what seemed to be exasperated fondness. ''That old dear. I allowed him to experience his youth again as his mental capacities diminished, but all he's done with it is to jabber.''

''And what's your reason for allowing me to experience the same thing?'' Kane asked, almost fearing the answer.

Sam shifted the data cards absently from his right to left hand. ''Isn't it obvious? I gave you a very minor demonstration of what might be yours if you rejoin the world, Kane.''

''You mean rejoin *you*.''

''You never did join me.'' Sam's friendly tone was suddenly edged with steel. ''You always acted on your own, following an individual agenda, even when we shared the same goal. Now I'm asking you to help me advance my ideals, and make my agenda your own.'' He paused and added meaningfully, ''And to join Tanvirah, as well.''

Without looking in Kane's direction, Tanvirah whispered, ''I made the offer. He refused.''

''I wasn't in the market,'' Kane stated. ''And even if you restore my hormones to the levels of when I was seventeen, I still won't be.''

He smiled with mock ingenuousness at Tanvirah.

"It might be a damn difficult choice, but I was even more stubborn at seventeen than I am now."

Sindri interjected impatiently, "You didn't answer his question about the plague."

Sam sighed. "It's not quite the horrible genocidal act you might think it is. I merely borrowed a few lessons from history. When a disease ravages a society, economics shatter, poverty moves in and trust in governments and fellow human beings dissolves."

"Not to mention," Kane said darkly, "new messiahs and messengers from God emerge from the chaos, especially if some kind of religious prophecies were apparently fulfilled during the plague times."

Sam gave him a fleeting, appreciative smile. "Exactly. In the Middle Ages, a century of progress was brought to a crashing halt by simultaneous outbreaks of the bubonic plague. When I inject my own virus into the various key points of time and place, I will effect changes just as major…but the nukecaust will be avoided, because the circumstances that led up to it will have been averted.

"There will be waste, of course, and that is to be deplored, but the plague victims will be mostly from the underclass of the stricken societies, those who contribute the least."

"The useless eaters," Kane drawled. "That old saw."

Sam chuckled. "But I want you, Kane, to be part of the Great Plan, especially as it moves into its final phase. If you're my ally, the temporal ripple backlash will be minimized. I will give you whatever you want. Just name it.''

Kane forced a contemptuous smirk to his face. "Can you give me back Brigid?"

When Sam's smile faltered, Kane stated, "What I want is not within your power. And even if you tried to convince me that it was, all you'd ever do is hold the possibility of returning her to me over my head, like a sword."

Sam began clicking the memory cards together again. "Then what can I do for you?"

Kane shrugged. "There are some questions you can answer, suspicions I've harbored for many years, that you can confirm or deny. I'd like to find out why you financed the Nirodha movement...what the significance of the entire Scorpia Prime alter ego and Tantric sex deal was all about."

Sam opened his mouth as if to reply, but Kane held up a hand. "But as much as I'd like to know those things, the fate of human civilization, maybe even of all humanity, rests with me. That's not something I ever bargained for. But I've come to accept it, and I'll do what I can."

With that, Kane moved with the blinding speed and the controlled explosion of near superhuman reflexes that had been his as a younger man. He hurled himself forward, shoulder-rolling between Tanvirah and Sam. He caught a fragmented glimpse of fearful desperation on the face of the soldier when he realized he was Kane's objective.

He tried to bring his autorifle to bear, but Kane rose smoothly to his feet right in front of him and the edge of his left hand lashed out, catching the man full across the neck. There was a mushy snap, as of a wet stick breaking, and the red-and-black-garbed trooper dropped dead after uttering only one choked cry.

Kane tried to wrestle the subgun out of the man's hands as he sagged, but they had reflexively tightened around it and he had no time to wrest it from his grip. He caught a blur of movement from behind him. Tanvirah launched an expert kick at his back, and he twisted aside, taking the impact on his hip. Pain shivered through him, but if her foot had struck solidly where it had been aimed, the impact could have cracked his spine.

Kane kept twisting, reaching out for the astonished Sam, putting his body between him and Tanvirah. She had started to launch another kick and checked the movement, shrieking in frustration. She stumbled, and Sindri chose that moment to cannonball his small body into her legs. She fell heavily, and Sindri leaped atop her. Kane knew from painful experience that Sindri was far stronger than he looked.

Sam tried to contort himself out of Kane's grasp, twisting and turning wildly. Kane turned with him, locking the man's left arm under his right and heaving up on it. Sam's lips writhed over his teeth in a grimace of pain. His nerve-numbed fingers opened and dropped the data cards.

Kane caught them, snatching them out of the air.

Maintaining the pressure on the captured arm, he forced the imperator down on the floor grille. "Stay there, messiah," he snapped. To show he meant business, he drove his knee into Sam's pointed chin, slamming him hard against the metal floor plates.

He whirled toward the computer consoles, noting as he did so that Tanvirah and Sindri were locked in thrashing, cursing combat. He swept his eyes across the machines and saw with a surge of relief that they were all networked. Swiftly he inserted the cards in the proper ports, praying they could be read.

Within a few seconds—which felt like a chain of interlocking eternities to Kane—symbols indicating the cards had been successfully uploaded flashed on the monitor screens. Kane then began inputting the spatiotemporal injection coordinates into the keyboards.

Even he was amazed by how swiftly and surely he moved. "Sindri!" he yelled. "Get over here!"

A hand suddenly closed around Kane's shoulder from behind. Fingers dug in deep, seeming to puncture flesh, muscle and bone. He was too engulfed by the pain even to cry out. Then a force hauled him violently away from the keyboards.

He didn't fall, but he staggered nearly the entire breadth of the circular walkway. He saw Sindri on his face, breathing hard with Tanvirah kneeling on his back, holding both of his arms in hammerlocks. And he saw Sam the imperator saunter toward him, carrying himself with the completely confident manner of a lion approaching its prey.

"You are such a fool," he said. "I was your salvation, your only hope, and you threw it all away." He shook his head in pity. "*All* away."

Kane leaped at Sam in a dropkick, throwing all of his weight against the tall, slender man. Both feet impacted against Sam's chest, but he merely took two stumbling steps back while Kane fell heavily on his back.

Before he could rise, Sam sidled in and caught hold of the back of his neck and squeezed. Kane choked off a scream of agony. The sensation was like being trapped between the jaws of a hydraulic bear trap. He tried, but failed, to pry Sam's fingers apart. Then he pistoned his fists into Sam's midsection as the imperator lifted him clear of the balcony's floor and twisted him around so they were face-to-face.

"You want to know why you were really implanted with the SQUID?" Sam asked pleasantly. The pupils of his eyes suddenly sparked with a familiar crimson glow, like pinpoints of fire.

Agony overtook Kane. He screamed in mindless pain and fury. Forgetting Sindri, even Tanvirah, he bellowed an animal wail of rage and pain, cursing the hot coals that seemed to fill the inside of his skull. He was unable to form words or even think a single cogent thought.

Sam released him and Kane fell limply to the floor, writhing and twitching feebly. The imperator toed him over onto his back, and Kane gazed up at him blankly, his nervous system overwhelmed. Sam reached up and pulled off his turban—revealing a naked cranium peeled of flesh, the skull bone open to the air. Sprouting from it were a series of tiny electrodes, studding it in an orderly pattern. Between the electrodes stretched flat ribbons of circuitry.

In a gentle tone barely above a whisper, he said, "That's why you were implanted, Kane...just like everyone will be one day...so we will be unified and I never need be alone again. No one will ever be alone again. All the units—the human brains in the world—will be linked to me. Chains, enabling my mind to take over that of another, to influence, to guide, to control, in almost total assimilation."

The pain in his head ebbed sufficiently so Kane could move and think again. He muttered, "That's a very old dream."

"Yes," Sam agreed. "Many others attempted what I have. But they never completely realized their dream of an orderly world, a controlled and unified universe. Until now."

Kane managed to shamble to a half crouch. Sam negligently drove a knee into his face. He heard and felt his nose cartilage collapse under the impact, and he fell over on his side. The pain was nothing compared to what he had experienced from the SQUID.

Sam continued, "Time will expand my horizons and build on the accomplishments of my predecessors."

"Predecessors?" Kane croaked, slowly trying to climb to his knees again.

Sam grinned, a very human grin, made horrific and macabre by his fleshless cranial bone. "Surely you've figured it out by now, Kane. Remember what I told you a long, long time ago, in another place altogether."

Kane wiped at the blood threading his face and tottered erect. He knew now who Sam really was. The imperator had confirmed suspicions he had secretly harbored, but dared not even consciously examine, for many years.

"I remember," Kane husked out. "You said that you're a program, not an individual entity." He made a statement; he didn't ask a question.

Sam started to nod—then cried out more in shock than pain when Sindri struck him from behind with the truncheon taken from the guard's body. He had performed a truly prodigious leap in order to do it. Sparks flew in a shower from the top of Sam's head.

Sam staggered forward—directly into Kane's left fist. He glimpsed Tanvirah grabbing Sindri and hauling him down to the floor, then a fountain of scorching rage erupted out of Kane. He moved to the attack, raining blow after blow on the imperator's face, trying to pulverize it, turn it into a bloody mass of pulped flesh. The imperator didn't bleed, and Kane hadn't really expected him to, although his pounding fists lacerated the prominent cheekbones and knocked out a couple of teeth.

Kane kept up the battering, driving his fists into Sam's body, then his face again in a flurry of hooks, right and left crosses and uppercuts. He was encouraged by the lack of neuronic energy pouring into his brain from the SQUID. Sindri had apparently knocked something askew, and Kane wasn't about to allow the imperator the opportunity to repair it.

Sam suddenly swung a fist from the hip, driving a blow into Kane's left side. The cracking of bone was audible, and sharp razors of pain slashed through Kane's torso. He doubled over, jackknifing around the fist. Slowly he fell, coughing up a mixture of blood and phlegm. The blow had been too swift, delivered with unerring accuracy and precision. Kane understood dimly that Sam had been learning while he was being pummeled. He had processed all the finer points of hand-to-hand combat. He knew exactly where to strike.

Kane lay doubled up around where the blow had landed, his eyes clouded with tears of pain. He panted through his open mouth, tasting blood. He waited for Sam to reach down and crush his larynx or kick him to death. Neither happened.

The imperator walked right past him and bumped against the rail. Kane gaped at him as Sam extended his arms and waved them through the air. In a voice high and wild with fear, he cried out, "I can't see! Tanvirah! I can't see!"

Kane almost laughed. The blow Sindri had landed on his SQUID network had damaged the optic nerve feed to his eyes. The imperator was blind. Tanvirah shrieked in horror and tried to hurl Sindri away from her, but he held on by double handfuls of her hair.

Kane forced himself to his feet, ignoring the grate of bone in his side. He lashed out with a straight-leg kick, catching Sam in the center of the back. Vertebrae crunched under the impact, but Sam didn't scream or plummet over the rail. Instead, his mouth opened but no sound came out. He jerked and fell, long limbs thrashing uncontrollably, like a puppet whose strings had been cut.

Kane guessed his entire network of neuronic energy was disrupted, but not necessarily permanently. He leaned against the rail to ease the pain of his shattered ribs and called, "Let her go, Sindri...time for us to implement the last phase of our own great plan."

Snarling, Sindri punched Tanvirah in the side of the head before letting her go. She flopped onto her back, arms and legs asprawl. Panting, Sindri staggered over to him. "You've uploaded the data cards?"

Kane nodded. "So you knew that's what I was going to do?"

Sindri snorted, then winced as he touched the welts swelling on the side of his face. "It was pretty damn obvious. I did everything I could to piss Sam off and make him careless."

"You did a fine job."

"You might say it's a calling, Mr. Kane."

"How well I know that." Kane forced a smile to his face. From the pocket of his bodysuit he withdrew the CD and handed it to Sindri. "Here you go. People's Exhibit A."

"And I guess I'm Exhibit B...providing I get to where you want me to go." Sindri moved along the rail in the direction of the computers, peering over the side into the pool. "How do you figure to inject me into the past?"

"The simplest way is to—"

Kane's words were drowned out by the stuttering report of the SIG-AMT. Tanvirah had pulled it from the soldier's hands and fired it in Kane and Sindri's general direction. She shrieked wordlessly as she did so, the recoil making her upper body shake violently. Bright brass arced from the ejector port and clinked at her feet. Sindri uttered a howl of fright.

Kane lunged forward, kicking himself off the balcony floor, the roar of the subgun a thundering drum roll in his ears. He saw bullets smash into the computer consoles, gouging through the plastic keyboards and tearing scars in the metal. He felt two sledgehammer blows against his back, which hurled him forward. He slammed into Sindri.

The little man toppled over the balcony rail, but he clung to Kane's hand and held it tightly for a long agonizing moment. The gunfire ended, replaced by the mechanical clack and snap of a jammed cylinder.

Sindri stared up uncomprehendingly into his face. Kane opened his mouth to speak, and blood vomited from his lips. Sindri uttered a short cry of disgust. By summoning all the energy left in his broken body, from toe-tip to the crown of his head, Kane managed to gasp out a half-gagged, imploring sentence. "When you get there, tell him—tell *me*—who the imperator really is. He's—"

He didn't finish saying the name when Tanvirah shrieked, hurling herself onto Kane. She pounded hysterically at his back with the butt of the autorifle. Kane's hand opened and Sindri plunged down, into the maw of the universe. When he struck the pool, the microcosm of infinity, a cloud of star sparks shot up like a stream of embers cast from a burning log. Then he was gone.

Kane hitched around and pushed Tanvirah away from him. She sat down hard on the floor, then crawled over to the spasming body of Sam. She cradled him in her arms, but he did not speak. His eyes were vacant, his gape-mouthed face a blank.

Tanvirah burst into tears, burying her face in her hands, sobbing as if her heart would break. Kane hoped it would. Gritting his teeth, he tried to make himself comfortable, but he knew that was an impossibility.

He ruefully eyed the raw, pulsing exit wounds on his chest. They were bleeding profusely, and he thought he saw bits of lung tissue mixed in with the scarlet flow, but he figured he would recover. He always did.

Then he chuckled at the absurd way his mind was constructed. It didn't seem capable of accepting death or defeat, even in the face of utter and complete finality.

As darkness crept in on the edges of his vision, he wondered how long he would be dead. Only time will tell, he thought.

Epilogue

Cerberus Redoubt

In the main operations complex, lights flashed and needle gauges flickered on the primary mat-trans console. In the anteroom, a droning hum arose from the gateway chamber.

Both Bry and Lakesh jumped in surprise. Brigid, seated at the main ops console, spun her chair away from the keyboard and stared at the armaglass-enclosed unit. "Is it a true matter stream carrier," she demanded, "or another quantum fluctuation like happened the other day?"

Swiveling his head around, Lakesh stared at the Mercator relief map spanning the entire length of one wall. Pinpoints of light shone steadily in almost every country, connected by a thin pattern of glowing lines. They represented the Cerberus network, the locations of all indexed functioning gateway units across the planet.

His eyes searched for any one of them that blinked steadily. A flashing bulb indicated a transmitting gateway, but there was none.

Bry announced stridently, "We've definitely got a matter stream, Lakesh! Coming into full phase!"

"How can that be?" Brigid asked, coming to stand beside Bry.

For a long moment, Lakesh didn't answer. He only shook his head in confusion. The main reason for his bewilderment was pure shock. Long ago he had altered the modulations of the Cerberus gateway unit's transit feed connections so its transmissions were untraceable. Nor could anyone jump into the redoubt's mat-trans, or send in so much as a molecule, either by accident or design—with one notable, relatively recent exception.

Recalling that exception kept his mind from working properly, and the bright flares, like bursts of heat lightning on the other side of the armaglass walls, distracted him further. The low hum climbed rapidly in pitch to a hurricane howl as the device cycled through the materialization process.

"We've definitely got a materialization," Bry said fearfully, pushing his chair back from the console on squeaking casters.

Staring at the flares of energy on the other side of the brown armaglass, Brigid said loudly, "Lakesh, you'd better get an armed detail in here."

The green-eyed woman's terse tone of voice freed Lakesh from his state of mental paralysis long enough for him to thumb down the call button on the trans-comm system. He half shouted, "Armed security detail to operations! *Stat!*"

His voice echoed hollowly all throughout the redoubt. A formal security force didn't exist as such in the installation. All of the personnel, including the recent Moon base émigrés, were required to become reasonably proficient with firearms, primarily the lightweight "point and shoot" SA80 subguns. The armed security detail Lakesh summoned would be anyone who grabbed a gun from the armory and reached the control center under his or her own power.

The electronic wail from the jump chamber faded, dropping down to silence. The bursts of energy behind the translucent slabs disappeared. Within a minute Kane rushed into the complex, wielding a nickel-plated Mustang .30, a memento of his escape from Area 51. He was wearing jeans and a black T-shirt, but no shoes, so he had apparently been relaxing in his quarters.

"We've got an unauthorized jumper," Brigid told him, nervously brushing her thick mane of red-gold hair back over her shoulders.

Kane snorted. "It's happened before, hasn't it?"

Bry said, "Yes, and it's never been a friendly visit from anyone, either."

Domi rushed in, double-fisting her .45-caliber Detonics Combat Master. The small albino girl followed Kane's hand signals and took up position on the left side of the jump chamber. She wore a short red jerkin that displayed most of her pearl-colored body. Her short, ragged mop of hair was the hue of bone, contrasting sharply with her ruby-red eyes.

Reba DeFore hustled in, looking both frightened and annoyed. A stocky, bronze-skinned woman, DeFore's usually tidy hair hung in disarrayed ash-blond wisps. Instead of a gun, she carried a medical kit. She hung back in the operations room, watching as Kane and Domi took up cross-fire positions on either side of the mat-trans unit, weapons held at hip level. Brigid stepped up to the platform and gripped the door handle. "No matter who—or what—is in there, don't shoot until I give you the go-ahead."

Carefully, Brigid disengaged the lock mechanism, lifted the handle and swung open the heavy door on its counterbalanced hinges. Most of the mist produced by the quincunx effect's plasma bleed-off had dissipated, so the figure slouched over against the far wall was easily discerned. Identification wasn't so easy.

Brigid stared at the small man-shape huddled on the hexagonal floor plates, then stepped in, dropping to one knee beside him. Despite the damp coating of blood half covering his face, she recognized the unconscious man. It took her two attempts but she managed to call out, "It's all right...I think."

Kane peered around the open door, stared in disbelief for a long second and half shouted, "Sindri!"

Sindri's eyes flew open, wide and wild. Convulsions shook him, racked him violently from head to toe. He dragged in a great shuddery breath as if his lungs had been deprived of oxygen for a long time. He clawed out with his right hand, finding Brigid's hands and closing his fingers around them, as if they were anchors to life. His glassy eyes asked a silent, beseeching question.

"You're in Cerberus," Brigid told him. "I'm assuming it's where you meant to end up."

Air rasped in and out of Sindri's lungs as he tried to sit up. He managed only a flailing spasm of arms and legs. Kane stepped in and pulled him up to a sitting position by the collar of his shadow suit, then dragged him out like a sack of corn, letting him use the table as support.

Lakesh and DeFore came in cautiously and joined Kane, Domi and Brigid, as they stared in dumbfounded silence at the little man. Despite suspecting they would encounter Sindri again, the notion that he would gate right into Cerberus covered in blood had never occurred to any of them.

"How the hell did you get here, pissant?" Kane snarled out the words.

Sindri leaned against the table edge, his eyes passing over the people and guns surrounding him. At length, he said hoarsely, "Mr. Kane, Miss Brigid. You probably won't believe this, but I'm overjoyed to see both of you again."

Lakesh stepped between DeFore and Domi. "And why is that?" he challenged. "Friend Kane and dearest Brigid told me you had the most ghastly fates for them in mind during your last meeting."

Sindri favored him with a bleak smile. "Yesterday's news. And I mean that in the most literal way possible."

He started to reach into a pocket, but Domi snapped her gun barrel up and he subsided. "Surely none of you think I can conceal a weapon in this outfit?"

"I think if anybody could," Kane snapped, "you'd be the one. Move slow."

Sindri did as he said, sliding out the slip-sleeved compact disc. Lakesh made a move to take it, but Sindri snatched it away. "No," he said firmly. "I have been charged to give this to Mr. Kane, and Mr. Kane only."

Brigid arched a questioning eyebrow. "Charged by whom?"

"That Mr. Kane will find out, after he reviews its contents."

Kane gazed at the disc distrustfully, as if he half suspected it was really a radioactive isotope. Gingerly he took it.

DeFore stepped forward, eyeing Sindri clinically. "I should get you to the infirmary and treat that wound."

Sindri shook his head. "No need. This blood isn't mine."

"Who does it belong to, then?" Domi demanded.

Sindri wiped a bit from his face and looked at it shining on his gloved fingertips. "I believe if you test it, you'll find it belongs to Mr. Kane."

Kane's jaw muscles knotted in angry frustration, and he took a threatening step toward Sindri. "I've had enough of this. Tell us how you got here, Sindri— and from where—or I'll do what Grant said he'd do the last time we were in each other's company."

Sindri's brow furrowed as if he were dredging up a memory. "Oh, right. Rip my arms off and hammer them down my throat. Where is the truculent Mr. Grant, anyway?"

"He is away at present," Lakesh responded gruffly. "I suggest you comply with friend Kane's request."

Sindri laughed with genuine amusement. "Very well. It's worth being pushed around just to see the looks on your faces. I came to be here through the venue of a spatial and temporal dimensional window, cutting across the continuum through a microcosmic pathway. It was put together by someone you know...he calls himself the imperator."

He paused, apparently enjoying the surprise flickering in all of their eyes. "However," he continued, "you know him best by his *nom de voyage,* the name he travels under...Colonel C. W. Thrush."

No one spoke or moved, or even appeared to breathe for a long, silent moment. Sindri made shooing motions with his hands. "Off with you, Mr. Kane. Time for you to find out what the future holds, and how you can get the hell out of the arrangement."

All the humor in Sindri's voice, eyes and manner disappeared, as he added, "And believe me, all of you have a very long way to go."

Take
2 explosive books
plus a
mystery bonus
FREE

DEATH LANDS®

Damnation Road Show

*Available in June 2003
at your favorite retail outlet.*

JAMES AXLER

DEATH LANDS

Damnation Road Show

Eerie remnants of preDark times linger a century after the nuclear blowout. But a traveling road show gives new meaning to the word *chilling*. Ryan and his warrior group have witnessed this carny's handiwork in the ruins and victims of unsuspecting villes. Even facing tremendous odds does nothing to deter the companions from challenging this wandering death merchant and an army of circus freaks. And no one is aware that a steel-eyed monster from the past is preparing a private act that would give Ryan star billing....